"Nice outfit..."

Way back in Kim's closet hung a blue satiny nightgown with matching robe. Kim had never worn it, but tonight she would. Because tonight was a night for lingerie.

The material felt slippery cool and wonderful against her still-heated skin. She pulled on the robe and checked her reflection. Mmm, perfect. The color matched her eyes and emphasized her slender figure in all the right places.

"Kim." She heard a soft knock.

Before she could change her mind, she marched to the door and flung it open. He was wearing soft shorts that showed off his powerful thigh muscles and a T-shirt that did the same for his biceps. His hair was wet and tousled, his skin golden, his eyes vividly brown surrounded by dark lashes.

"What's the occasion?"

"Tonight."

"Kim." His voice was low, throaty, that tone that got her so worked up, undoubtedly perfected on dozens of women. She knew what was coming.

"Can I come in...?"

Dear Reader,

If you're like me, you grew up crushing on the bad boys. Not the really bad boys, not the ones likely to end up in jail, but the guys who were cool, funny and charming, a little—or maybe a lot—irresponsible, always dating someone new and always out of reach.

I've grown past wanting that fantasy in my life, but I haven't grown past wanting to explore it in my books. *Long Slow Burn* features Nathan, on the surface a charming, smooth guy with a few endearing faults that keep him approachable. Underneath he's a sweet kid with a decade-long passion for a shy older woman who thinks of him as a pesky little brother.

After she sees him half-naked, Kim is shocked to realize he's no longer sixteen, and it's not long before Nathan has turned not only her head, but her heart, as well.

Look for *Hot to the Touch*, the last book in my Checking E-Males miniseries, available in June 2010. And don't forget to visit my website at www.IsabelSharpe.com.

Cheers!

Isabel Sharpe

Isabel Sharpe

LONG SLOW BURN

TORONTO NEW YORK LONDON
AMSTERDAM PARIS SYDNEY HAMBURG
STOCKHOLM ATHENS TOKYO MILAN MADRID
PRAGUE WARSAW BUDAPEST AUCKLAND

Recycling programs
for this product may
not exist in your area.

ISBN-13: 978-0-373-79610-6

LONG SLOW BURN

Copyright © 2011 by Muna Shehadi Sill

www.eHarlequin.com

Printed in U.S.A.

ABOUT THE AUTHOR

Isabel Sharpe was not born pen in hand like so many of her fellow writers. After she quit work to stay home with her firstborn son and nearly went out of her mind, she started writing. After more than twenty novels for Harlequin—along with another son—Isabel is more than happy with her choice these days. She loves hearing from readers. Write to her at www.IsabelSharpe.com.

Books by Isabel Sharpe

To Adam Ziles, web designer *par excellence*, who gave me Kim's career, and to Jessie Gemmer, future brilliant architect, who gave me Nathan's. I could not have written this book without their considerable expertise and always-willing, cheerful assistance.

Prologue

MARIE HEWITT WIPED toast crumbs off her fingers, thinking that plain toast with jelly was a depressing thing to have for breakfast at any time, but when there was a plate in the middle of the table loaded with doughnuts, Danish and a particularly appetizing raspberry cream-cheese coffee cake, plain toast with jelly was like time in prison. Sometimes Marie thought she should make friends with her hips, call them voluptuous, and be done with it.

She looked enviously around the table at her skinny companions chowing down on fatty pastry that would have absolutely no effect on their figures. Kim Charlotte Horton, Darcy Clark and Candy Graham had joined her table, as usual, in the seventh floor meeting room at Milwaukee's Pfister Hotel for the March gathering of Women in Power, an association of female business owners.

"So who has news this month?" She turned to her right, where Candy was biting reverently into a crumbly blueberry muffin. Candy's transformation had been astonishing over the past month. Gone was the long-suffering martyr, pining for her horrible ex-boyfriend. Finding true love had made her glow like she was radioactive. "How's the party-planning business going?"

"Ten to one it's been taken over by the wedding-planning

business." Dark, beautiful Darcy smirked across the table, playing her familiar cynical-about-love role.

Candy didn't blink. By now they all knew Darcy's bark might sound nasty but there was no bite. "Justin and I are having a fall wedding, small and informal. We'd rather spend our money on a Paris honeymoon."

"Oh, wow." To Marie's left, Kim's tired blue eyes had turned starry at the mere mention.

"Paris. You lucky dog." Even Darcy looked wistful.

Marie couldn't help feeling smug. She'd drag Kim and Darcy into true love, too—Darcy kicking and screaming until she admitted how much she wanted it. As the founder of Milwaukeedates.com, the city's premier—if she did say so herself—online dating service, Marie had made a New Year's resolution to match up her three closest friends from Women in Power. She'd been able to cross Candy off last month after she and Justin Case got engaged on Valentine's Day. Kim was up next; her thirtieth birthday was next month, April fifteenth, and Marie was determined she'd have something to celebrate. A surprise party, which she and Candy needed to get busy planning, and with any luck, a romance, too.

Then would come Darcy, the real matchmaker's challenge. "Darcy, how is Gladiolas doing?"

Darcy made a face that couldn't conceal her pride. "Milwaukee's restaurant scene is getting more crowded and competitive, but we're hanging in there."

Candy snorted. "Justin and I tried to get in last weekend. Not only were there no reservations available, but a crowd was waiting. I'd say you're doing more than hanging in there."

"I don't take anything for granted. Restaurants spring up and die like weeds. If I could stand doing anything else, I would." Darcy shrugged and hoisted her coffee. "I'd rather hear about Kim and her proposal for the new Carter International website. How's that going, Kim?"

"Okay. Not great." Kim smiled bravely. She'd been

working her butt off at her solo company, Charlotte's Web Design, for the past five years and hadn't yet gotten where she wanted to be. Kim was looking at this bid to design a new website for the crystal and china megacompany as her last chance before giving up her entrepreneurial dream. "I've had some ideas but nothing amazing yet. Carter is marketing this new line, Carter2, at a younger, more casual crowd, so I have to incorporate a funkier feel into their existing upscale image. So far it's not working."

"You'll get this!" Candy smacked the table determinedly. "You are so talented. They have to hire you."

"Thanks, Candy." Kim reached for another doughnut; Marie chewed on a grape and forced herself not to do the same, though the coffee cake was still calling her name. She'd think skinny hips. She'd think toast.

"How's the new roommate working out?" Darcy asked.

"It's been…interesting." Kim bit into the doughnut.

"In what way?"

"Well." Kim washed her bite down with orange juice. "He's a guy."

The table erupted into laughter.

"Say no more." Darcy rolled her eyes, a smile still on her face. "Toilet seat up, toothpaste cap left off, dishes piling up in his bedroom."

"Oh, you've lived with him, too?" Kim kept her gaze deliberately innocent while the rest of the table cracked up again. "Nathan is okay. He's my brother's age, three years younger than me, but it sure seems like more."

"Men mature more slowly." Darcy quirked a dark eyebrow. "They're generally not done until about age forty-five."

Quinn's age. Marie shook herself. She needed to stop thinking about her friend Quinn Peters, who looked like George Clooney and acted like Don Juan. Though at least he wasn't fattening.

"Is Nathan cute?" Candy cut off a small piece of Danish and put it on her plate.

"Yes, but…" Kim wrinkled her nose. "He's one of those

guys who had so much fun partying in college he never stopped. He and my brother still spend too much time drinking and trying to score."

"Oh, *that* type." Darcy grimaced. "Men with the depth of a toddler pool. Keep your distance."

"Trust me, that won't be a problem." Kim ate the last bite of doughnut with obvious enjoyment. Marie forced herself to look away, then found herself gazing at the cake again and had to turn away from that, too. Damn toast. How about *curvaceous* hips?

"What does Nathan do again?" Candy asked.

"He finished the course work for a master's in architecture at UW Milwaukee, but can't make himself finish his thesis project. He's surviving on odd jobs, barista in the morning at Alterra, bartender in the evening at the Hi Hat, delaying real life as long as possible is my guess." She shrugged. "I put up with him as a favor to Kent. And his help with the rent."

"I say we toast new beginnings for Kim." Marie lifted her coffee, wishing she hadn't just said "toast." "Here's to you getting the Carter job."

"Hear, hear." Darcy and the others raised their cups.

"And…" Marie smiled at Kim. "I've been thinking about another new beginning for you, not lucrative, but a lot more fun."

Kim stopped wiping sugar off her fingers. "What do you mean?"

"Ha!" Candy started laughing. "I know that look, Marie. You turned it on me in January."

"And look what happened to her. Trapped. Chained. Ruined." Darcy shook her head in mock despair.

Marie winked at Candy. "Kim, you set your thirtieth birthday as your deadline for Charlotte's Web sinking or swimming. I'm thinking it's also a good milestone for finding a man."

"Oh." Kim straightened in her chair. "Well, actually I'm thinking—"

"I'd be thinking *run* if I were you," Darcy said.

"She's not you." Candy grasped Kim's forearm. "Go see Marie, she's amazing. Dating is just what you need to jazz up life. I had a blast, and of course, I found Justin."

"And got your very own engagement ring stuck in a pizza." Darcy snorted.

Candy's smile only got wider. "Right then pizza was as good as black velvet to me. You think you want everything a certain way, but when the guy is right, none of the showy stuff matters at all."

"Very true." Marie beamed proudly at Candy. "You have learned well, Grasshopper."

The women burst into giggles. Even Darcy.

"So what do you think, Kim? Come see me?" Marie pulled out her iPhone and called up the calendar. "I even have someone in mind for you."

Kim looked taken aback. "Oh, well, I'm—"

"Ooh, tell us about him." Candy leaned forward eagerly.

"Troy Cahill. Sound familiar?"

"Oh! Yes! Perfect!" Candy all but bounced in her seat. "Oh gosh, this is so great. He's Justin's best friend and his coauthor on the interactive computer manual. We can go on double dates and—"

"Down, girl." Darcy playfully restrained her. "The sparkles from that diamond have gone to your head."

"No, seriously." Candy shook her fingers as if they were burning. "And he is sooo *hot*."

Kim laughed, her blush making her eyes brighter. Shyness might make Kim easy to overlook at first, but her smile or the occasional glint of mischief in her eyes gradually made the blond girl-next-door beauty more obvious, as well as her strength. "I was already thinking I'd—"

"Friday, Kim?" Marie smiled approvingly at the blush. The timing was right. "Morning?"

"Yes! Friday!" Kim threw up her hands. "I've been *trying* to tell you all that I have been thinking about dating. Because of my birthday, and then after seeing Candy so happy. Nine-thirty?"

"Nine-thirty, Friday." Marie chuckled, entering the appointment into her iPhone. She had picked out Troy for Kim initially, but another profile had also caught her eye, a recent sign-up, Dale Swallow. Unfortunate name, but an interesting guy. She could see him being good for Kim, helping challenge her with new experiences to grow her confidence. There was more to Kim under that reserve and shyness, and Marie had a feeling the right man could get at it. Besides, Marie wasn't sure Troy had made enough of an effort yet to get over his old girlfriend.

Either way, Kim was coming to see her without having put up a fight, and Marie could find her the happiness she deserved. This was going to be a piece of cake.

Piece of cake. *Mmm.*

She gave in and lifted a slice of coffee cake onto her plate.

Goodbye toast. Hello *womanly* hips.

1

"HI, YOU MUST BE KIM." Marie's red-haired receptionist extended her hand for a shake. "I'm Jane."

"Hi, Jane." Kim smiled politely, refraining from pointing out that they'd met a couple of times before. The first time when Marie moved into these offices, and Kim, Candy and Darcy had brought over flowers and champagne for an impromptu celebration. Then two weeks ago, when Kim had come by to pick up Marie for lunch. "Think it will ever be spring?"

"According to the calendar next week. But given that it's Wisconsin…" She gestured to the counter across from her desk. "Help yourself to coffee, tea or hot chocolate. Is it snowing?"

"Not accumulating, but it's coming down, yes."

"Enough to foul up traffic and remind us it's still winter." Jane rolled her eyes, blue behind narrow black glasses. "Marie is finishing up with someone. She'll be done soon."

"That's fine. I'm early." Kim poured a cup of coffee she didn't need, since Nathan kept their apartment stocked with fresh-roasted beans from Alterra, and splashed in some milk. She was early because she'd been pacing nervously around her apartment all morning, too keyed up to get work done and not in the mood for anything else. Finally she'd figured it was better just to get going, drive slowly and hope for delaying traffic, which the snow had made possible.

Kim had been thinking about trying online dating for a while. She'd delayed, waiting for the perfect time, hoping Charlotte's Web would take off so she could come into a relationship from a position of confidence and financial security. However, with her thirtieth birthday looming, she realized a lot of years had gone by without a "perfect time," and that if she won the Carter bid and was no longer constantly teetering on the brink of insolvency, she might be too busy to date. Marie pressing her for an appointment now had clinched it.

"You can go in." Jane pointed back toward Marie's office, from which a younger woman had just emerged. "Marie's got a treat for you."

"A treat?"

Jane waggled her brows. "One of our new listings. Adorable."

"Oh." Kim laughed uncomfortably, ducking her head when the woman Marie had been meeting with passed behind her. Being here made her feel exposed, as if she was announcing to the world that she couldn't get dates the normal way. Whatever normal was these days. Probably being here. She moved toward Marie's office, wanting away from Jane's black-framed stare. "Thanks, Jane."

"Nice to meet you finally."

"Right." She pushed into Marie's office. So flattering when people forgot they ever laid eyes on you. "Hey, Marie."

"Kim, how are you? Come on in." She beckoned warmly, elegant as always in a black pantsuit with cream accents and tasteful gold jewelry.

"Thanks." Kim stepped into the cozy office, decorated more like someone's favorite room than a place of business. Shelves lined two walls, with books, decorative pottery pieces and plants set at attractive intervals. Trust Marie to keep clients relaxed and comfortable in whatever way she could. "You've done fabulous things with this room."

"That's right, it was completely bare when you were in here before." Marie waved her toward one of the overstuffed chairs in front of her desk, and took the other one. "Have a seat, make yourself comfortable. I see you got coffee already."

"Not that I need to be any more jittery." She perched on the chair's edge, mug in one hand, Milwaukeedates.com paperwork clutched in the other.

"Trust me, everyone is nervous doing this. What did you think of the forms? Have any trouble?"

"Not really." She held them out to Marie. "I'm not into the whole self-pimping thing, but I did my best."

"Self-pimping? Interesting choice of words." Marie took the papers, glancing over at Kim before she read them. "I'll start with your description of yourself, then we'll talk about the guy you'd like to meet. Okay with you?"

"Sounds good."

Marie read while Kim got fidgety, sipped coffee, decided she didn't need more caffeine, held the cup down in her lap, got fidgety, sipped more coffee...

"Okay." Marie shifted position, frowning slightly. "Your profile. You've described yourself well here...."

"But?"

"But." Marie put the papers down and met her eyes. "You make yourself sound a little dull."

"I am a little dull." She held up her hand when Marie started protesting. "I don't wear makeup, I don't own sexy clothes, I rarely go out. Men who want that whole hot party-girl thing aren't going to want to waste time on a date with me."

"Most men only want that kind of woman in fantasy." Marie leaned forward earnestly. "Here they ask for honest women, loyal women, women with brains and with a sense of humor. You've got all that, but you make it sound as if you have nothing to offer. 'I stay home most of the time. I don't like crowds or noise.'"

Kim shrugged. "I want to be honest about who I am."

"Understood." Marie held up the page and shook it vigorously. "But this is maybe half of who you are."

Kim tried to keep from bristling, without much luck. "How would you change it? With some dating euphemism? Like when Realtors say 'cozy and quaint' and mean 'cramped and dingy,' instead of 'shy' I should say I'm 'serene' or I have 'hidden passion'?"

Marie dimpled a too-innocent smile. "Why, that's exactly what I was going to suggest. 'Hi, I'm Kim. Serene with hidden passion.'"

Kim's cranky outrage wilted into laughter. "Ew."

"We'll move on for now. Tell me about your past relationships. The main ones. What the men were like, what happened, etc."

Ugh. Kim wiggled farther back into the chair. "Well, let's see. First boyfriend, Sam, in high school. Geek like me, quiet, we both had horrible skin and a love for all things computer. That lasted three years. We broke up when we went to college."

"Because…"

"Our relationship had gotten too predictable and we both wanted to grow."

"Understandable. Were you sexually involved?"

"Yeah." Kim blushed. "Or something like it. High school, you know."

"I do. Who came next?"

"Josh, in college. We dated for a year, then he ended it. He was a physics and philosophy double major and didn't have time for a girlfriend."

"Ouch." Marie grimaced sympathetically. "Nice when you come first, huh?"

"Yeah, it didn't feel great." Kim adjusted the hem of her sweater, wanting to change the subject, but knowing Marie wouldn't let her off the hook. "I survived."

"After that?"

"Oh, well…" She took a sip of coffee that suddenly tasted bitter.

"Hmm." Marie narrowed her eyes. "Something not so great."

"Tony." Kim let her head drop back against the chair. "Big, handsome jock, the kind of guy I'd get a crush on but never thought would be into me."

Marie lifted her eyebrows. "*I'm* not surprised he was."

"Yeah, well, I was suspicious, but he kept coming around." She put her mug on Marie's desk. "He was charming, persistent and surprisingly interesting to talk to. I got sucked in, started dressing better and wearing makeup. I went on meds to clear up my face. I looked good and felt great, and thought, *Oh boy, the birth of New Kim!* I loved the attention, not only from him, but from his friends. Seemed like wherever we went, they were watching me. I thought I was hot stuff."

"You are." Marie held up Kim's profile again. "You're selling yourself way short here. You should be—"

"Wait." Kim shook her head, throat tightening. "Let me finish. I finally trusted him enough to let him in, to care about him. One night after he'd taken me to some horrible, loud party where I drank too much to be able to stand it, we went back to his place. He lived off campus, and his roommate wasn't there. We had sex all over the apartment all night long. Incredible sex, I-didn't-know-it-could-be-like-that sex."

Marie's frown crept back. She obviously couldn't figure Tony out any better than Kim had been able to. "And this was bad how?"

"Turned out he had a bet with his friends that I'd be better in bed than I looked. Apparently he considered himself an expert at being able to tell which geeky girls were hot in the sack."

"Ah." Marie's lips tightened. "I can see why you're not keen on the phrase 'hidden passion.'"

"Then it got worse."

"Oh, Kim."

"Since he won the bet, he had to beat his chest all over campus." Kim screwed her eyes shut. "I had guys lining up to ask me out for weeks after, thinking they'd get what he got. I'm sure it never occurred to them I'd actually started to like the pig and that's why I slept with him."

"I'm sorry."

Kim opened her eyes, hating the quaver in her voice the story could still bring on. "I got over it. Mostly. But now I avoid any guy who seems more concerned with what a woman represents than who she is. That whole 'score at any cost' mentality."

"Your brother and new roommate."

"Bingo." She pointed emphatically at Marie. "Kent probably inherited his roving dick from Dad, who constantly cheated on Mom until he left her. I know there are better men out there. I just want to make sure I get the right kind. So if I sound boring on my profile, and my picture is plain, tough. I don't want to attract another shallow jerk. I want someone to love me for me—no makeup, happy in a quiet life at home, geeking out with my computer."

She finished, a little out of breath, and waited for a reaction. Marie sat quietly, watching her as if she was trying to make up her mind about something.

"Okay." Marie got up with her usual grace and went around behind her desk. "I get what you're saying. I had two men picked out for you before this meeting. I still want to show them to you, and I want you to look with an open mind. If you're not interested, you can go online and choose whatever profiles you want. Just bear in mind that sometimes when we feel fear or aversion, it's not necessarily good instinct talking. It can be habit or baggage instead. Very hard to tell the two apart. Deal?"

Kim reached for her mug, fingered the textured porcelain and then took a sip. She'd only have to look. Nothing more unless it felt right. "Okay. I'll check them out."

"Good." Marie tapped a few letters on the keyboard. "Here."

Kim got up stiffly; she must have been tensing her body ridiculously tight. Not many people had heard the story of Kim and Tony, at least not from her. Since college she'd told only Kent, trying to make him understand why she hated the way he and his friends talked about and treated women, but he'd just insisted she didn't understand.

Yeah, no kidding.

"This is Troy."

Kim found herself looking into a pair of the deepest, darkest eyes she'd ever seen, jumping off the screen under a strong forehead and tousled dark curls. Handsome. Very. Wearing a Green Day T-shirt over broad, developed shoulders.

Immediate panic kicked in. She didn't want to go out with him. "He's nice looking. Sexy."

"He was adorable when we met. Gentle and very sweet. Smart, too. Works in IT, so you have computers in common. He owns a house in Whitefish Bay not far from the lake and lives there with his dog, Dylan. Solid career, and he's writing a book with Candy's fiancé, Justin, so they can vouch for him, too. I think he's worth giving a try."

Kim tilted her head noncommittally, sick with nerves.

"Take your time, Kim. This is not a speed test. You can stare at him to your heart's content in the privacy of your own home or ignore him completely. It's up to you. You have all the power in this situation." Marie tapped a few more keys and Troy's midnight brooding eyes disappeared. Kim felt immediate relief. "Here's the other man I thought might interest you. His name is Dale."

"Dale." She stared at the ordinary face filling the screen, and the pang of relief turned into a buzz of excitement. Light brown hair in a basic short cut, brown eyes behind chic frameless glasses that made him look professor-smart. He wore a dark suit that sat well on his shoulders—all she could see of him. His expression was serious, but not grim. His eyes looked kind, and his lips quirked as if he was about to smile.

"He works for Johnson Controls as a consultant. Does a lot of traveling, all over the world. He's charming, educated, well-read, into yoga, skiing, sailing. Very interesting to talk to. I liked him."

"Skiing? Sailing?" She snorted. "Not really my speed."

"Honey, you're twenty-nine. You can't possibly have figured out everything about how you fit into the world. Maybe when you're ninety, but even then I'd have my doubts."

Marie had a point. Kim gazed into the warm brown eyes on the monitor. Something about this guy...

"Think about it. I can set up dates with both of them if you want, and if they want."

Kim imagined herself sitting across the table from Troy even for an hour. She wasn't sure she could do it. That handsome face would completely disconcert her. She'd babble, stutter and spill drinks.

"Kim." Marie's hand was comforting on her arm. "I know this is pushing you out of your comfort zone. Putting yourself out there is very hard. For you and for every single person that comes through that door, and if it's not, there's something wrong. Troy and Dale may not be the guys you pictured when you thought about signing up, but you don't have to marry either one of them. You don't even have to do more than look, exchange an email or have a quick cup of coffee."

"True." She wished that made her feel safer.

"It's a place to start. When you left your full-time job at Soka Associates five years ago to start Charlotte's Web Design, you took an enormous leap of faith, much bigger than going on an experimental date." She gave Kim's arm a squeeze. "This will be easy in comparison."

Kim nodded, experiencing a jumble of mixed reactions: fear, excitement, pride and an overriding desire to run home and hide in bed. But if she always gave in to fear she'd still be miserable at Soka. Still be dating Sam. Still the same old pimply, dowdy Kim.

Marie tapped a few more keys; Dale's face disappeared from the monitor but lingered in Kim's brain for a few pleasant seconds before Troy's dark eyes and lean features supplanted his.

Kim had come a long way. What hadn't killed her had made her stronger, and there was no reason she couldn't continue to change and grow, as Marie said, even if, God forbid, Charlotte's Web failed. She wanted a relationship, and she'd lose nothing by meeting with these two. Call it practice, if that made the hours easier to cope with. And if she babbled and stuttered and spilled, so be it. No animals or small children would be harmed in the having of these dates.

"I'll do it." She spoke impulsively, started to take the words back, and found she couldn't, because she didn't want to take anything back; from now on she wanted to take everything forward.

"Both of them?"

Kim nodded firmly, her face flushed. "Both of them. I'm ready."

2

"HEY, NATHAN."

"Mmph?" Nathan opened one eye. Kim. What was she doing in his bedroom? Undoubtedly not what he wanted her to be doing in his bedroom.

Wait. He wasn't in bed. He was on the couch in her—their—living room. What the—

"Did you remember to get wine on your way home?" Hands on her hips, lips pursed. "For my book club meeting tonight?"

Wine? Oh, no. He must have fallen asleep. She'd asked him this morning to get some; his fog-brain did remember that much. "I don't think so."

Kim's face set. "No problem. I'll get it."

"No. No." He sat up, rubbing his eyes, and shook his head, trying to clear it. Wine. She'd wanted him to get some on his way home from…where? "I'll get it. I said I would. Wait, what time is it?"

She looked at her watch. "Almost four-thirty."

His memory came back. He'd gone out after his bartending job at the Hi Hat Lounge last night, stayed out until four, gotten to work at Alterra Coffee at six, then stumbled home and slept through his four o'clock appointment with his faculty advisor, during which he was to have reported on progress he hadn't made. He was supposed to buy Kim's wine on the way back.

Nathan bounced off the couch, got an instant brownout and had to bend over until his vision cleared.

He was never, ever drinking tequila again.

"How long have you been asleep? Didn't you have an appointment with Dr. Stephanopolous?"

"Um. Maybe."

"Oh, no." She used that tone he hated most. That what-am-I-going-to-do-with-you tone that meant all she saw was her little brother's loser friend. He couldn't tell her about the panic that gripped him when he tried to work, the compulsion to jump up and run, the inability to focus, the instinct that putting more work into what he'd planned was shoving bad after worse.

Sometimes he thought he was going nuts.

"I'll call and straighten it out. Then I'll get the wine." He staggered forward into the pizza he'd bought after work and half finished before nodding off. *Squish.* A tepid slice stuck to the bottom of his bare foot. When he shook free, the sauce-slathered crust dropped back to the plate but the mozzarella clung. He hopped a few times, lost his balance and fell back on the couch, his cheesy foot sticking into the air.

Why always in front of this woman? If she laughed, he'd join her.

She didn't laugh. She sighed.

He hated those sighs. "Help, cheese is trying to eat my foot."

"Nathan." Amusement in her voice this time. Good. He could usually get her to laugh. Someday soon he hoped to earn respect along with that laughter. Maybe affection. Maybe more.

She disappeared and came back with a paper towel, her hair in an endearingly sloppy ponytail, her slender, toned body hidden under baggy gray sweats and a shapeless sweater. "You are truly something."

"Aren't I?" He grinned up at her, the oh-so-charming, cocky boy-man she expected, and took the towel to wipe his foot clean. "Thanks for the rescue. I have to call Dr. S., then I'll get your wine, I promise."

Dreading the next installment of his advisor's disappointment, he strode over the crooked, scarred hardwood floors of the narrow hallway to his bedroom, painted a vibrant blue by Kim before he'd moved in early in the month. She'd done amazing things with blasts of color here and there, but the apartment had definitely seen better days. As far as Nathan was concerned, however, any place Kim lived was paradise. He still couldn't believe fate—or rather his previous landlord selling the building—had made this miracle possible.

After searching through piles of laundry and stacks of paper, his phone appeared on the floor next to his drafting table. He made the call quickly to get it over with, then found Kim in their old-fashioned kitchen, whose drab colors she'd ambushed with bright red canisters, colorful bowls of fruit and intricately patterned decorative tiles.

"What's that smile for?" She'd picked up his pizza plate and glass and carried them to the sink. Why hadn't he taken the time to do that? Fifteen seconds wouldn't have made his screwup with his advisor worse, and it would have kept Kim from having to treat him like a little boy again.

"You won't believe me." He nudged her out of the way at the sink and took over washing. "Dr. S. forgot our meeting. He couldn't apologize enough."

"Are you serious?" She stopped drying her hands on a red towel. "You're not kidding?"

"Would I lie to you?"

"I don't know."

"I wouldn't." He gave a final rinse to the pot he'd used to heat stomach-soothing oatmeal for breakfast, and set it upside down in the drying rack. "I told him not to worry, that I'd waited outside his office only fifteen minutes. Twenty, tops."

Kim shook her head in exasperation. "I swear, you are

the luckiest person on the planet. Totally self-indulgent and it never catches up to you."

"Self-indulgent? Me?" He pretended comic outrage, though the barb hurt. Comments like that from Kim only bolstered his determination that while they were living together she would come around to seeing him differently. Yes, he'd always been disorganized. Ask his mom how often he'd left homework materials at home in the morning and at school in the afternoon. But he was plenty smart, and had been a good student all his life until the previous semester, when the panic and mental blocking started. "I was exhausted and fell asleep. That's human nature, not self-indulgence."

"Exhausted from being out until four in the morning. That's self-indulgence."

"I was at a friend's bachelor party." He tossed down the sponge he'd used to wipe the sink, and leaned against the counter so he could watch her. "You can't leave those early. It is written."

Kim scrunched up her face. "Where?"

"In *The Man's Guide to Being Manly.*"

"Aha." She spooned flour into a metal measuring cup. "I knew that book existed somewhere. Did you write it?"

He puffed out his chest, flexed his biceps. "You need to ask?"

"Oh, um, of course not." She put away the flour, consulted her recipe, dumped a stick of butter into the mixer bowl with some sugar and turned on the battered yellow machine. She seemed tense, had been for the past few days. He hoped she hadn't had another setback on the Carter bid. He didn't understand her thirtieth-birthday deadline for giving up on Charlotte's Web Design. Seemed an artificial stopping point to him. But then he hadn't been struggling for five years, day in and out, to keep his dream alive the way she had.

"Can I help?"

"Wine."

"Yes. Wine. I'm on my way. I have your list." He patted his pockets frantically. "Somewhere."

She picked up the paper from the counter, where it lay in plain view, and smacked it into his hand, leaving flour smudged on his palm.

"Oh, there." He waved cheerfully, groaning inside, took the elevator down and jogged through the chilly March wind to the liquor store, a couple blocks east on Oakland. If he ever managed to do something macho and smooth around Kim she'd probably have a heart attack from the shock. Luck didn't ever seem to be on his side where she was concerned.

Wine bought, he strode briskly back toward home, carrying the four bottles. His cell rang; he fumbled in his pocket, shifting the wine to his hip. It was Kent, who'd probably punch him if he knew the thoughts Nathan had regularly about his sister.

"Hey, Kent."

"How'd it go this morning? Did you make it out of bed?"

"Barely. You?"

"Barely. I was nearly late to a meeting." Kent chuckled. "John will remember that party for the rest of his life. Those women were incredible."

"They were." If you were sexually attracted to Barbie.

"Any of them would make me very happy for at least an hour. Maybe two. Poor John's given up that chance forever." Kent laughed harshly. "Same woman, day after day, for the rest of his life. He's had it."

Nathan chuckled dutifully. He was used to Kent's bluster, not unlike the talk Nathan's four older brothers and father indulged in. Lately, though, he wondered how much of it was really Kent and how much was sour grapes after his New York girlfriend dumped him.

"Oof, I need more coffee." Kent yawned loudly. "Anyway, here's the deal. Kim's friend Marie called. She's throwing Kim a thirtieth-birthday surprise party and wants us to help."

He liked that idea. Kim needed more fun in her life. "How?"

"You'll have to ask her. From me she wants childhood memories and all that." His voice shifted into a caricature of a fussy female. "Let's put together a *super fun-filled scrapbook!*"

"No way."

"I got her number and told her you'd call her. Ready?"

"Hang on." Nathan put the bottles down on the sidewalk, found a pen in his jacket but no paper so he scrawled Marie's number on the liquor store bag. "Got it, thanks."

"Basketball Sunday?"

"I'm there." He hung up, tore the edge off the bag and dialed Marie. "Hey, this is Kim's roommate, Nathan. Kent called me...."

"Wow, that was fast." The voice was rich and friendly. "What did he tell you?"

"That you need my help with Kim's party."

"We do, we do. I haven't yet met with my partner in crime, Candy, but we've talked a little. We'll need information about Kim so we can come up with the party's theme."

Nathan winced. *Theme?* All you needed for a party was people, a room and a keg. "Okay."

"We'll pick Kent's brain for her friends and stories, but there might be one or two personal items you can find or steal, since you'll have the most access to her. Maybe stories you can coax out of her. Are you willing to do that?"

Scrapbooking couldn't be far behind. But Nathan would be happy for any excuse to interact with Kim. As long as nothing involved him using glitter. "Sure."

"Terrific. Is this the best number to reach you at?"

"This is my cell, yeah."

"Excellent. Thanks for getting back to me so fast, Nathan. This will be great to do for Kim. She's such a sweetheart."

He agreed with that and hung up, not sure how he felt about stealing personal items—like what?—but hearing about Kim's life and memories was part of his plan for getting to know her better, anyway. He turned—nearly forgetting the wine—and started back toward home. Parties meant presents. This would be a great opportunity to do something really special for her. Something she'd notice and appreciate, and be touched by. Something to make her think of him in a new light.

What that could be he had no idea, but he had time.

Five minutes later he'd carried the bottles safely into the house and unloaded the reds, put the whites in the refrigerator. Kim was sitting at the Shaker-style natural-finish table, scooping balls of dough onto a baking sheet.

"Can I help with anything?"

"No, thanks, Nathan." She smiled tightly. "I've got it."

"C'mon, there must be something." He lifted his hands to show them empty and willing, anxious to make up for his earlier bungling. "I'm no chef, but I'm not inept, either."

She considered him. "How are you at putting snacks into bowls?"

"Expert."

"Without eating them all?"

"Oh." He made himself look pained. "I can try."

"Good enough." She smiled, pointing to a can of nuts, bags of chips and pretzels, and bowls, all on a tray on the counter.

Nathan pulled up a chair opposite and started his task, glancing at Kim once in a while. She was definitely on edge, her expression inward and thoughtful. She was too serious, too reserved. He loved goosing her into life, making her laugh. She needed someone like him around.

He poured pretzels into the last bowl. "I'm done here. What else can I help with? And don't say you have it all covered. I've got time and there's more to do."

"Okay." She pushed a third baking sheet toward him. "You can help make the cookies."

"Sure." He imitated her motions, scooping up dough with a teaspoon and pushing the blob onto a cookie sheet lined with a silicone mat. Homemade cookies in his childhood had meant store-bought slice-and-bake dough from the supermarket, so this was new to him. "You do realize what I'm sacrificing here, Kim."

"I can guess. Making cookies isn't manly, either?" She shot him a look. "Is anything manly that doesn't involve drunken oblivion or getting laid?"

"Of course." Nathan paused his cookie spooning. "Yelling obscenities at referees and umpires counts, too."

Kim let go with a good giggle that time, the one he loved best, the one that turned her cheeks pink and softened her features. "What else?"

"Let's see. Crushing beer cans on your head. Belches that wake the dead. More intimacy with the TV than with your girlfriend…"

She rolled her eyes. "It's a miracle marriage ever happens."

"No, no, there are other, serious parts to the *Man's Guide* that females can appreciate."

"Like?"

"Like…" Nathan leaned toward her across the table, taking his first chance. "A Manly Man always swears to love, support and protect his woman for his whole life."

"Huh?" Kim did not look impressed. "Support? Protect? Your woman? That sounds more like *cave*manly."

Hmm. That did not go the way Nathan had envisioned. Her eyes hadn't gotten misty, nor had infatuation lit them up. She hadn't sighed and said, *Oh, Nathan, that is so romantic.*

The seduction of Kim Charlotte Horton would take trial and error. Growing up with four older brothers and a chauvinist father hadn't prepared Nathan for approaching a smart, independent woman like her. He wouldn't give up, though. Hell, he'd just started trying.

She took her sheet to the oven, opened the door and put the cookies in. He didn't mean to pay close attention when she bent over, but while he respected the very ground she walked on, to deny himself the pleasure of that sight would be pure masochism.

Why had this woman hit him so hard and never let go? First time he'd seen her he'd been following Kent into his house their freshman year in high school, Kim's senior. Their family had just moved to Milwaukee from somewhere in Ohio. She'd been standing framed by the doorway between the living room and dining room, arguing with her mother, her face flushed, her eyes snapping blue heat. Nathan, all of fifteen, had literally stopped in his tracks. She wasn't the kind of woman whose beauty struck you right off the bat, but something had sure struck him like a boulder between the eyes. Kent finally had to yank on his arm to get him to move. That's how it had been right from the beginning. And the years hadn't changed those feelings, or replicated them, no matter how many other women Nathan had tried to find them with. Now his goal was to figure out this crazy fantasy or turn it into reality.

She came back to the table, pulled the next baking sheet toward her and settled into her seat with a defeated plop. Something was definitely not right. His instinct was to tell her more jokes, but his instinct when it came to Kim was usually wrong. Maybe his best bet going forward would be to do the opposite of whatever came naturally.

He cleared his throat, feeling as if he were about to audition for a part he wasn't right for. "How was your day? Did you get a lot done on the Carter proposal?"

"Another dead end." She made a silly face, trying to hide her disappointment. "I like some things about the current design. It's balanced, good colors, chic feel, but it just doesn't pop."

He wished he could come up with the perfect solution to take the frown off her face. He'd offer to look, but had already learned she was intensely private about her work in progress. "It's a solid start, though?"

"Yeah, I guess." She looked miserably down at the perfect mounds of cookie dough on her baking sheet.

Was that all that was bothering her? "Something will come to you. You're very talented."

"Thanks, Nathan." A real smile then. "It's just nerve-racking with the deadline looming, both for the bid and for Charlotte's Web. What about your day?"

"My day." He rubbed the back of his neck, wishing he hadn't had that fifth drink at 3:00 a.m. "It started late last night, ended early this morning. In between was some very good tequila and some very bad judgment."

She laughed. "Sounds like a typical night."

That was the problem. To her that did seem typical. She didn't understand that this self-destructive part of him wasn't all there was. He was trapped right now in a cycle he didn't understand how to get out of. Yet. Though he knew he would. In the meantime there was more of him to show her: that he was a good listener, a loyal friend and that he cared about her more than she knew. Probably more than was rational or reasonable.

The timer went off and she jumped to extract the first sheet of perfectly browned cookies. He lifted his nose like a puppy. "Mmm, those smell good."

"Don't they?" Kim sniffed rapturously. "Mom's sugar oatmeal. Plain, but wonderful."

She stood there, sparking uncharacteristically edgy energy. Nathan's instinct was to go with the cookie conversation. Therefore he'd do the opposite. "Something's up besides the website issues. Want to tell me?"

She stared down at the hot baking sheet, looking serious and shy and even more delicious than the cookies. "What do you mean?"

"I'm not sure." He found himself gripping the spoon hard enough to bend it. "But something is different about you the past few days."

"You're very perceptive." She said it as if it was a surprise. She took the cookies to the counter and started sliding them onto a cooling rack, her back to him. "I went to see Marie on Friday."

Was this about the party? "You had lunch with her?"

"No, I went to the Milwaukeedates.com office."

Small alarm bell. He pushed another ball of dough onto the sheet. "Why?"

"I'm going to start dating."

"No." He realized how that sounded when she turned, startled. "No…way, really?"

"I know, shock, right?" She made a wry face before she went back to the cookies. "Little mouse-girl wants herself a man."

"That's not what I was thinking." This was bad. Nathan had a negative image to overcome with her; his only hope was to take things slowly. If Kim met some guy right away and was hot for him from the beginning… "You're not a mouse. More like a sleepy lioness."

"Hmph." She flushed with pleasure even as she sent him a scowl. "I don't think so."

"I do." He dipped the spoon into the bowl, trying to act casual. "Any good prospects?"

"A couple."

"Sounds promising." *Sounds horrible.* "What are they like?"

Kim left the baking sheet on the stove, ran water over the silicone mat, wiping it down carefully. "One is an author and computer geek."

He wanted to groan. The guy sounded ideal for her. "Good things."

"I don't know.…"

"No?" He tried not to sound hopeful. "Why not?"

"He's absolutely gorgeous."

Oh, just effing great. "This is a problem?"

"I don't like guys like that."

Nathan managed to unfreeze his face. "Yeah, we absolutely gorgeous guys can be real jerks."

She laughed, flicking water at him.

"What?" He blinked innocently, scraping up the last of the dough from the bowl. "What about the other one?"

"Dale? He seems pretty great."

No. Dale was not pretty great. Dale sucked. Nathan was absolutely sure of that. "Yeah? What's his deal?"

"He's some kind of consultant. Travels a lot. I wrote to him already. He wrote back right away." She came over to pick up Nathan's filled sheet; he could smell her flowery scent under the sugary vanilla aroma in the kitchen and wanted to devour her. "He's vacationing. In Jamaica."

Jamaica. This was bad. Nathan couldn't afford to take Kim to Jamaica. Nathan could barely afford to take Kim to Applebees. "He's probably there buying drugs."

"Nathan!" She swept his baking sheet over to the oven.

"Who goes to Jamaica alone for any other reason? Or no, I've got it." He pushed back his chair, turned it to face her. "He's there with his wife. Or his fourteen-year-old girlfriend. Or both."

"You are a hopeless cynic." The timer went off. Kim took out the second cookie sheet and put his batch in.

Yeah, a hopeless cynic, who happened to be struck dumb by his first sight of this woman over ten years earlier. A woman who still hadn't looked back. "I know how men think because I am one."

"You're not all of them."

He couldn't argue with that. "I'm going out with Kent and Steve tomorrow tonight. Want to come?"

"Watch you all get shit-faced and try to get laid? No thanks."

"Kim." He stood up, wanting some advantage, any advantage, even something that seemed like advantage. The invitation had come out of his mouth in desperation. Because he was desperate. "I haven't 'gotten laid' like that in quite a while."

"Not for lack of trying."

"How do you know?"

"I hear from Kent."

Nathan gestured in frustration. Kent exaggerated. Her brother never used to be so swaggering until he'd come back from New York and started hanging around with Steve, the Master Swaggerer. "That's not all I'm about. I've never tried with you."

She gave him a withering look. "Like you would."

"Why not?"

She laughed, then saw he was serious; her laughter died and she glanced at him uneasily. "I'm not exactly your type."

"No?" They were going to bust at least this part of the myth right now. "What is my type?"

"Bubbly with big boobs and a bent for blow jobs."

Instinct told him to take the joke further. So instead he caught a stray piece of her hair, stroking its soft length between his thumb and index finger, hoping she'd experience an unexpected and highly sensual shiver. "What if I told you my type was blond and shy with hidden passion waiting to be—"

"Hidden passion?" She yanked her hair back as if he were about to set it on fire.

Crap. She was not experiencing anything like an unexpected sensual shiver. "Someone else said that. There's no way I would say anything so stupid."

"Geez, Nathan." She wasn't laughing. He wasn't, either.

"You're selling me short. There have been many women I've dated who aren't bubbly and who don't have big boobs. Many." He gazed at her earnestly. She started looking cornered, folded her arms across her chest and stepped away from him. *Oh, no.* Scaring her was not what he wanted to do at all. He frowned. "Well…one, anyway. Maybe."

She laughed in nervous relief and he grinned, cursing under his breath, wishing he had the guts to stay serious with her, wishing he had the nerve to set her straight. But it was still too soon. He needed time to win her. He thought he'd have plenty. But if she was going to start dating, he'd need to regroup, find a way to get her to think differently about him much sooner than planned.

Because otherwise, he could lose even the hope of her, and after ten years of wasted time, he just wasn't willing to do that.

3

MARIE WENT DOWN THE stairs from Roots Restaurant to the Cellar bar. Quinn Peters would be waiting there for their usual Friday night "meeting." She'd call it a date, but she'd promised herself to keep any and all romantic thoughts about Quinn firmly under control, under wraps, underground. No point being a masochist by indulging in such fantasies.

She was late tonight. Ten minutes before she was due to leave, her delightful ex-husband, Grant, had called. He rarely did, but whenever his number showed up on caller ID, it was a guarantee Marie had some teeth-clenching time ahead of her. Tonight had been no exception. The louse had the nerve to ask if she'd consider returning the ruby-and-diamond channel-set ring he'd given her for their tenth and final anniversary, the one Marie called the Guilt Ring because Grant had already been having an affair with Lizzy, a woman nearly half his age.

Part of Marie wanted to give the ring back, preferably by jamming it down his throat. She wasn't, and might never be, at a place where she could happily wear it again, so why not let it shine on someone else's finger?

Because the other part of her, maybe not the most mature and gracious part, didn't want to give him anything he wanted. Ever. Because he'd taken from her a good chunk of self-confidence, and though she'd come a long way, she was still struggling to get the rest of it back.

After she'd hung up the phone it had taken her half an hour to calm down to the point where she'd be able to face Quinn calmly and cheerfully.

Her stomach did a little flip. There he was, sitting at the long wooden bar, one empty seat beside him in the otherwise crowded room. Temperatures had flirted with fifty degrees that day; everyone seemed to be emerging from winter hibernation, restless for spring.

"Hi there." She climbed onto the chair next to him, keeping her smile bright, hoping he couldn't tell she'd been crying. They'd settled into a comfortable weekly routine of meeting for drinks and dinner. At first she'd been surprised he'd want to spend that much time with her, especially on Fridays, a prime date night. Before they'd become friends, they'd both been casual regulars at the bar, and Marie had been fascinated by his success with women. His relaxed charm hooked 'em nearly every time. The fact that he looked like George Clooney didn't hurt.

"Marie." His welcoming grin always turned her a little giddy. She knew better than to react that way to Quinn, but her inner whatever-it-was insisted on rebelling. Luckily, she'd stopped short of falling seriously since he'd told her how much she reminded him of his sister.

Pop goes the ego…

"What are you drinking tonight?" Not that she needed to ask. "Oh, gin martini, something new and different."

"Why mess with perfection?" He lifted his glass to toast her. "What'll you have? My treat tonight."

"Your treat?" Marie hung her purse on a hook under the bar. "Why, did something good happen?"

"No, actually, something bad."

"Oh, no." She turned with concern. He didn't look upset— he didn't look anything but gorgeous, as usual—but in her experience men could hide their feelings better than women. "What is it?"

He shrugged. "I don't know."

"Uh." Her eyebrows shot up. "You don't know?"

"No, but I hope you'll tell me."

"Quinn, how many of those have you had?" She touched the base of his glass. "Something bad happened to you and *I'm* supposed to know what it is?"

"Not to me." He flagged Joe, the dreamy-eyed bartender, on her behalf. As independent and competent as Marie was, moments of being taken care of like this were delicious. "Something bad happened to you."

Marie gaped at him. "What gave me away?"

"You were late, you're moving more slowly than usual, your body language is tense and you're wearing heavier makeup around your eyes."

"Sherlock, you impress me."

"Thank you."

"Marie, good to see you." Joe put a coaster on the bar in front of her, his arm muscles ripped and rippling. He must spend half his life in a weight room. "What's it going to be?"

"How about a Manhattan?"

"Manhattan it is." He gestured between Marie and Quinn. "Will you want to order food now or wait awhile?"

"Are you hungry, Quinn?" Marie put a hand to her stomach, still churning from her recent fury and frustration. "I can hold off."

"Same here. We'll wait, Joe."

"No problem. Your drink will be right up, Marie." He tapped the bar smartly and turned to reach for a bottle of bourbon.

"So you get to decide." Quinn's touch was gentle on her forearm. "Do you want to talk fun stuff to cheer you up or do you want to tell me what happened?"

Marie bit her lip. She hadn't been planning to spill, but the idea of unburdening appealed to her. Her ex had this way of making her question everything she knew to be right and true. "Grant called."

"Oh, that sounds uplifting."

"Like a too-tight WonderBra." She rubbed her aching forehead. "He wants me to return the ring he gave me for our tenth anniversary, when the marriage was already over but I didn't know it yet, so he can give it to his second wife for their fifth."

Quinn's easy, sympathetic smile turned to granite. "He what?"

"He figured I'd want to get rid of it, I guess." She laughed at her ex's typically insensitive and self-centered logic. "I see his point, but—"

"Are you kidding me? What point? He has none." Quinn looked murderous and James Bond tough. "A gift is a gift. Not a loan, not a ransom and not a weapon. Your ex has the emotional IQ of a clam. Except for all I know, clams are very empathetic, and he doesn't even rate that high."

She managed a smile, relieved when Joe put her drink down and she could take that first icy gulp. The intensity of Quinn's anger was thrilling. Brave knight defending the damsel in distress. Thrilling and dangerous, because against her best instincts, that level of passion had her wondering how much this sexy knight would summon for his real lady. "Thank you, Quinn."

"I hope you're furious as well as upset."

She shrugged. "I don't wear the ring. I hate everything it represents, but it is beautiful. Maybe it should be enjoyed by someone."

"Then give it to Goodwill. Sell it on eBay." He gestured too hard with his glass and splashed gin on the bar, but didn't appear to notice. "Don't let that cheap, cheating bastard have it back."

Oh, Quinn. Marie took a turn with a comforting hand on his forearm, chiding herself for thinking his emotions had everything to do with her. Quinn had plenty to be furious about from the contents of his own baggage cart. His wife had cheated on him, married the other man, cheated on him, too, married the third one.… Who knew how long that twisted cycle would go on? "You're absolutely right. I shouldn't even be considering sending it back to him. In some ways it would be a relief to get rid of the thing, but then I'd torture myself thinking of *her* wearing it."

"Unless…" Quinn turned slowly toward her. As always, she had to clear her mind when he set that wicked grin on full blast.

"Uh-oh, what's that look for?"

He put down his drink and startled Marie by cupping her chin to bring her head closer, putting his fine, fine lips next to her ear. "Unless you send the ring directly to his wife with warmest wishes."

"*Why* would I do that?" Shivers had gone through Marie's body that had less to do with the vibrations of his deep voice and more to do with him being so close and touching her face.

Crazy girl.

"So you can make sure she knows where it came from and what kind of truly special and generous guy Grant is to want it back, just for her."

Marie giggled, her bad mood dissolving in the masculine scent of his aftershave and the titillating thrill of his attention. "I think imagining that situation is all the revenge I need, at least right now."

"Wise woman." He turned back to his drink.

"Thanks, Quinn. It helps to be able to share this with someone who understands."

"Believe me, sweetheart, I do." He leaned over, pressing his shoulder to hers.

The intimacy became too much; Marie had to move away, reminding herself that he was a compulsive player. Reminding herself how lucky she was to be able to claim his friendship for the past couple of months, a relationship that undoubtedly had lasted longer than any of his recent romantic brushes with women. "Now that we've dismissed my clam of an ex, how was your week?"

"My week was dull."

"How so?" She put on her most sugary smile. "No hot babe action?"

He scowled at her. "Marie..."

"Only six or seven this week? Three the most you could get in one night?"

He shook his head. "You are too much."

No, she wasn't enough. She patted his shoulder. "Sorry. You know I love to tease you about your...expertise."

"I did know that." He hunched his shoulders, let them drop. "It's actually been a while."

"Really?" She wasn't sure what to do with his serious reaction. Usually he joked right along with her. "How come?"

"The chase is losing its appeal."

Marie frowned at his profile. She'd never seen him like this, defenses nearly breachable. "Why do you think that is?"

"Primarily because of what I was catching."

"Germs? Viruses? STDs? What?"

He chuckled. "That's why I love you, Marie. You are smart, funny, compassionate and truly disgusting."

"Thank you, dear." She felt a blush rising and was mortified, which made her blush hotter. Men of his ilk should not be allowed to say "I love you" unless they meant it. "Go on about leaving the chase. I really do want to hear why you think it's not satisfying anymore."

"Well." He finished a sip, put his glass down, smoothed the edges of the napkin under it. "I'm thinking it might be time for a deeper connection. One that's longer lasting. Maybe a rela—"

"Uh-oh."

"A rela-a—" He clutched at his throat, made a horrible choking noise. "Rela-a-a—"

"—tionship?"

"Thank you." He mopped at his brow. "One of those."

She rolled her eyes and laughed at his act, feeling sick underneath. She shouldn't be making this about her, but if

Quinn got a girlfriend, she could lose him, would probably lose him. She'd have to face how much he'd come to mean to her. And why she was no longer putting any serious thought or effort into matching him up with Darcy. "Congratulations, Quinn. This is a great step forward."

"Thanks." He moved restlessly in the chair. "So when do you take *your* great step forward?"

"Me?" His question startled her; she laughed shortly. "I'm not interested in getting married again."

"Did I say married?"

"No, I know, I know." She waved his comment away, wishing he'd change the subject. "Right now I'm not interested in any of it."

"Hmm." He tilted his head, eyebrow quirked suggestively. "Not in any of it?"

Marie's face caught fire again. What would he do if she said she was dying for sex? Probably recommend a friend. Some dumpling-shaped guy more appropriate for her. "I'm happy alone. It's going to stay that way for a good while longer."

"Okay, then." He emptied his martini, put the glass down, signaled to Joe. "I'm having another drink. You want one, too?"

She felt rebuked and wasn't sure why. "Not yet. Maybe food?"

"Sure. Menu, too, Joe? Thanks."

The couple beside Quinn got up and left. A new couple sat down, arms around each other, heads together, giggling. They were probably in their late twenties, a dozen years younger than Marie, more than fifteen younger than Quinn. Marie wanted them to be exactly that carefree and happy together for the rest of their lives, and it saddened her that the odds weren't great.

"Hey." She punched Quinn playfully. "You want to tell me why you shut down all of a sudden?"

"Sorry." He turned in the chair so he was facing her. "I'm on edge tonight."

"I 'fessed up earlier. Your turn now."

"Nothing really." He shrugged. "Probably just that I'm ready for spring and spring isn't ready for me."

She rolled her eyes. "Honey, it's March. This isn't Florida. You've got months yet."

"That I knew."

"What else, Quinn? There's something."

"I was just thinking." He twisted his mouth. "That maybe we could have done some relationship-type things together."

Joe put down the second martini and menus—perfect timing, because Marie's heart stopped until she realized what Quinn must have meant. "You wanted to compare notes on dating?"

Quinn thanked Joe and handed her a menu. "Yes. Compare notes on dating. Misery loves company, right?"

His facial muscles had loosened, but his voice still held an edge. She wished he would confide in her. Maybe a conquest had gone wrong? A woman had turned him down? Maybe two? Enough to make him lose confidence?

She couldn't imagine Quinn anything but confident. Especially with women.

"I can't go down that road, Quinn." In any other difficulty she'd be first in line offering him support and a figurative shoulder, but she wouldn't be able to stand hearing anything about him trying to date seriously.

"It's fine." He buried himself in his menu. "So how's the matchmaking business going with Kim?"

Marie slumped in defeat. When all else failed, bring out the change of subject. Okay. She'd go with that. She shouldn't be wasting energy wishing he felt comfortable enough with her to share whatever it was. That was for another woman someday, apparently sooner rather than later.

"Kim is terrific." Marie glanced at her watch. "As a matter of fact, she's out with Troy right now."

"Troy…"

"Cahill. Friend of Justin."

"Justin…"

"Candy's fiancé."

"Got it." His face cleared. "Candy and Justin, last month's meddling."

"*Matching,* not meddling." Marie rolled her eyes. "They're deliriously happy."

"Weren't we all."

"Oh, you cynic." She smacked him with her menu, surprised by this dark side of him tonight, and wishing she could help with whatever had caused it—short of going back in time and preventing him from marrying The CheaterBeast. "We had to go through what we went through for some reason. The trick is to figure it out and then work up the courage to move on."

"Here's to getting there." He lifted his glass.

"However long it takes." She hoisted hers; they both drank.

"You think Kim and Troy are a good match?"

Marie frowned. "I'm not sure. Kim is beautiful and very talented, but shy and a little down on herself. Troy is a very good-looking, well-put-together, wealthy man, and I think she's a little intimidated. I'm hoping she gives herself a chance to shine. She has no idea how sexy she is."

"Hmm." Quinn smirked at his drink. "That reminds me of someone."

"Yeah? Who?"

He twisted to look at her, then for some reason started laughing.

"*What* is so funny?"

"Never mind, you wouldn't get it. Just tell me, Marie. What advice would you give Kim about this problem?"

"Why?"

"I want to pass on your wisdom." He dug out his Black-Berry and pulled up a blank email. "I'll write it down and send it to her."

"Are you serious?"

"Absolutely."

"Okay." Marie looked up into the decorative hanging of tangled metal roots over the bar, trying to clear her head, muddled by bourbon and by Quinn's mood tonight. "Let's see. I'd tell her to go back though her life looking for messages she received about her sexuality and her self-esteem, and see if there's a pattern she can identify that could be informing how she feels about herself now."

"…feels…about herself…now." He put in the period with a flourish. "And?"

"Undoubtedly the message that she isn't worthy is coming from some judge figure in her life, probably a parent. She needs to tell that judge that she'll be deciding her own feelings from now on."

"…from now…on."

"And then she should dress to kill, look in a mirror and promise to give herself positive feedback every day on how she looks and who she is and what she deserves."

"…what…she deserves. That it?"

"She should probably go to therapy and talk the whole thing out, but this will help if she's honest with herself, yes."

"Excellent." He selected a recipient and punched the send button. "She'll be very surprised to hear from me."

"And pleased, I hope?"

"Me, too." He shrugged, putting the BlackBerry back in his pocket. "Want to order dinner?"

"I do." She tossed back the rest of her drink and picked up a menu, hunger signals finally able to be heard through the decreasing clamor of her emotions. Helping people feel better about themselves always made her feel better about herself, too.

She and Quinn chatted easily for the rest of the evening, all the bizarre tension completely dissipated. As usual after their Friday night meeting, she felt refreshed and revitalized on her walk home to her beloved Victorian in the same quirky Brewer's Hill neighborhood as the restaurant.

Inside her front door, she flicked on the light and said hello to her gray tabby, Jezebel, who'd come to greet her by weaving around her legs, making walking as difficult as possible. On the way up to her bedroom on the second floor, Marie sorted through the day's mail, ditched most in the recycling box near her desk, and powered up her laptop. After changing into her beloved sloppy, nonbinding and infinitely comfortable sweats, she sat at her desk and waited for Jezebel's predictable jump into her lap for the evening's kitty-worship.

She opened her email program while she scratched soft ears and brought Jezebel's rumbling purr to life. New emails: five. One from a college roommate, one from Mom and Dad...

Marie's eyes jumped down the list. One from Quinn? How did he get home so much faster than she had?

Her phone rang and she did a comical back and forth, phone to email to phone, before grabbing the receiver and checking caller ID. Candy. She'd take it.

"Hey, woman, what's up?"

"Ugh." Candy's melodramatic exasperation made Marie smile. "I just came back from the cocktail party from hell. The caterer was late, someone stole half the booze, one guest drank the other half and threw up, you name it."

"That does not sound fun." She touched her mouse, staring at Quinn's email, then snatched her hand back.

"Anyway, I'm looking ahead and life is going to be a little calmer for a week or two, so we should get serious about planning Kim's party."

"Right. We should." She swiveled her chair away from the monitor so Quinn's note wouldn't tempt her while talking to her friend, but it was as if it was sending out rays that burned her back. "I've already enlisted her brother, Kent, and that Nathan guy to help."

"Perfect. We'll need pictures of her at various ages, maybe

a few personal items, like, I don't know, some favorite stuffed animal or toy, old favorite outfits, diplomas, awards, anything like that. Her mom might have some stuff to contribute. We should also find out her favorite foods, beverages, all that, too. And figure out where we want to have it."

"We can do it at my office or we can—"

"Ooh, I forgot to ask, how did her meeting with you go? Did she like Troy?"

Marie tsk-tsked. "Client confidentiality, Candy. You can ask her."

"Aw c'mon. You can't even—" A deep voice sounded in the background, then Candy sighed. "Justin says I shouldn't snoop."

"You shouldn't."

"I hope she finds someone. She's so sweet."

Marie scratched under Jezebel's chin. "Ah, but I'm betting there's a vixen in there somewhere."

"A *vixen!*" Candy whistled. "Has anyone used that term in the past twenty years?"

"So I'm old." She rolled her eyes. "Go jump on Justin and leave me alone."

"Mmm, good idea." Candy sighed blissfully. "So I'll plan and you set our spies in motion. Oh, and I had a great idea for an early birthday present from the three of us, you, me and Darcy. Next Saturday I want to try out a salon where I might get my wedding hair done. I think we should make it a spa day, invite everyone and then pay for Kim."

"I love it! I was thinking along the lines of sexy underwear to inspire her on the dating quest."

"Ha!" Candy giggled. "That is too perfect. Let's do both."

"Done." Marie gave in, twisted around and peeked. She hadn't dreamed it; the email was still there.

Candy chatted a minute more, then Marie made her escape and shamelessly spun the chair back to her computer, Jezebel giving a brief *mrrf* of protest. Marie clicked open

the email from Quinn, scanned the words, caught her breath
and read them again, her brain whirling in confusion.

Go back though your life looking for messages you
received about your sexuality...

Why had he sent the email to *her?* A blind copy? A car-
bon? A mistake? She peered at the header. He'd sent it to
her directly. And she'd been sitting right there at Roots; he
hadn't sent it twice. What the hell?
That reminds me of someone I know. He'd been talking about another woman who didn't realize how sexy she
was.
He couldn't be talking about Marie.
She hit Reply, typed quickly.

Did you send this to me by mistake? Or is this a blind
copy?

Then she hit Send and got up from the desk, pushing a
very annoyed Jezebel off her lap because there was no way
she'd survive sitting there waiting for him to respond. She'd
go completely mental.
Her email chimed. She whirled around in the middle of
the room. *Already?*
Of course, it could be from anyone.
She rushed to peer at the screen. It was from Quinn. A
simple response, straight to the point.

Answering both questions: Absolutely not.

BLIND DATES WERE THE devil's work. There was no other explanation. Torture of this magnitude should be prohibited by the Geneva Convention. Kim checked her watch for the fourth time, standing just inside the entrance to Coast, an elegant bar and restaurant on the shore of Lake Michigan. To her left, the dramatic, white "wings" of the Milwaukee Art Museum expansion rose into the blue sky, appearing to pierce a pair of clouds hanging overhead.

So far Troy was two minutes late. Which wouldn't be bad except that she'd gotten here five minutes early. Seven minutes standing here imagining how horribly the evening could go. How awkward it could be. How disappointed he might be in her.

Kim let out a sound of disgust. What was wrong with her? She wasn't usually glass-half-empty like this. But if Troy was half as gorgeous and successful and wonderful and kind as everyone said, she was afraid he'd show up having walked across the lake. Kim wanted someone as flawed and shy and regular as herself. Like Dale, who wasn't classically handsome, but had such warm eyes on screen. They'd been emailing back and forth since she first got up the nerve to write to him a couple days after she'd seen his picture in Marie's office. For someone on vacation he sure spent a lot of time online. Whenever she wrote, she heard back within an hour, morning, afternoon or night.

She loved writing to him. Shyness didn't matter when you had all the time you wanted to compose sentences, to find interesting and witty ways to express yourself. Kim could take all night if she felt like it, get up and pace and think until every thought, every word was just the way she wanted. In short order she and Dale had gone from where-did-you-grow-up and what's-your-favorite-movie to how-are-you-feeling and what-do-you-believe-in?

His answer still sang in her head. *I believe in God, in country, in dancing until dawn and in loving a woman until the last breath leaves my body.*

Kim had nearly melted onto her keyboard.

She moved aside for another couple entering the restaurant, and checked her watch again. Four minutes late. *Come on, Troy.* She wanted this first-meeting misery over with. His emails had been shorter than Dale's, and businesslike. He'd wanted to meet her right away, not waste time chatting online, where so much could be imagined or misunderstood. He was smart. But it meant their initial face-to-face would be so much more awkward. When she finally met Dale she'd feel she already knew him.

"Kim?"

Kim spun around. Oh, my Lord. Troy. As gorgeous as he was online. No, more so, because his dark eyes were alive and therefore twice as vivid. He was tall. She knew that, but six foot four didn't register as dramatically on screen as it did in the flesh.

"Troy. Hi."

"Hey, nice to meet you." He held out his hand, warm, dry and strong. Hers was cold, damp and trembling. "I was waiting inside at a table, then realized we hadn't mentioned where we'd meet so I came looking for you."

"Oh." She laughed stupidly, too rattled to do more than glance at his face and away. His presence was overpowering. "I should have checked."

"Not a problem. I found you. Let's go sit." His easy grin made her want to run the other way. He was obviously not finding this nerve-racking at all. Some people had no idea how lucky they were to be born without the shyness gene. The simplest things were so difficult for her. Like meeting a perfectly nice man and talking to him.

She walked next to him through the light, airy space to a table by the window facing the lake, already sure this wasn't a man she could have a relationship with. Still, if she got through the date with self-esteem intact, that would be something to celebrate. The next dates would be easier, most notably the one with Dale on Monday. That one really mattered.

Wait, so maybe it wouldn't be easier. Why was she doing this again?

They sat, Troy waiting until her butt hit the chair before he took his seat. So he was a gentleman as well as perfect.

He folded his hands on the table. "I think we know someone in common besides Justin and Candy."

"We do?" She put her purse down and braced herself to spend the next hour having to look at him.

"My neighbor Steve was in your brother's class at Marquette High. I graduated before he got there, but I used to see Kent hanging around next door."

"Oh. Yes. I know Steve." She nodded politely. Steve was a chauvinist jerk. He'd always had this weird hold over Kent that she didn't understand.

Troy quirked a dark brow, eyes dancing. "Not one of your favorites?"

"Um." She couldn't help smiling. "Not exactly."

"My sister isn't wild about him, either. Maybe he wears better on guys."

"Probably."

A tall, slender and unfairly gorgeous waitress came over, smiling directly at Troy. "What can I get you?"

"Kim?" He gestured to her. "What'll you have?"

"Oh, um, a beer?"

The waitress rattled off a list of brews and waited expectantly.

Kim grabbed the last name. "I'll have a Spotted Cow."

"And you, sir?"

"That sounds good to me, too."

"I'll have those right out." She shot a killer smile at Troy and swept away.

Awkward silence. *C'mon, Kim, think of something....*

"Well." Troy adjusted himself in the seat. "What were we talking about?"

"Oh…" Kim hadn't the faintest idea, because her brains had turned to scrambled eggs. Guys like Troy had intimidated her since adolescence, when she'd been victimized by the "popular crowd" he undoubtedly belonged to. Though it was unfair to put him in a fifteen-year-old box.

"So…what's Kent up to these days? He's in New York, right?"

"No, he's back." She had to look away, gazing at the restaurant's deck where patrons could sit in warmer weather, and out at the lake beyond, then steel herself to meet Troy's midnight eyes again. "He got laid off last fall and came home to Milwaukee."

"Damn. Has he found a job yet?"

"A couple of months ago, with M&I Bank."

"Good for him."

"He was happy." She smirked. "So were my parents. He was living with them for a while."

Troy laughed. "Tell him I said hello."

"I will." She looked down at the table, hating the silence, worrying about what to say next. "He plays basketball. Do you?"

"I do." By some miracle Troy looked really interested. "Does he have a game going?"

"Yes." Kim perked up, encouraged by his reaction. "Sunday afternoons. They're looking for more people. Do you want his number?"

"I'd love it." He dug out his cell. "Go ahead."

She rattled off the number; he put it into his phone.

"Here we go." The waitress set down their beers. "Will you be ordering off the menu?"

"Not just yet, thanks." Troy picked up his glass and held it toward Kim. "Cheers."

She clinked with him and took a long sip, feeling cattily delighted that he hadn't so much as glanced at the gorgeous waitress. And having been able to do Troy the favor of connecting him with her brother, she felt less like she was out on a date with a movie star and more like he was one of the gang.

"Tell me about this book you're writing, Troy."

He answered easily, with his usual charm and poise, but she no longer let it throw her, and by the end of their second beer and a shared appetizer, they were giggling together like old friends. He even brainstormed a few ideas for the Carter website, though she found them too masculine for the look she thought Carter wanted.

"Ready to go?" He stood, having taken care of the bill despite her offer to split it.

"I'm ready, yes." She preceded him out of the restaurant and they walked together to the garage where they'd both parked, chatting about how great it felt to have warmer weather. Once there, he was gallant enough to make sure she got safely to her car. "Thanks for a great time, Troy. I enjoyed meeting you."

"Same here. We should do this again sometime."

She had to force herself not to snort. According to Kent, guys said that regardless of whether they meant it or not. "I'd like that, yes."

Dating ritual: complete. But the evening had been a success because she'd had fun even though he was unbelievably gorgeous. And if that sounded weird, it was just Kim being Kim.

"Great." He backed away a few steps and raised his hand in farewell. "I'll give you a call."

She couldn't resist. "You don't have my number."

"Oh, geez." He rolled his eyes and came back sheepishly. "Smooth, huh?"

She shook her head mock-disparagingly, liking him more. Troy the Magnificent had done a dorky thing. "I've completely changed my mind about seeing you again."

He cracked up, opening his cell. "Don't blame you."

She gave him her number, said good-night, then grinned all the way home. Hey, guess what? She'd lived through a date with a totally hot guy. How about that?

And maybe back at her apartment, an email from Dale would be waiting on her laptop. If this kept up Kim would start thinking she was some kind of megababe.

She arrived home and let herself in to find Nathan sprawled on the couch in the dark, watching the giant high-definition TV he'd brought from his old place and set up in her living room. Honestly. Men must have done all the prehistoric cave paintings, because otherwise what would they have to stare at all evening?

"Hi, Nathan." She walked past him, heading for the laptop in her room and her latest fun email from Dale. Two men in one evening? She was getting greedy.

"Kim. Hey." He sat bolt upright and turned off the set. "How was your date?"

Wait, he'd turned off the set? She backtracked and peered at him through the dim light. Was he feeling okay?

"Hello?" He frowned at her, snapped his fingers. "Your date?"

"The date was fine." She couldn't help another grin, coupled with a giggle. Maybe the beers helped her giddiness along, but she didn't think that was all. "Great, actually."

"Yeah?" He didn't look thrilled. "I thought this guy was too gorgeous."

Kim shrugged, picked up one of the throw pillows from the couch and punched at it to fluff it up. "Yeah, well. Apparently not."

He got up and stretched. "You going to see him again?"

"Very possibly." She twirled the pillow between her

fingers, trying to act supremely casual. Gorgeous guy after her? Sure, why not?

"What about this *Dale* guy?" Nathan said the name as if it were a disease.

"I'm seeing him Monday." Kim tossed the fluffed pillow up in the air, her hands ready to catch it.

Nathan grabbed it out of the air and threw it back onto the couch.

Startled, she looked up at him. He was staring at her oddly.

"Wh—" The word didn't make it out the first time and she had to clear her throat to try again. "What? Why are you staring at me like that?"

Had he always been that tall? That broad? Maybe the twilight in the room made him more impressive. Against the glow coming through the unshaded windows he loomed large and male, not threatening, but…she felt nervous, edgy, as if she should step away from him. Why should she? Nathan wasn't dangerous.

He just seemed it right now.

"You're really doing this dating thing, huh?" His voice was gruff, not his familiar casual tone.

She had plenty of sassy in-his-face responses, starting with *Don't you think it's about time?* Moving on to *Why, you think you're the only one who needs sex?* But all she could do was stare at his darkened face, trying to read his mood.

He swallowed audibly. "Kim…"

This was weird. Too intimate somehow. All wrong with Nathan. "You don't think I should be dating?"

"No. No, you should be. Absolutely."

"So where's the problem?"

"There is no problem." He reached out and touched her shoulder. He'd touched her before, but this felt different, as if she was supposed to find meaning in it. All she found was more confusion. "I hope you find someone great. Someone who treats you like the amazing woman you are. Someone who respects every part of you, everything you do and believe, and everything you want."

Was he making fun of her? He didn't sound as if he was, but more than once she'd bought into some sincerity act and had it bite her on the ass when he cracked up with a *gotcha*.

She gave a stuttering laugh. "Well. Okay then. Thanks, Nathan."

"Right." He backed away. "I'll just go back to *my* hot date. With Miss St. Pauli Girl."

Kim took an impulsive step forward. What the hell? Now he did sound annoyed. And sulky. What was with him?

He turned and went into the kitchen. Through the pass-through she could see him by the refrigerator light. Seconds later, a bottle top rattled to the counter—where he would undoubtedly leave it. "Want a beer?"

"I had some earlier. I'm going to my room."

He emerged from the kitchen. "Rushing to see what Jamaica Dale has written?"

Kim bristled, since yes, that was exactly what she was going to do, and it was none of his business. "Actually, I'm tired. I'm going to read for a while."

"Uh-huh." He tipped the beer up to his mouth, a shadowy figure leaning against the doorway between the living and dining rooms.

"What is with you tonight?"

He lowered the bottle, gave her a look she couldn't see in the dim light, but said nothing. His silence made her nervous, which, combined with her irritation, made her want to jab at him, get some reaction.

"Why aren't you out on your night off, trying to get some? It's Friday, prime hunting. The dewy-eyed does must be out in force."

He pushed himself away from the wall, pausing to put his beer on the end table. "Is that what you think of me? That my life is all drinking and sex?"

Nathan didn't talk like this. He was always making fun

of himself, his sexual prowess, his TV habits, his love of a good beer or two or three. He must be teasing. Setting her up again. It just didn't sound like it.

"No, I'm sure there are one or two waking hours during which you think about something else." She held up a hand to count off fingers. "Like when you're thinking about food. Or sleep."

He started toward her. She stepped back, stifling a giggle. This was more like it. She teased, he pretended to get angry, it was all part of their game. Like family. Like siblings.

"*Or* I'm sure sometimes you think about how to get away from the woman you just did, in case she actually expects conversation— *Oh!*"

He'd lunged, grabbed her wrists and pinned them up against the wall over her head. His face loomed closer. For one completely absurd second she thought he was going to kiss her, and she caught her breath, heart beating wildly. This wasn't their game. He was changing the rules.

"Is that really what you think of me?"

She laughed, waited for him to join in, to let on that this was a ho-ho-funny joke on big sister Kim.

Nothing. She tried to pull her hands down, but let them be when he tightened his grip.

"Nathan, what are you doing?"

The apartment seemed eerily silent around them. No traffic noises outside, no pedestrian voices. She swore she could hear the sound of her blood rushing through her veins.

"It's not all about parties and women for me."

"Okay. I mean, I know. I mean…I'm sure it's not." Her voice was breathless. She didn't know whether to tease him or humor him. She wanted him to let go, but she couldn't seem to make herself tell him to release her.

Because…?

Because she knew he would.

Gah, she didn't even want to admit it. Nathan, big goofy jovial Nathan, had turned into this…*caveman,* and she was getting off on it. If this turned out to be a *gotcha* game, it wasn't funny. Not even close.

"I think about lots of things." His voice was low and even. He could probably hear her irregular breathing. This was crazy. *This was Nathan.* Except it wasn't.

"Yeah?" She was whispering. Couldn't even summon a normal tone. *Damn it, Nathan, what are you doing?* "What other things?"

He narrowed his eyes, glanced down at her lips. Kim shrank back against the wall, her heart still pounding. What had gotten into him tonight? What had gotten into *her*? "I'm waiting."

Nathan took in a long, nearly silent breath. "Sometimes when I wake up in the middle of the night and it's quiet, or sometimes during a daydream, I think about what it would be like to—" He stopped as if he were about to choke on his words. "I think about…"

Kim held her breath.

His body suddenly relaxed. "You know, how long it's been since I last had sex."

She burst out laughing, sounding like a manic hyena. The release of tension was part relief, part disappointment. Yes, *gotcha*. He'd done it again. She should have seen the punch line coming. But this time, truly, she'd thought he was going to tell her something real, something important. And she'd surprised herself by dying to know what it was.

"I'm going to my room, you complete nutcase. Good night." She escaped through her door, wedged it shut, and then collapsed against it with a long breath.

Nathan?

No. No-no-no. A bizarre aberration, a bizarre and *temporary* aberration. Going out with Troy and corresponding with Dale must have made Kim into a hyped-up nymphomaniac, or convinced her all men would find her irresistible. Thank God Nathan brought her down to earth by teasing her.

She crossed her room swiftly, flung open her laptop and opened her email program. At the top of the list, a reply from Dale, giving her that great, giddy rush. A quick check of the time on his note showed he'd answered only half an hour after she'd sent hers early that afternoon. Did he take his laptop to the beach? She couldn't imagine. Too much sand. Maybe poolside? She wished she was there with him. Jamaica. How exotic and romantic.

Dear Kim,

As always, I was so happy to hear from you. Your emails are such a bright spot. I can hardly wait to meet you on Monday. Tomorrow is my last day here. The temperatures have been ideal, and I'll miss the tangle of flowers everywhere, the smell of the sea, breakfast on the balcony overlooking the Caribbean... But think what a lovely view I'll have across the table from you! Worth coming home for a chance to try out some in-person conversation. I have no doubt that we'll hit it off. You sound like a fascinating and very lovely woman.

Today was another long bout of indulgence. Tennis in the morning with a guy I met here, a relaxing afternoon on the beach and a little shopping before dinner. I bought you a souvenir. Not to worry, it's nothing fancy.

Can't wait to hear from you again.

Dale

Kim gave a big sigh and dropped her chin onto her hand, gazing dreamily at the words on the screen. Her world had righted itself. Dale sounded so great. She couldn't wait to meet him. She just wished he didn't keep saying how amazing she sounded. Not that she was chopped liver, even Troy had said he wanted to see her again, but...she really didn't want to disappoint Dale.

She got up from the computer and went over to her mirror,

peered at her face, her hair a plain blunt cut past her shoulders, makeup very basic: mascara and lip gloss. She'd worn plain black pants and a blue sweater tonight, nice clothes, but maybe not those a "fascinating, very lovely" woman would wear. Would she make a bad first impression? Would he expect something more from the way she sounded online, where she could choose her words so carefully? Where it was easy to be bold?

She turned to the side, held her hair up with both hands, trying to see how she'd look with it back. To one side? Parted differently?

Dropping her arms, she scowled at herself. Who was she kidding? She couldn't let even this tiny amount of dating success go to her head. She was who she was, and men had better appreciate her that way, or not at all. Because she wasn't changing for anyone.

Except maybe herself.

"SORRY I'M LATE. I was picking out flowers for the reception." Candy landed breathlessly into the seat opposite Kim, next to Marie. They'd gathered at Jane's Sandwich Shop in a Fox Point strip mall for lunch before trying out the salon next door, La Bellezza, which Candy was considering using on her wedding day. "Kim, what did you think of Troy?"

Kim exchanged glances with an amused Marie. "Hi, Candy. Nice to see you. How are you doing?"

"Sorry, sorry." She shoved her purse and shopping bag under the table. "Hi, Kim. Hi, Marie. It's good to see both of you, I'm so glad we planned this afternoon, you're both looking great. Kim, how was your date with Troy?"

Kim laughed. "He's a great guy. I enjoyed his company."

"And? And?" She pounded the table. "Details, woman. Are you going to see him again?"

Kim felt herself blushing. "He *said* he wanted to, but—"

"Awesome!" Candy gave a thumbs-up. "This calls for a drink. You both with me?"

"Sure, why not." Marie grinned, casual but still totally put-together in loosely clinging pants and a tunic top. "I'm not doing any work on a Saturday afternoon. Kim?"

"I always have work I *could* do, but…" She shrugged. She'd done some that morning after her ballet class, starting a redesign on a site for a local bestselling author who wanted her image changed about every six months. Fine by Kim; she got paid. Her other jobs she could hold off for a half day with no problem. The Carter bid was still the same thorn in her same side. "Count me in."

On cue a plump blond waitress came by. "Hi, ladies, can I get you something to drink?"

"Absolutely." Candy grabbed the wine menu and handed it to Marie. "Choose a bottle of something for us, Marie."

"Yes, ma'am."

"Thanks." Candy shook back her chestnut hair and clipped it into a ponytail. "I have a feeling we're all going to love this salon. Justin's mother has a friend who'd heard about it clear over in California. I guess she has family here who say it's absolute pamper heaven."

"Works for me." Marie pointed at the drink menu for the waitress. "We'll have a bottle of the Washington State Chardonnay, please."

"Pamper heaven sounds great." Kim forced enthusiasm into her voice. She'd agreed to come today, but the whole chic salon thing was better suited to women such as Marie and Candy. Kim had been to a fancy salon once before, when her friend Becky got married, and had found the women snooty, the skin and body treatments of dubious benefit, and the products wildly overpriced. She could use a haircut, that would be nice, but for a basic trim she hardly needed La Bellezza. Or its prices.

Instead she'd look at it as a great excuse to spend girls'-day-out time. That was worth plenty. She'd do whatever was cheapest and try not to panic over the cost.

"Kim, have you heard from Dale?"

"Yes." She kept her eyes on her menu and miraculously

managed not to blush yet again. "We've been corresponding pretty regularly. I'll finally meet him on Monday."

"How does he sound?" Candy asked.

"Pretty fabulous. He's in Jamaica right now. I guess he travels a lot. He's been all over the world. The Far East, Australia, the Middle East, Europe, everywhere." She closed her menu, still not having decided, and smiled wanly while her friends made appropriate ooh and aah noises. "We've been having great chats."

"But?" Marie, always the perceptive one.

"I'm…not sure I'm being myself, exactly. I mean I'm flirting with him, and it's really fun, but online it's easy and safe, and not real. I can't be that person. I'm afraid when we meet he's going to be disappointed."

"Troy wasn't disappointed," Candy said.

"He had no expectations. I probably made my life sound more exciting to Dale than it is, and probably made myself sound more sophisticated. I'm probably worrying over nothing. He does seem sweet."

"I don't see the problem." Candy winked at Marie. "But I do know the solution."

Marie was grinning. "Uh-huh."

Kim glanced warily between them. "What's going on?"

"Candy and I have an early birthday present for you. And Darcy, but she couldn't get away from the restaurant today."

The waitress arrived with their wine and Kim had to wait while the bottle was opened and a half inch was poured for Marie to try.

"It's the perfect solution. You are worried about how you'll come across and we're going to a beauty salon in an hour." Candy gestured toward her, top to bottom. "We're giving you a makeover."

"*Me?* I don't think—"

"Well, we do." Marie nodded her approval of the wine; the waitress went around the table pouring. "It's perfect. A new haircut, makeup and you'll feel like the woman you think you're only pretending to be."

"And since we'll all be tipsy and don't have anything else going on, we're taking you shopping afterward for a first-date blow-him-away outfit." She lifted her glass. "Casually sophisticated. Sexy without being obvious."

"What do you think, Kim?" Marie asked in her gentle therapist voice. "Of course, we won't force you."

"Oh, yes, we will." Candy giggled when Marie glared. "Okay, we'll *encourage you strongly,* how's that."

"I don't think I'd be comfortable—" Kim broke off. Something deep inside her was shimmering with excitement. Too often she said no to anything that took her out of her comfort zone, and her comfort zone had always been pretty damn small. Maybe she needed to start saying yes more often. Maybe she already had. Yes to trying for the Carter job. Yes to dating.

Yes to a makeover at one of the city's best salons?

"It's not going to be that drastic, Kim." Marie tossed her menu on the table. "Not like you'll shave half your head and get a nose ring."

"Or spend future dates talking human sacrifices." Candy giggled behind her hand. "And showing off the tattoos on your—"

"You'll still be you," Marie said. "You, with a little extra pizzazz."

"I don't know." Kim wrinkled her nose, took another sip of wine, excitement skipping through her. She wanted to say yes, but she couldn't make herself do it yet. "I hadn't planned on this. I'm not really the spontaneous type."

"Try being that way just this afternoon."

"We won't pressure you into anything you don't want to do, Kim." Marie gave Candy a warning look. "We'll have lunch, and you think about it. You don't have to decide until you're sitting in the salon chair. You have time."

"Okay." The shimmers wouldn't leave her alone. She imagined herself in some low-cut slit-up-to-there black dress, breasts pushed front and center, sultry makeup transforming her into the kind of sophisticate she'd always admired. Parading in front of Troy, watching his jaw drop. Parading in front of Dale. Ditto with his jaw. While she was at it, parading in front of Tony, the jerk jock who'd messed with her head in college. Hey, Tony, how geeky did she look now? Parading into the apartment in front of…Nathan.

Kim reached for her wine again, took a shaky sip. She did not need to be worrying about what *he* thought. He'd always been another little brother to her, and Kim was and always had been the big sister he never had.

The three women gabbed on through lunch, the bottle of wine and coffee, then walked next door to the salon, giggling over everything and nothing. Candy opened the front door and gestured Kim through, but not before Kim saw her exchanging crossed-fingers with Marie. The two were undoubtedly trying to figure out how to get her to agree to try a new look.

She caught a glimpse of herself in a mirror in the entranceway. Cheeks flushed by wine, eyes snapping with excitement… She looked radiant. But plain. Her eyes could use definition. Her hair could use shaping.

Marie was right. Kim wouldn't be changing, not really. Though by agreeing to sign up for Milwaukeedates.com she was already changing. Finding the courage to date a guy like Troy, to flirt with a man like Dale. So maybe rather than a Band-Aid to help her feel better about herself, a makeover could be another step in that evolution. She'd certainly been feeling differently lately on the inside. Why not see if she could show something different on the outside, too?

Because she'd feel like a phony. On those introvert days when she didn't want to leave her house or talk to anyone, where she'd disappear into her world of design to escape having to put effort into human interaction. The haircut and makeup wouldn't fit that woman.

"Hi, ladies. Welcome." The receptionist had makeup so lush she resembled a painting of a woman.

There was no way Kim could do that to herself.

They were led to dressing rooms to change into robes and slippers, then offered snacks and bottled water. First, they got hot stone massages: heated, oiled stones used to smooth out kinked muscles. Facials second: steamed, scrubbed, moisturized. Showers third: Swedish stalls with a luxurious embarrassment of showerheads. Shampoos fourth, then Kim sat in the chair looking at herself in the mirror, hair a sodden tangle, skin tingling from the treatments, muscles relaxed, head still buzzing pleasantly from the wine.

This was the life.

"Hi, I'm Jenny. What would you like to do today, Kim?"

"I just want a trim?" She hadn't meant to make it a question. "Or...I don't know."

The woman held up a length of her hair and gazed into the mirror. "That's it?"

"Oh. Well...maybe more?"

"If I could suggest something."

Kim had a feeling Marie and Candy had put her up to this. "Okay."

"You need a shorter length with a bang to bring out those dynamite eyes and those incredible cheekbones. They're lost in this length. Minimal makeup. Your skin is gorgeous on its own. Women would kill to have your pores."

"Oh. Thank you." Kim tried to look pleased. She was very glad she had never thought to worry about her pores, and doubly glad to know now that she wouldn't need to worry about them in the future.

"Will you let me try? I think you'll be pleased with the result."

The Kim parade began again in her mind. Sexy cut, sexy outfit, sexy Kim. Troy, Dale, Tony...

And again, Nathan, holding Sexy Kim's wrists above her head in the dark room, his wide body hovering over hers.

She met the stylist's eyes in the mirror and gave a firm nod, lips pressed tightly together.

"Do it."

5

KIM TOOK THE ELEVATOR up to the third floor in her building, grateful it was empty and that Nathan would be tending bar at the Hi Hat Lounge. She was anxious to get inside her apartment without anyone seeing her, to have private time to take in her new look.

What had seemed exciting and right while she sat in the chair had turned exciting and right and scary as long clumps of her hair succumbed to the scissors. She'd ended up with a deftly highlighted, chin-length bob with slanted bangs. The makeup, which she insisted be applied with a light hand, emphasized her eyes and cheekbones, and colored her lips into sensual splendor.

She looked great. And very different. Older. More sophisticated. Sexier. To her embarrassment, Marie and Candy had squealed loudly when she'd emerged into the lavish lobby all done up. Then they'd carted her off to roughly twenty million stores—at least it felt like that many—to find the fabled outfit that would make men fall at her feet.

They'd found it. Or rather, Marie and Candy found it—and insisted on buying—a low-cut white cashmere sweater and a clingy, deep rose skirt. With matching shoes. Another couple of pieces Kim bought for herself with their approval. They'd insisted she keep on the purple scoop-neck minidress with an Empire waistline that did flattering things to her figure and image, and the black pumps they declared gave her legs enough punch to knock guys out. Kim wasn't sure. On the way back she'd passed several men and not one had keeled over.

She giggled, blaming the wine. After the shopping, Marie had insisted another drink was in order. Kim would probably be hungover before dinner. Nice.

The elevator doors opened and she walked down the shabby hall to her door in the unfamiliar heels, which hadn't tripped her yet, but she was sure it was only a matter of time. Her key hit the lock and turned. Whew. Safe haven. She scurried inside and froze, one hand clutching the doorknob.

Nathan. Not at work. Standing in their living room. Wearing nothing but a towel.

Oh, my God. He had the body of an Olympic diver. He had hair on his chest. He was a *man*. A real one.

Oh, my God.

"Kim." He was staring as if he'd never seen her before, either. "You look incredible."

She had no idea what to do or what to say. The heat in his eyes was unmistakable. He hadn't fallen at her feet yet, but he looked as if he might.

Or maybe kneel there. Put his arms around her thighs and press his face to—

Kim, get a grip.

Letting go of the doorknob was a good first step. Next, she put down her packages, which contained her old clothes and the rest of the new, including a little black dress very much like the one in her parade-in-front-of-men fantasy. She couldn't imagine when she'd wear it, but once Marie and Candy saw it on her, that was that.

"Why aren't you at work?"

"Traded shifts. I'm going later. What did you do to yourself?" He hadn't stopped staring. She didn't think he'd even blinked.

"I went to a salon. With friends. And then shopping." She

dragged her eyes away from his muscled chest and arms and from his predatory gaze, but they dragged themselves back.

He was handsome. Not just cute. Handsome in a more real way than Troy's dark perfection. His brown hair was still wet, and bits of it stood on end all over his head, making him look sexily disheveled. His jaw was smooth-shaven. The scents of soap and aftershave even made inhaling in the same room arousing.

Nathan was *hot*.

He walked toward her, stopped six feet away when she put up her hand, warding off the unknown.

"Kim." His voice was deep, husky. "You look like a completely different woman."

"No. No, no. I'm not." Immediately, she wanted her long hair back, wanted to run to the bathroom and wash off the new face. She did not want to look like one of the women Nathan collected. She didn't want him attracted to her for that reason.

Wait, she didn't want him attracted to her for *any* reason.

"Hey, hey. No. Of course you're not." He was speaking uncharacteristically slowly, as if the sight of her had run down his brain. Blood draining somewhere else? She glanced at his towel; she couldn't help it. No, thank goodness, nothing that obvious. "I just said you look different. You look incredible."

So do you.

She couldn't say that. Up close his body was even more beautiful and even more disconcerting. His skin looked soft and touchable, the muscle tough and sensually masculine.

"Thank you. You look very…" She gestured vaguely to his torso, eyes down somewhere by his knees. "Clean."

When he didn't respond, she lifted her eyes and immediately wished she hadn't, because his gaze gripped hers and held on. She'd seen men's bodies before, had admired men's bodies before, but had never wanted to touch and taste like this. Was it the wine? The makeup? The outfit? Was she going to turn into someone as shallow in pursuit of the opposite sex as Nathan?

Look at him, practically drooling just because she'd changed her appearance. What about last night? She wasn't worth drooling over then?

He'd pressed her to the wall, leaned close, but no, not drooling; it was all a big ha-ha joke on her. Good thing she hadn't known what that body looked like under his clothes or she would have been even more tempted, and then humiliated by the *gotcha*.

She had to break this crazy spell.

"I'm going to change and wash this stuff off. You hungry? I assume you're going to want to put something on besides a towel for dinner?"

He blinked, as if she'd woken him from a trance, and gestured to his lack of outfit. "Yeah, I was in the shower and remembered I don't have any…clean underwear."

The look on his face was so boyishly sheepish that she was able to forget the body. Yup. Still Nathan. So, fine. They'd had a weird connection on some other level than they were used to, that was all. For a few seconds they'd been attractive strangers to each other. Now back to normal.

"Go commando then. Stir-fry tonight? I found a recipe for orange-beef with broccoli that sounds great. I could use help if you feel like it." She walked past him, aware she was babbling. "You finished in the bathroom?"

"It's all yours."

She spun around and eyed him like a disapproving schoolteacher. "In this bathroom that you are all finished with, will I find dirty clothes on the floor and the bath mat not put back?"

"Um…" He made a beeline for the bathroom door, holding her off with an outstretched hand. "Be right out. I, uh, forgot to shave twice."

Kim laughed, completely back on track. After he came out with an armload of his clothes, she went into the bathroom, which was humid and fresh, and filled with the same scent she'd smelled on Nathan, but which she would now and for-ever after ignore. She washed the makeup off, glad when the mirror showed her drippy familiar reflection, though with the new hair. She dried her face and went back to her room to change into her sweats and sweater.

The sweats went on, baggy sweater went on. She stood for a moment in the old, comfortable clothes, then went to her full-length mirror for a long look.

Impulsively, she changed the sweats for jeans, pulled the sweater back off and dug in her bureau drawer until she found a soft blue cardigan, which she paired with a white, scoop-neck shirt. Another look in the mirror. Her cheeks glowed from their scrubbing, her eyes matched the sweater—but they'd lost their vivid shape.

She strode to the bed, where she'd thrown the bag of overpriced cosmetics, bought under the careful scrutiny of Marie, Candy and the lady at Macy's whose makeup, Kim thought privately, made her look like the bride of Dracula. She grabbed the soft brown eye liner, smudged on the barest amount, then curled her lashes and darkened the tips with mascara.

Back to the mirror. Turning this way, that way, touching her new shorter hair, making sure she didn't look as if she'd made herself up to look sexy for Nathan, because she was doing this only for herself. And for Dale and any guys she'd be dating in the future.

Feeling a little giddy, she made for the kitchen and started getting out ingredients: knives and cutting boards, steak, broccoli, an orange, scallions, garlic, soy sauce and sesame oil, cornstarch for coating the beef, and rice, which she put on to cook so it would be ready when they were.

"I'm no longer indecent."

Nathan's voice made her jump. For heaven's sake, she had to stay comfortable with him or she'd never survive the next few months. "Well, that's good."

"But you are still beautiful."

She scowled at him. "What, you want to borrow money or something?"

"Actually." He stood next to her at the counter, too close. "I am short for rent this month."

"Really?" Her mouth went dry; the wine rebelled in her stomach. Nathan sent her a look that made her cringe in shame. "Sorry, right, sorry. You were kidding."

"Geez, Kim. It's great to know you have such a high opinion of me." He nudged her to show he was teasing. "Put me to work."

"Can you slice the steak?"

"How do you want it?" He reached across her; his upper arm brushed her collarbone; Kim jerked back, then was annoyed at herself for reacting. "Thin slices?"

"Yes." She stepped away from the counter, peered at her recipe, taking a minute to calm down.

"Want a beer?" He opened the refrigerator.

Maybe that would relax her, though she wasn't sure she needed any more alcohol today. "Okay."

"Coming up." Nathan popped the tops off of two St. Pauli Girls and handed her one. "To your health."

"Thank you." She clinked bottles without looking at him, took a long sip. "Mmm, that hits the spot."

"Uh-huh." He took his place at the kitchen table with a cutting board, knife and steak, and started slicing. "Tell me something I don't know about you, Kim."

"Huh? Why?" She put her beer on the counter, opened a drawer for the Microplane grater and went to work on the orange rind.

"Why not? Tell me your best childhood memory."

Kim set the orange down and twisted to look at him. This wasn't the type of conversation she'd come to expect from Nathan. "Are you serious?"

"Yes, I'm serious. Why shouldn't I be?"

"I don't know." While she thought how to answer, she piled fragrant rind onto a saucer, picked up a scallion and stripped off a wilted outer leaf. "Okay, I can think of two favorite memories."

"Tell me."

"We-ell." She felt shy sharing with him, and wasn't sure why. "The first is when I was eight, my dad made me a dollhouse for my birthday, an incredible one. Three stories, taller than me. It was fully furnished, too, electric lights that worked, and a little doll family in residence. It was the most magical thing I'd ever seen. I played with it constantly."

"What happened to it?"

"When I went to college Mom sold it." Kim's voice thickened with nostalgia. She reached for her beer and took a long slug.

"Without *asking* you?"

"She told me she was doing it." Kim began chopping the scallions into half-inch lengths. "It was around the time of the divorce, my sophomore year. She was moving into a smaller place. I didn't have the heart to insist she keep something she had no room for and which I'd never play with again. It was some other girl's turn to enjoy it."

"I'm sorry."

Kim shrugged, surprised at how the memory moved her. "We all have to grow up sometime."

"Ha. *I* never bothered."

Laughter caught her. She turned and found Nathan behind her with a board of neatly sliced steak. "Meat's done. What's next, boss?"

"Coat it with cornstarch?"

Nathan frowned dubiously. "Um…"

"Put cornstarch in a plastic bag, add the slices and shake."

"That sounds like serious fun."

She laughed at his enthusiasm, feeling at ease again. He seemed able to rattle her and smooth her out within a very few minutes. Nice little roller coaster.

"You said there were two childhood memories." He

reached for the yellow box of cornstarch, poured some into a plastic bread bag. "What was the second?"

"Are you going to tell me yours afterward?"

"Are you kidding me?" He interrupted a swallow of beer to stare scornfully. "I don't share anything with women but body fluids."

"Nathan!"

He grinned. "I will tell you whatever you want to know, Kim. Finish yours first."

"Hmph. But okay." She scraped the chopped scallions onto a plate, pulled the broccoli toward her. "My second favorite memory was the first time my dad took me to the ballet."

"Your *dad* went to the ballet?"

Kim rolled her eyes, then caught the twinkle in his. "Why do you pretend to be such a boor?"

He seemed caught off guard. "I don't know what you mean."

"More of a boor than you really are, I mean."

He grinned, easy and in control again, and shrugged. "Habit."

"Bad one."

"Could be." He added meat slices to the bag of cornstarch. "Your dad sounds like a cool guy."

"Great dad. Dismal husband." She gave the broccoli a particularly vicious whack with the knife. "He didn't do much to keep the home fires burning. In fact, he was out lighting them everywhere else."

Nathan stopped shaking the bag. "Kim, I'm sorry."

"Thanks." She whacked off another floret, not sure why she'd told him. She hadn't told many people. Her best friend in high school. Boyfriends. Marie. And now Nathan.

"But he took you to the ballet."

"He did. The *Nutcracker* at Christmas. I was about seven. Mom wasn't into that kind of cultural experience, but he felt it was important. I loved the dancing so much I begged to take lessons."

"And you still do."

"I stopped for a while. But I started up again last year at Danceworks with a Saturday morning class. I really missed it."

She finished with the broccoli. Nathan shook up the last batch of meat slices and dumped them onto a plate with the first half.

"Your turn, now."

"For what?" He came up behind her, opening the cabinets above her head. His chest pressed against her upper back. His arms circled her, one resting on each door.

Kim tensed, holding the chef's knife suspended over the cutting board, her body reacting to the contact with his. She wanted to lean into him, wanted his arms to slide down from the cabinets and wrap around her.

She was completely insane. The parallel with Nathan, her father and Tony wasn't too hard to figure out. Womanizing father, womanizing boyfriend, lust now for womanizing roommate? No. Not returning to that pattern.

She put the knife down, wiggled around and got right into his face. "What are you doing?"

He didn't blink, looked down at her calmly, close enough that she could kiss him by rising on tiptoes. "Getting crackers. What are you doing?"

Her face flamed. He didn't feel anything being this close? Didn't realize what he was doing to her? "You're crowding me."

He didn't move. "Yeah?"

She poked him in the chest and pointed back to where he'd stood before. "I'll get the crackers. You go over there."

"You smell good."

"Over. There."

"You look even better."

"Go. *Now.*"

"Yes, ma'am." He ambled back to the cornstarch-powdered meat. "I finished this. Do you want me to chop garlic now? Measure seasonings?"

She took a moment to reach for the crackers, wanting to sock him. She was a jittery mess of adrenaline and hormones, and he felt nothing?

Think Troy. Think Dale. Think dating, not lust. Think relationship, think communication, think all the things that were much more important than desire. Besides, she'd known Nathan since senior year, lived with him for three and a half weeks, and only in the past couple of days had she started seeing him differently. It had to do with her awakening to members of the opposite sex. She wanted love, not Nathan.

"You measure out the soy sauce and sesame oil, I'll chop the garlic, then we're ready to cook."

Bravo, Kim. She was in control here. She had the power. She'd learned from her father, from Tony, from her brother, how men like to play with women to make themselves feel attractive. This had nothing to do with her. To Nathan she was a female body. But to Dale she was Kim Charlotte Horton, someone worth getting to know.

"Now tell me your most special childhood memory."

"Kim." Nathan looked supremely pained. "Because sharing special memories is not in *The Man's Guide to Being Manly* I'll have to swear you to secrecy."

"You can trust me."

"I know." He smiled, an open, dazzling smile that would have made her toes curl had she been in that mode still. But of course, she wasn't; she was cured of any illusions about her new and very unfortunate awareness of Nathan.

"Let me guess your secret." She rid her fingers of the garlic smell by rubbing them on a stainless spoon under running water. "I'm thinking you had a Barbie at age twelve."

"Hey." He capped the soy sauce, looking convincingly bewildered. "Who told you?"

"I have my sources." She dried her hands. "Tell me more."

"Let's see. Special childhood memory...probably when

I finally got my first dog at age thirteen, and realized I had someone to talk to who really understood me."

He was grinning as if it was a joke, but Kim sensed something deeper lurked underneath. "You were lonely."

"Nah." Nathan picked up a sponge and wiped down the counter. "I had four brothers and plenty of friends."

He was lonely. Lonely surrounded by people, a worse kind of lonely than being alone. She'd been there, too, the only introvert in a boisterous, extroverted family. Sometimes she felt as if she must have been found on the doorstep.

But why would Nathan be lonely? She'd met his brothers over the years, and they seemed the same kind of high-fiving chest-bumper he was. Apparently Nathan hadn't blazed his own trail the way she had. Not that she'd had much choice; she simply couldn't function at the high energy level of the rest of her family.

She reached under the counter, brought out their largest skillet and started it heating on the burner next to the rice. "What was your dog's name?"

"Lloyd. After Frank Lloyd Wright."

"Is he still around?"

"Nope." He drained his beer, opened the refrigerator for another. "A car got him a few years after I did."

"Oh, Nathan." She stared helplessly, holding the bottle of canola oil poised over the heated pan. "I'm sorry. You never got another one?"

"I was off to college soon after I lost him, and my last apartment didn't allow them." He popped off the top of his second beer and half raised it to his lips. "Why, you want a puppy here?"

"Um. No." She poured in the oil, added the beef and stirred. He stood close, watching. She didn't let him get to her this time, but browned the beef, then the broccoli, mixed them with the orange rind, scallions and seasonings, let the dish simmer, and pronounced it done.

They ate at the kitchen table, talking comfortably as they'd done every night since Nathan moved in. Kim made herself focus on Dale, anticipating the email that would be waiting dependably on her laptop.

They did the dishes side by side, Kim rinsing, Nathan loading the dishwasher, then Nathan washing pans and knives, Kim drying. She did the final cleanup while Nathan got ready for work.

"I had fun tonight." He came back into the kitchen, looking sharp in his all-black bartending outfit.

"Me, too." She grinned at him fondly.

"I think you like me."

"Of course I like you." She dried her hands, hung the towel back in place. "I wouldn't have let you live with me if I didn't like you."

"No-o-o, I think you *li-ike,* like me." He adopted a nerdy, nasal tone, waggled his eyebrows, then shot out his hands and hooked his thumbs through her belt loops. "Admit it, you have a crush on me-e-e."

"Ew!"

"C'mon, bay-bee." He gave a ghastly bucktoothed grin. "Admit it, I'm irre-*sis*-tible."

"Get over yourself, Urquel." She could barely speak through her giggles.

Nathan twisted to look at the stove clock, still holding her at the waist, then turned back, all goofiness gone.

"I have to go." He pulled her close. "Don't wait up for me, sweetheart."

"Nathan…" She rolled her eyes, put her hands to his chest, then pulled them away abruptly, hating the way she responded to the hard muscle there and the fake tenderness in his voice. "You are completely—"

He gathered her to him, pressed his warm lips to her forehead, lingered a beat longer than was brotherly, then pulled back, hands splayed at her waist. "See you tomorrow, Kim. Sleep well."

She nodded, unable to produce any sound.

He released her and left the kitchen. The front door

opened. Closed. The apartment felt suddenly tomblike, missing his vitality.

Kim stood for a full minute, forlorn and off balance, her forehead still registering the feel of his lips.

After the hell she went through with Tony, she'd seen a therapist who'd said everyone had a core belief about him or herself formed in childhood, and that Kim's was that she was not good enough. Unless she changed that belief, she'd keep seeking out experiences that reinforced it.

In other words, she felt like dirt, so she went after people who made her feel that way. Tony or Nathan, who treated women casually, like playthings, were exactly the types to reinforce that message about herself. Now he lusts, now he's brotherly, now he couldn't care either way. The biggest mistake she could make would be to take any of it seriously.

There. She drew in a breath, let it out. Decoding confusing feelings was half the battle. Understanding her reactions gave her power over them.

She went into her room, turned on her laptop, needing the latest email from Dale to stabilize her. Unlike Nathan, he made her feel special, precious, anything but worthless. If she was ever going to become the strong, confident woman she wanted to be, inside as well as out, she needed to start believing that in earnest.

Her email program came up. There. A note from Dale, reassuring her of his steady, sincere, appropriate interest, as always. She scanned his words, her heart warming at his thoughtfulness and affection. He'd written from the airport in Montego Bay just before he took off, saying he'd email again when he landed in Milwaukee. He couldn't wait to see her, the hours until Monday seemed so long, but he'd be busy the next day getting settled in, and wanted to be fresh and at his best. She'd hear from him, though; she could count on that.

Yes. She could. This was the kind of man she needed.

She'd focus on that, and on the certainty that as soon as she met Dale, all the excitement over her sexy, unreliable room-mate would disappear.

6

"NATHAN? IT'S MARIE."

"Marie, hi." Nathan adjusted his cell phone next to his ear and pulled over to park on Humboldt Avenue in Milwaukee. The guys were meeting at the Kern Park courts for Sunday basketball. "What's going on?"

"Got a minute?"

"Sure." He turned off the car, unbuckled his seat belt and stretched his legs. "Kim's party?"

"Uh-huh. I talked to Candy yesterday and Darcy this morning and we're all in agreement."

"About?"

"Her birthday is a Saturday this year so we'll have it right on the day, April fifteenth, at Candy's house in Shorewood."

Nathan tried to imagine Kim's reaction. Would she enjoy being the center of that much attention? He guessed her friends knew her better than he did, though he hoped to change that. "What do you need from me? Besides stories. I've already started getting those."

"Anything good?"

"She had some incredible dollhouse when she was a girl, and she loves ballet." He ran his finger over the steering wheel, thinking the words didn't come close to doing her stories justice, or the emotions that went along with them.

"Ballet I knew about, will have to research the doll-house."

"That's long gone."

"Oh, too bad. Get whatever else you can. Pictures of it, maybe? We want to put up a wall of Kim, showing her evolution from a sweet little girl on toe shoes to the hot mama she is today. Have you seen her new look?"

"Last night." He still hadn't recovered.

"Doesn't she look great?"

"She does." He kept his voice casual, not anxious to have Marie figure out that Kim's new look had made his job of keeping his hands to himself, at least awhile longer, pretty much impossible.

"I think so, too. I'm thrilled for her. Back to the party. We'd like to ask you for three things."

"Shoot." He didn't mean to sound wary, but girl-parties could get rough on a guy.

"One, see if she has any photo albums around, and get a variety of pictures. I called her mother and she doesn't think any are stored with her."

"Pictures. Okay." A sharp thud on his window made him jump. Steve, trying to get his attention. Nathan pointed to the phone and shook his head.

"Second, we need something she loves, cherishes, can't live without, besides her computer. Something with great personality. A stuffed animal, some keepsake, a doll, a china figurine, something like that."

Nathan rolled his eyes. He wasn't wrong to dread the girlie thing. "I'll see what I can do."

Steve rapped again. *"Dude."*

Nathan scowled at him. Steve was a good basketball player, but he could be a real asshole. Nathan didn't understand why Kent hung around with him so much. "Got that. And the third thing?"

"You're not going to like this."

"Uh-oh."

"We need her underwear size. Bra and panties."

Nathan froze in the car. His mind immediately went places it shouldn't. Kim, with that fantastic new haircut, blue eyes bold in her face, wearing nothing but tiny bits of white lace. "Un-derwear?"

"We're buying her naughty stuff."

He let his head fall against the back of his seat, suppressing a groan. "Like…what kind?"

The second the words were out of his mouth, he wished them back in. *What kind?* Could he be any more obvious that he was dying to picture her wearing them?

"We're not sure yet. Any ideas, Nathan?" She was teasing him, he could hear the laughter in her voice.

"No." He lifted his head from the headrest and dropped it forward onto his fist. For God's sake. He should have made a joke and suggested something his great-grandmother would have worn, like bloomers. Or a girdle.

Except Kim would look sexy even in that.

"Yo, Nathan." Steve again. Making the sign to roll down his window. Nathan was tempted to send back a sign that meant something entirely different, but shook his head instead.

"Okay, Marie. I'll get right on all that. If you need anything else, let me know."

"We will. Thanks so much, Nathan."

He turned off the phone. Well. It looked as if he was going to have to go through Kim's underwear drawer. If that didn't turn him on wildly…

He responded to the latest impatient knock from Steve by getting out of the car. "Chill, dude. I was on the phone."

"We're on court three."

"And that couldn't wait five minutes because…"

Steve lifted his hammy fist and gave Nathan the exact sign Nathan had been tempted to use earlier. "Come on. There'll be four of us today. This guy Troy is coming. Friend of Kent's."

Troy. The "gorgeous" guy, the one who went out with

Kim, the one who wanted to see her again? The one who'd see her made over and totally hot?

Not caring if Steve was following or not, Nathan slammed his door and strode toward the basketball courts. He needed more time. He'd flustered Kim a little by flirting the night before, but he couldn't tell if she'd been disconcerted because he affected her or because she thought he'd lost his mind, and felt sorry for him.

Court three came into view, and on it a tall man shooting baskets, making most of them. Dark curly hair, solid build, a graceful athlete. He saw Steve and Nathan coming onto the court, caught the ball and smiled. White teeth. Looked like a movie star.

Crap.

"Hey, I'm Troy." He strode toward them with an easy gait, held out his hand and shook.

Seemed nice, too. Double crap.

"I'm Nathan."

"Steve." Steve stuck out his hand, peering up suspiciously from his five-foot-seven-inch stocky frame. Steve had issues with tall men. And pretty much everything else.

"Hey, Troy." Kent, hurrying onto the court behind them, tall, slender and blond like his sister, his Kim-blue eyes hidden behind dark glasses. "Good to see you, man. You met these two useless males already?"

"I did." The two shook hands. Troy wheeled around and shot the ball; Kent covered him. Nathan and Steve joined in, pairing off in teams: Nathan and Troy, Kent and Steve. An hour later, they were done, Nathan and Troy having dominated the game, Kent and Steve satisfying themselves by insulting their opponents with unrestrained obscenity.

The smell of testosterone hung thick in the air.

"Brews at Wolski's?" Steve pointed to each man in turn.

There was general agreement. They walked to their cars, drove down Humboldt and parked on Pulaski Street by Wolski's Tavern, a Milwaukee neighborhood institution famous for its I Closed Wolski's bumper stickers. The classic interior held dart boards, games and good, cold beer.

The guys ordered plenty and stood clustered by the bar.

"Whoa, check that out." Steve lifted his square chin toward the corner behind Nathan, who didn't need to see to know blond hair and large breasts were involved.

Kent turned around for a lingering leer. "Oh, yeah. I could seriously enjoy some of that."

"I saw her first, dude."

Nathan glanced behind him. Pretty girl. Aware of their attention by now, pretending she wasn't, tossing back her hair, smiling widely, leaning forward to talk to her friend. Then a quick sidelong shift of her eyes, making sure they were staring.

"She totally wants it." Steve was practically slobbering. "Nathan? I'm going in. You up for the friend?"

He shook his head. "Not interested."

"What is with you?" Steve cuffed the back of Nathan's neck. "You are turning into a wuss."

Nathan shrugged. Troy was watching him curiously.

"Seriously," Kent said. "You haven't been on the hunt in a while."

"Ever since you moved in with Kim." Steve made a lewd gesture. "You getting some there?"

"Hey." Kent slitted his eyes, puffed up his slender chest. "You're talking about my sister."

Troy's eyebrows lifted at Nathan. "You live with Kim?"

"I lost my lease. She had room. Favor to Kent." He drank more beer than he wanted, feeling dangerously exposed.

"Convenient." Troy nodded, not taking his eyes off Nathan. "Nice woman."

"Yup." Nathan took another gulp, wanting to sock Troy in the nose except he seemed to be a good guy.

"What is wrong? She have you all domesticated?" Steve sneered. "Sewing little curtains for the place?"

"Nah." Troy shook his head. "She's not like that."

Troy being protective: bad sign.

"Shut up, Steve." Kent was disgusted. "Troy's right, Kim isn't like that."

"What you need, Nate, is some action." As usual, Steve was completely unfazed by their disapproval. He gestured toward the blonde. "Those women over there are calling your name."

"I don't think so." Nathan drained the rest of his drink.

Even Kent was staring at him now. "What is up, Nate?"

Nathan shrugged. "Just not into it."

"Whoa, emergency situation." Steve signaled the bartender. "Another round here. Though maybe we should do shots."

"Not me," Troy said.

"Okay, I know the problem." Kent held up his hands, commanding attention, upping the drama. "I've seen the symptoms before."

"VD?" Steve offered.

Kent turned to Nathan. "What's her name?"

Nathan saw that one coming. What would Kent do if he told him? He blurted out the first name that came into his head. "Angelina."

"What, like Jolie?"

"Yeah." Nathan accepted his new beer. "Like that."

"What's the problem?" Troy was watching him again, as if he knew Nathan was lying. "She's not into you?"

"I don't know." He already regretted saying anything. "I don't really want to talk—"

"Make your move already, boy-man." Steve drained half his second beer. "Her reaction will tell you what you need to know."

"Does she know you're into her?" Troy asked.

Nathan twisted his face, wishing he'd never brought this up. "Not…really."

"Oh, no, no, no." Steve shook his pale head repeatedly. "She can't know. Not ever. Once you admit to a woman you want more than sex, you might as well hand her your balls for her collection."

"I get that." Troy chuckled drily. "My old girlfriend never gave mine back. I had to grow a new pair."

"I had one like that back in New York." Kent whistled silently. "Gruesome. I was almost glad I got laid off so I could get the hell away."

Nathan swallowed uncomfortably. He didn't like the turn of this conversation. All his rosy dreams about Kim were becoming tainted by these idiots' view of reality.

"What are you guys, men or fairies? Never admit that stuff." Steve scowled at each of them. "Insert tab A into slot B, repeat as needed, but keep her guessing at all times."

Nathan thought about the way Kim had been the night before, unsure, vulnerable. Yeah, he'd kept her guessing, but sooner or later she, or any normal woman, would get sick of those games. Then there was the fact that Steve was perpetually single, which didn't make him a great source of dating advice. "Seems like a pretty shitty thing to do to someone you care about."

"*Care* about?" Steve shook his head. "You are whipped, boy. Just put on your apron, bend over and take it from her. That's all you're good for."

Uneasy laughter followed.

Nathan dug out ten dollars from his wallet, slapped it into Kent's palm. "This is for my beer. I'm outta here. Thanks for the game."

Steve gave a wide-eyed, girlie pout. "Running home to Kimmy?"

"Nah. It just stinks in here."

He left, ignoring whatever lame comeback Steve shouted after him. Let them hang on to macho misery. Even a month ago he'd have been right there with them, commiserating, laughing at Steve, but with him, too. He'd have gone willingly to chat up the blonde's friend. But that constant shallow Hi-I'm-Nathan BS conversation didn't seem real anymore. It seemed pathetic. As did Steve.

Nathan was going to step up his plan to show Kim he felt very differently about her than she did about him, see if he could build on the confusion he'd seen in her eyes last night, see if he could introduce some of the desire he felt for her into her reactions to him, make her aware of him at least physically—then maybe more.

Kim would be going out on her first date with that Dale guy the next night. If Nathan had anything to say about it, she'd be leaving their apartment thinking only of him.

COUNTDOWN TO LEAVING FOR DATE with Dale: half an hour. Kim wasn't dressed. Well, she'd been dressed, in what she thought was the perfect outfit, five or six times. This one too casual. That one too dressy. This one too sexual. That one not sexual enough.

She hated this. Life had been so peaceful and wonderful when she wasn't hunting for a man. Now look at her. She'd gone completely insane with stress and nerves, her self-esteem was shaky—in short, she was losing it.

Why had she let Marie talk her into joining Milwaukee-dates.com? Why had she let Marie talk her into going out with Dale? Why had she let Marie and Candy talk her into getting a makeover?

She stared at herself in the mirror, at the long, slender rose skirt paired with the sweater top. This was the third time she'd tried on the outfit Candy and Marie bought for her, and she loved it. She looked great in it. But it might look as if she was trying too hard to impress him.

What if they had no chemistry? What if he was horribly disappointed? What if she was?

Kim rolled her eyes at her reflection, forcing the bursts of worry out of her mind.

Marie and Candy hadn't convinced her to do a damn thing she hadn't wanted to. If she was a frantic mess right now it was her own fault. No doubt the second she sat opposite Dale and smiled into his eyes, everything would fall into place. Even if he didn't turn out to be the love of her life, at least they'd have a nice evening. Look at all they had to talk about: Jamaica, his childhood, her childhood, their tastes, favorites, everything. Two entire lives ready to be mutually discovered. It was a beautiful thing.

So she'd stop right now being timid and muddled, and sail through this like the goddess she was intent on becoming. Never mind that she looked pale, that her eyes were large and haunted, and that her mouth was rigid with tension.

Okay? Okay.

What's more, she was going to stop fussing with what she'd wear and how she looked and just go. Now. Out into the kitchen, have a glass of water, maybe talk to Nathan for a while, and not act as if Armageddon was around the corner. She hadn't been remotely this nervous for her date with Troy. Probably because Troy—who hadn't yet called, surprise, surprise—hadn't seemed remotely suitable as a boyfriend. Dale, yes. But she'd done fine that night and would do fine tonight, too.

Confidence, confidence. She straightened her shoulders, nodded firmly to herself and left the room, high heels making an unaccustomed clacking sound on the apartment's hardwood floors.

"Wow." Nathan was leaning in the doorway between the dining and living rooms, same as the other night, only now the lights were all on, and she could see him easily. His eyes slid over her in a way that made every nerve ending spring to life.

Not again.

"Think it's okay?" She didn't know what to do with her hands, so stood with them hanging awkwardly at her sides, then rounded them, feet wanting to turn out into ballet first position.

"It's more than okay." He twirled his finger in a circle. "Turn around. I want the three-sixty view."

She rolled her eyes, kicked off her shoes for comfort and turned slowly around. "Not too fancy?"

"Where are you going?"

"Mimma's Café."

"Nice." He didn't look impressed. He looked crabby. "Swanky place. You're dressed fine."

Kim narrowed her eyes. "What's bugging you?"

He looked startled. "Nothing. Why?"

"I don't know, you just don't have much..." She searched for the next word. "Enthusiasm."

That wasn't the right one.

"No?"

"Not that you should be all whupped up over my love life." She spotted a thread on her skirt and reached to remove it.

"I'm jealous."

Kim straightened abruptly, then saw his smile and couldn't believe she'd thought he was serious. Or that some silly, egotistical part of her had wanted him to be. *Nice, Kim.* "I'll just bet."

"You look beautiful. He's going to get the world's biggest hard-on when he sees you in that outfit."

"Nathan." She blushed, laughing.

"I'm serious." He took two steps toward her, hands on his hips. "I think I'm getting one."

"Stop that." She fought the urge to move back when he took two more steps. This reflex flirting he did was really disconcerting. Maybe he was trying to bolster her confidence, but it only unnerved her. A lot.

"What time are you meeting him?"

She looked at her watch. "I have to leave in twenty minutes."

"Time for a beer to relax you? Or a shot of something stronger?"

"It's that obvious I'm tense?"

Another slow step, then another. "If I touched you, I think you'd break."

"Yeah?" Her voice lowered. She was holding her ground, holding his gaze. That crazy warmth was spreading through her again. What was she doing? "Then you better not touch me."

"You're sure?"

"I'm sure." The sound barely came out of her mouth. He was one step away. He could touch her if he extended his hand.

She wanted him to.

Kim!

The outfit. The makeup. The anxiety of the date. She'd turned into someone she no longer recognized. It was thrilling, intoxicating. She had power.

He extended his hand toward her; she stayed motionless, standing tall, breath catching in her chest. His finger landed on her mouth, a soft kiss of a touch. She had an absurd impulse to open her lips, take him in and taste. But that seductive power was not in her. That power was in people like Tony, in her brother and his friend Steve…and in Nathan. And how.

She moved her head back from his finger; he dropped his arm, looking slightly stunned. As she had been, too. Whatever was growing between them couldn't be allowed to mushroom any further. From now on she'd concentrate any and all of this strange new sexual energy on men she might actually want to have a relationship with.

"See? I didn't break."

"No, you didn't." His smile was slow and easy. "But you still look like you're going to."

She shrugged. "All I need is to survive this date."

"I'll give you good odds on that."

"Okay, then." She brushed past him into the kitchen, poured herself a glass of water to cover her rattled state.

"Need some dating pointers?"

"Pleez."

"One, don't eat garlic unless he does."

"Give me a break." She plopped in a couple of ice cubes and drank half the glass.

"Two, don't bring up radical political or religious views."

"Yes, Daddy dearest."

"And don't put out on the first date, especially not in the back of his car."

She nearly spit water into the sink. "Bet you wouldn't give that advice to *your* first date."

"Absolutely I would." He grinned in the doorway, arms folded over his chest. "Whets the appetite for date two."

"Oh, for—" She dumped the ice into the sink. "You are too much."

"And make sure he pays."

"Why should he? I have plenty of money. And last time I checked it's the twenty-first century."

"No." Nathan rubbed his chin. "Man pays on the first date."

"Yes, sir." She glanced at the clock; adrenaline was starting to work overtime again. Maybe she should leave earlier than planned in case there was traffic? "Any more advice?"

"Relax."

"Oh, yeah, that's likely." She left the kitchen for the living room, put on her heels, took a few steps to accustom herself again to the new height, visibly shaky with nerves. She gathered her coat, purse, directions to the restaurant… What else? Was she missing something? She hated this near-panicky feeling.

"Ready?" He was waiting by the door.

She crossed to him, touching her jacket pocket to make sure she had her car keys. "I hope I find parking."

"There's a lot by the restaurant."

"Good. Wait." She touched her mouth. "Did I forget lipstick?"

"No."

"Do I have my phone?" She rummaged though her purse. "I think it's here, I just—"

"Kim." His hands landed on her shoulders.

Her fingers closed around her phone. Whew. "What?"

"Breathe."

"I'm breathing."

"Slow it down."

She tried. "Like this?"

"You're breathing too high. Here." He put his palm to her abdomen. "Breathe from here. Keep your chest still, shoulders relaxed. You know, be a dancer."

"Right." She felt her breathing shift lower and slow.

"Good?"

"It helps."

"Of course it does. Now close your eyes."

She closed them. His hand was warm on her stomach, guiding her breath.

"Feel better now?"

"Some." She did. But she was also aware of him again, in that hot way she didn't want to be. Could smell his aftershave, sense his body's size and nearness even without seeing it.

"Make yourself heavy." His fingers left her abdomen, moved to the back of her neck and started a slow massage.

"Ohhh." Delicious. Muscles she didn't realize she was holding tight succumbed to the gentle pressure. Muscles worried about the date, muscles overused from sitting too long at the computer, muscles afraid she'd lose Charlotte's Web and have to return to the hell of an office like Soka Associates.

"Better?"

"You have no idea."

His hands were magic, finding the pain and tension, easing it away. Her neck, her upper back, her shoulders. Heaven.

"When you're sitting with him, if you feel tense, just think of me doing this, touching you this way." His voice was low, hypnotic, and very close. He barely had to make sound and she could hear him. "Think of my hands on you, Kim. Think of how they made you feel."

Mmm... Wait, that was the last thing she should be thinking of when she was with Dale. The last thing. The very, very...*mmm.*

He hit a particularly wonderful spot at the base of her neck; she arched back, her lips parting to emit a soft moan of contentment. The hand at the base of her neck stopped massaging, cupped the back of her head. She froze instinctively. Nathan muttered something she couldn't catch, and her head was pulled up.

Her eyes shot open. Too late. His lips were a centimeter from hers. Then not even that far. She braced her hands against his chest, tried to push away. At the same time she registered the beautiful soft-firm pressure of his mouth, and the dark burst shooting through her, which had nothing to do with nerves this time. *Oh, my God.*

Nathan pulled back, grinning like the devil himself. "There."

"What was that for?"

"To give you that just-kissed glow."

"Glow? What the hell are you talking about? I'm not glowing, I'm pissed." She glared at him. Smug jerk. "That was completely out of—"

He pulled her against the hard length of his body, his arms overpowering her resistance—at least she was pretty sure that's why she was still standing there being kissed again. And how. She didn't get away from him until he released her, leaving her limp and confused.

"Geez, Nathan, what gave you the right to—"

"Go look."

"What?" She pushed him away, dangerously stirred up. "Go look at what?"

"Yourself."

"Why would I want to do that?" She scowled at him. "You need help, buddy."

"You have to fix your lipstick, anyway." He hadn't stopped grinning. Not for a second. "And you can see for yourself. Like a lightbulb."

"What is like a lightbulb?"

"You glowing."

"Oh, right." She snorted. "You are a cocky, arrogant, appalling excuse for a man."

"Okay. But go look. And tell me whether you'd rather

show up for this Dale guy, looking like you do now, or like you did ten minutes ago?"

"Give me a break." Growling, she marched into the bath-room and met her own eyes in the mirror.

Yes, her lipstick was gone. But also gone were her pallor, the worry from around her eyes, the tension in her forehead and mouth.

Oh, God. He was right. The son of a bitch was absolutely right.

She was glowing.

7

Seven o'clock

Mimma's was beautiful. Excellent service, great atmosphere, every table filled. The menu was varied; the portion sizes, from what Kim could see at other tables, were enormous. Dale was everything she'd hoped. Maybe a little shorter and softer around the edges than she'd imagined, but decently attractive, and therefore just right.

Except… She'd walked in the front door where he was waiting and recognized him right away. Insides fizzing with excitement, she'd put on a huge smile. Here he was, the man she'd been emailing for so many days, the man who already felt like a friend, and who could become a whole lot more than that. He'd caught sight of her and she'd had the agony of seeing a flash of disappointment on his face before he recovered.

Her worst nightmare. Even made up and dressed well she wasn't what he wanted? What had he expected? She hadn't even opened her mouth yet.

They sat at a table in one of the dining rooms—Mimma's was huge—and the waitress came by within moments to welcome them and offer drinks.

Dale hadn't hesitated. "Double Scotch on the rocks," he'd said, then turned expectantly to Kim.

She guessed ordering a Miller Lite wouldn't cut it. What was a sophisticated drink? *Think chic, classy...Sex and the City.*

She ordered a cosmopolitan.

Now they were studying the menus in that horrible silence that settles over strangers deciding whether to talk or get the business of ordering dinner out of the way. Kim could barely take in the choices, hoping her cosmo would show up soon. Not only was she off balance from Dale's disheartening reaction, but she couldn't get the feel and taste and memories of Nathan's kisses out of her head. Or her fury that he'd done something so personal and affected her so strongly, when his intention all along had been to fluff her up for another man.

The silence at the table was becoming truly painful. Kim grabbed the name of a ravioli dish off the menu and smiled her most alluring smile. "Tell me more about Jamaica, Dale."

Not that she wanted Nathan to kiss her for himself, of course not. It was the principle of the thing. Kissing shouldn't be wasted on gimmickry.

"Ah, Jamaica." Dale glanced up, returned his gaze to the menu. "Home to the world's best coffee, reggae music. *La dolce vita,* my friend.

"Nice." It wasn't as if Nathan meant anything by the kisses, either. It was just more of his horrible arrogance, treating women like objects. If you were going to kiss a woman, it should be because you really wanted to. Because you really felt something. Not for some stupid impersonal reason. "Do you go there often?"

Where was her drink? She didn't usually go for the hard stuff, but tonight she'd need all the help she can get. Trying to impress one guy while wanting to murder another took a lot of energy.

"Whenever I can, whenever there isn't somewhere else calling my name." He smiled and his nice brown eyes crinkled in the corners, which she'd always thought was very sexy. Maybe she was just too tense to succumb to his chemistry tonight.

"Where have you traveled to recently?"

"Ha. Where *haven't* I?" He took off his frameless glasses, which made his eyes larger and closer. He really had beautiful eyes. She should be able to happily stare into them for quite a while. Someday. Maybe not tonight. Tonight she saw only Nathan's eyes, smug and triumphant, while she'd been falling apart. "Most recently London, Beijing and a brief stay in Rome."

"That sounds incredible."

"It is. I'm very lucky. And very good at what I do."

"I'm sure you are." In Nathan's view, women were completely interchangeable one from the other. Kim couldn't imagine how many women thought his act was put on for their benefit and inevitably were disillusioned. She felt sorry for all of them.

"I work hard for it. Job security is so important."

"Mmm, yes, it really is."

The silence stretched again. She searched her brain for some intelligent and fitting topic, but came up with nothing other than what she might hurl at Nathan's head when she got home. He couldn't get away with treating her as if she were one of his bimbos. She'd totally set him straight on that.

"Tell me about Kim. How's she doing?"

"Oh." She jerked her brain guiltily back to the date, wondering if she was supposed to talk about herself in the third person. *Kim is fine, thanks.* "Well, let's see. Right now I'm a little frustrated. The Carter project I told you about, which is so important to me, is still not going as well as—"

"I don't want to hear about that." He waved her career away like it was dust. "It's you I want to know. Tell me what you're feeling right now."

"Oh." What was she feeling? Besides wanting to sock Nathan when she got home? "I'm looking forward to getting to know you better."

"Oh, yes. That will certainly happen." He didn't sound

certain. Was she blowing this? If she blew this because Nathan had so flustered her, she was definitely going to sock him when she got home. *Where the hell was that drink?*

As if she could sense Kim's near-despair, the waitress appeared. "Here we go. Cosmopolitan and a double Scotch."

Thank you, God.

"Excellent." Dale took a sip, swallowed, tasted again. "Single malt. The Macallan? Ten-year?"

The waitress nodded, smiling. "That's exactly right."

He grinned triumphantly at Kim. "I'm an amateur expert."

"I'm impressed." She smiled casually, when actually she was floored. She didn't think there was anything she could identify by one sip. Coke maybe. Nathan could probably name every beer on the market.

Stop thinking about Nathan.

"Are you ready to order?" The waitress stood poised.

"Absolutely." Dale started to point to the menu, then apparently remembered his manners and gestured to Kim. "Ladies first."

She couldn't remember what ravioli she'd selected last time, and blindly ordered the first one she saw and a salad, then noticed she'd pointed to lobster ravioli, which was a lot more expensive than her first choice. Oops. Dale didn't blink, ordered gnocchi in a blue cheese sauce, and fried calamari. Then took such elaborate care choosing a bottle of wine that Kim succumbed to an admittedly large first gulp of her cosmopolitan, telling the alcohol to please hurry up and relax her so she could salvage this evening, which Nathan had put in such jeopardy with his—

She had to stop. If she wanted this date to work, if she wanted a chance with someone steady and dependable and interesting like Dale, she had to get Nathan out of her head.

There. Done. He was gone. Forever.

Dale finally seemed satisfied with his choice and the waitress collected their menus and was off. And there they were again. In silence. Kim took another gulp of her drink.

"How are you finding Milwaukeedates.com, Kim?"

"Fun." She clutched the drink. Why bother putting it down when she desperately needed its company? "Since Marie is a friend of mine it was a natural choice when I decided to start dating."

"It seems like there are a lot of quality people on the site."

"Oh. Yes. I guess Marie is very…conscientious." *Quality people?* She wasn't really sure what defined a quality person. Trappings? Education? Kindness? What really mattered to Dale? Whatever it was, she might not have enough of it.

Another pause, which Kim filled with a slow sip of her drink. How could two people have so much to say in email and nothing to say in person? Was it just nerves? She had been sure they'd be easy friends, at the very least. Maybe the idea of Dale as a perfect relationship was all in her head, all her fantasy.

All the same, it was a really, really nice one, and she very much wanted it back.

Eight o'clock

THIS NIGHT WAS GOING to go on forever. All Nathan could do was sit in the living room he shared with Kim and hope she was having the worst night of her life. Hope she was sitting at the table thinking about him as hard, and as sexually, as he was thinking about her.

Kissing her, even surprise-attack kissing, even pretending it was some cheap trick to make her relax for her date, had been like no kissing he'd ever done. Lust had been part of it, sure. But also a pull from deep in his chest. A pull that made him kiss her again, even after she'd made it clear the first one hadn't been welcome, because there was no way, having kissed her once, that he couldn't do it again.

Remembering was torture. Sitting here without her was

torture. But he was obviously a masochist, because all he'd done in the hour and a half since she'd left was sit here without her and remember.

He flicked listlessly through TV channels. Nothing appealed. He'd tried to force himself again to do some work on his thesis, a design for low-income "green" housing with a Leadership in Energy and Environmental Design—which everyone called LEED—certification at the platinum level, the highest possible. But while he could put the necessary ingredients together—south-facing windows for light and heat, trees sheltering from the north, passive and active solar features, wastewater treatment—the result never satisfied him.

Eventually, as always, frustration overcame him, and by now predictable fears. His professors had been excited about this project. He'd been confident, probably cocky, thinking he could improve on something that had been done before: design maximally green housing developments more cheaply than developments using traditional methods. First he hit snags. Then boulders. Now mountains, grown by uncertainty that fed on itself until nothing he did felt right, and his computer—where he'd spent many constructive hours, sometimes so absorbed he'd miss meals—that computer now felt like his enemy.

He needed to go out. There was no way he could spend another hour imagining all the fun Kim could be having with some other guy. A guy she was really excited about, for chrissake. Nathan needed to be out having fun of his own. If he lay here like a dead jellyfish any longer, he'd start thinking Steve was right, that showing a woman you cared was like giving up your balls. He wanted to keep his, in the fond hope that someday he'd need them again.

Fifteen minutes later, he'd called his usual crowd. John was home, but doing some prewedding thing. Everyone else was either busy or didn't answer. He didn't try Steve.

He'd go out on his own then. Not the first time, probably not the last. Lonely guy walking into bar. There were worse things. Like lonely guy sitting alone in his living room, watching TV, pining after a woman who was out with someone else.

He dragged on a jacket, went out into the damp, penetrating chill that was too often March in Wisconsin. In his secondhand Hyundai, he drove to Water Street downtown, home to bars filled with people in their twenties checking each other out. He'd been successful there many times, met some wild and willing women, and had a great time.

Tonight he wasn't sure what kind of time he'd have, and what kind of mood he was in. Maybe finding female company was the best cure for what ailed him. Have a few beers, then a few more, chat up some hot women. Probably just what he needed. Give him some pride back, anyway. Make him feel less vulnerable. He hated that feeling. He and vulnerable didn't have much to say to each other.

Brocach Irish Pub was packed tonight, just the way he liked it. He squeezed in, absorbing the noise, the energy, the heat and scents of bodies and beer. This was his element. Up at the bar, he ordered a beer, drumming in time to the music, looking around for a likely playmate. In the corner, a brunette in a low, tight tank top, talking with her friend. Nice. His beer came. He paid and took a gulp, then another one. Started toward her. She glanced over his way and he smiled. She smiled back. Bingo. He reached her, nodded like the oh-so-cool guy he was.

"Hi there, I'm Nathan." He had to shout to be heard.

"Natalie." She giggled. "Nathan and Natalie!"

"Has a nice ring to it, huh?"

"What?"

He pitched his voice to cut through a hurricane, his head starting to ache. "I said it has a nice ring to it."

"Your phone has a nice ring?"

"No, Nathan and Natalie."

"What about us?"

He shook his head, thought about what to say next. *Can I buy you a drink? Want to get out of here and go someplace where we can talk?* He didn't want to say either. He wanted Kim.

Damn it.

Natalie was looking at him expectantly. Someone jostled him from behind and he nearly fell into her.

"Sorry."

"It's okay."

They stood again. Natalie started giggling. Nathan had to say something. Or shout something. "So what—"

"Buy me a drink?"

Buy her a drink. He should be celebrating. Steve would be. She liked him! He was in! Hurray! He had a chance to get some!

All Nathan could think was that if he bought her a drink he'd be stuck talking to her. He shouldn't have come. "What'll you have?"

"What?" She lurched away from the wall to get closer.

"What are you drinking?"

"Anything." She burst into giggles and he wondered how badly off she'd be after another drink.

"Yeah. Sure. Be right back." He headed for the bar, was blocked by a couple of guys in one direction, blocked in another. To hell with it.

He turned and left. He wouldn't be good company for Natalie or any other human being tonight. His heart wasn't in it.

His damn heart wasn't even in his chest. It was beating lamely over at Mimma's, with Kim.

Nine o'clock

THINGS HAD GOTTEN BETTER. Much, much better. Kim's cosmopolitan had been followed by a couple glasses of wine from the bottle Dale ultimately had emptied, then he'd had a brandy and she'd had tea, unable to absorb any more alcohol, especially that potent. During dinner, conversation had flowed, finally, though, granted, Dale had done most of the talking, about his travels, about his work, about his life. Kim read somewhere that men talked about themselves a lot on the first date, in essence auditioning for the part of boyfriend, so she wasn't entirely surprised, and didn't hold it against him. If he wanted to see her again, there would be plenty of time to talk about herself.

Dale pocketed the receipt for the meal, which he'd insisted on paying for. "Would you like to take a walk, Kim? Nice brisk night. A little sobering up isn't a bad idea before we get back into our cars, either, huh?"

"I'd love it." She got up from the table and put on her jacket, glad she'd worn her warmest one. Fresh air sounded wonderful. Making the evening longer than going straight home after dinner sounded wonderful, too. She wasn't ready to come back to earth and face Nathan. Though if this much booze didn't make her brave enough, probably nothing would.

They walked out into the chilly night air of Brady Street and headed east. The glow of alcohol lingered, making her warmer, making the night romantic and the neighborhood more enchanting than it was. Something about strolling along with a date was more relaxing and liberating than being imprisoned opposite him in a restaurant.

"I have a confession to make, Kim."

Her smile started slipping. "Confession? Uh-oh. What is it?"

"At the beginning of the date, when I saw you…"

She slowed her steps. She knew what had happened when he saw her. He'd wanted to turn around and walk out. "Yes?"

"You weren't what I expected."

"Oh." She didn't know what to say to that. She was sorry? "What was different?"

"You were—I don't know how to say this."

Oh, no. She thought they'd had a nice evening, even if it had taken a while to get going. Had he not enjoyed himself? "Just say it. I won't break."

Oh, she wished she hadn't said that. Her lips immediately started remembering the soft press of Nathan's finger. *If I touched you, I think you'd break.*

Stop.

"In your picture on Milwaukeedates.com, you were shy and sweet-looking, easily approachable."

She stopped dead, forcing Dale to swing around to face her. "And I'm not now?"

He gestured toward her. "You look so…done up."

Oh, Dale. If the streetlights went out around them, the street wouldn't go dark, because Kim's smile would be enough to light it. "The irony of what you just said…"

"What do you mean?"

She couldn't believe how stupid she'd been, worrying about her appearance like that. After they'd been emailing with such openness and frequency. "You seemed so sophisticated, Dale. I was intimidated, and afraid you'd be disappointed if I showed up looking like the girl next door."

"Disappointed? That's crazy." He lurched forward, grabbed her to him in a hug. "I picked you exactly because of how girlish and sweet you looked. Like the Ivory girl. Simple and uncomplicated, and beautiful."

She hugged him back, laughing and nearly crying at the same time. Exactly what she'd told Marie she wanted, why she hadn't played herself up in the profile. He liked her for *her,* without the paint and polish. What kind of idiot had she been, thinking she should change herself to get the kind of guy she wanted?

He drew back, caught her chin in his hand. "Next time, don't wear any of that, okay?"

She nodded, not able to stop smiling. "I won't."

"We'll go somewhere casual. You can wear jeans. Okay?"

"Yes. Yes. Okay." She laughed, laughed again. This evening was turning out perfectly!

His fingers tightened on her chin. His face sobered. He pulled her toward him, covered her lips with his.

Oh, dear.

She banished the immediate comparison, kissed him back wholeheartedly. He broke away, rested his forehead against hers. "I can't believe I found you, Kim."

This was the man she knew. The romantic from his emails. "Yes, it's amazing."

"You're my dream come true. My angel of mercy."

Ooh. Words like that worked better in emails; in person they sounded borderline over-the-top. But okay. It was a first date. People always said stupid things on first dates. She had, she was sure.

He kissed her again with a few lashings of his tongue that weren't quite what she was in the mood for. Then he staggered back, breathing heavily. "Kim."

"Yes?" She couldn't help being alarmed. Was he having a heart attack?

"I can't believe this." He clutched at his chest.

Oh, God. She'd taken CPR, but it was a while ago. "Dale, are you—"

"I forgot to give this to you." He fumbled in his jacket and brought out a small box. Whew. Not heart attack. Too much brandy plus her present in his breast pocket. "It's a little something I picked up in Jamaica. I told you."

"Oh, Dale. You really—"

"Ah, ah." He waggled his finger like a disapproving parent. "Don't say I shouldn't have. I wanted to."

"Thank you. You're very sweet." She opened the box, and gave an inadvertent "oooh" of pleasure. Inside lay an exquisite pair of earrings, coral carved into tiny roses. "Oh. Dale. They are so beautiful."

"From one of the finest shops in Montego Bay."

She was bewildered by his generosity. "This is too much."

"Nothing's too good for you." His voice was low and full of emotion. "I know this will sound crazy, Kim. After a few emails and one date, it's crazy. But I really think I could fall for you."

Ten o'clock

HOW THE HELL LONG did it take to have dinner, anyway? Not that this Dale creep had taken her to a place where you had your entrée dumped in front of you and sucked it down in ten minutes. No, he'd taken her to Mimma's, and would probably spend on her as much as Nathan made in a week.

At this rate, they'd probably stay there a week.

How short could you cut a fancy dinner date if you weren't having a good time?

Shorter than this.

Crap. He'd recently traded lying on the couch for pacing and drinking beer. His latest, Bass Ale tonight, was just about ready to be tossed into their recycling bin. Then it was time for another. After his outing to the bar had been ludicrously unsatisfying, he'd driven by Kent's apartment. Not there. Monday night? What was so special about Monday night when it wasn't even Packers season?

What was Kim doing now? What if Dale had taken her home? What if she didn't come back until morning? Nathan would go nuts. He'd never survive. He'd have to drink himself into a stupor, buy sleeping pills and take enough to knock out a rhinoceros. Otherwise he'd sit here—or pace here—pain burning a hole in his chest, missing her. That old devil vulnerable. Not a feeling he was used to.

Maybe he'd better move out now. Maybe he'd better give up this losing battle before it destroyed him. Before his balls left him to find a real man.

But how could he leave after those kisses?

Jeez, listen to him, he was becoming exactly the wuss Steve accused him of being. Mooning around after a woman. Lovesick moose, that was him.

He turned into the kitchen and pulled out another beer. Might as well get completely hyphenated. The hangover couldn't be any worse than what he was feeling now.

Nathan paused just as he was about to open the bottle. What if she was trapped in a long evening? What if she was having a terrible time? It could happen. She shouldn't come back to the house and find Nathan staggering drunk. That could ruin any advantage he might have gained by the explosive chemistry of their kisses.

She had to have felt that; he hadn't been kidding when he said she'd been glowing. Did she do that for every guy who kissed her? Was she doing it for Dale? It had taken everything in Nathan to act as if it was nothing special. Maybe he shouldn't have bothered trying.

He flipped open the beer defiantly, went back into the living room, popped a Slipknot CD into the player and turned the volume up loud. Heavy metal filled the room: angry, throbbing violent sound, perfect for his mood. Couldn't do his work, couldn't get the girl…

Oh, yeah. He raged around the living room, now playing air guitar, now drums, lip syncing along to the throat-busting vocal track.

This was more like it. No more moose for him.

He executed a jumping kick and a couple of most excellent air-guitar-playing spins that landed him at the entrance to Kim's bedroom.

He stopped playing, stood in the doorway.

Kim wasn't here. He was supposed to look for pictures, a keepsake and…her underwear.

The first song, "Execute," ended. The next one started with a guitar riff and growling monotone vocals.

He retrieved his beer, walked into her room, turned on the light. The air smelled like Kim, like the perfume she'd been wearing when he kissed her. His groin reacted. He wanted to kiss her again. Like crazy.

Oh, man, he should not have had this many beers. His inhibitions were nonexistent. If she showed up now he'd probably attack her. She was so beautiful. So sexy. So—

Okay, didn't he say enough of the moose?

Yup. He said that. He did.

Pictures. He scanned her bookshelves vainly, put his bottle down on her desk and guiltily tugged open the door to her closet, not wild about the violation of her privacy. Inside, hanging clothes on one side, neatly organized shelves on the other. If she had albums they'd be here.

He found one on the top shelf, with a black, red and white geometric cover. He brought it to her bed and sat, opened to the first page. Baby Kim. He put the book down, went out into the living room and hit Pause to silence the music. He couldn't look at such innocence listening to heavy metal.

Back on her bed, he looked again. Kim had been an adorable baby. Big blue eyes, chubby cheeks, a smile that practically split her face in half. He turned another page, grinning almost as foolishly. Kim again, a more solemn little girl, standing close to her plump, pretty mother's side, blond hair to her chin. Kim, Kent and a handsome man who must be the cheating father. Kim in ballet slippers and a pink tutu.

Another page turn and he stared for a long time. Kim, standing beside her dollhouse, smiling proudly. She wasn't kidding; the little palace was amazing. Three stories, tiny yellow shingles with gingerbread trim, what looked like a slate roof, shuttered windows, chimneys and balustraded balconies. Another shot, of her and the house's interior. Inside, tiny fireplaces, chandeliers, elegant wood and metal furniture graced each room. Nothing plastic. Nothing cheap.

Impulsively, he slipped pictures from the pages: the dollhouse shots, Kim as a baby, as a little girl and ballerina. From her desk he scrounged an envelope to protect them.

Keepsakes? Another brief search in the closet turned up a small pink shoe box containing a pair of small, well-used toe shoes. Her first pair? He fingered the worn satin gently, imagining her girlish determination, her grace. What had it taken for such a shy girl to dance? He imagined her coming alive on stage. He'd like to have seen that.

He replaced the lid, and took the box and the envelope of pictures into his room, shoving the former under his bed and sticking the latter under a pile of books on his drafting table. Heading back toward Kim's room, he felt the silence in the apartment closing in on him, so he punched off the pause button and let Slipknot deafen him the rest of the way to the most dangerous part of his mission: Operation Underwear.

He stood in front of her dresser for a few seconds, nodding to the beat, feeling even more like an interloper than when he was ransacking her closet, then resolutely tugged open the top drawer. Bras. Lacy ones, plain ones, all kinds of colors, red and black, beige and white, some with polka dots, one leopard print. Nathan groaned. He'd never be able to look at Kim again without imagining one of these wonders under her clothes.

This was going to kill him.

He lifted out the leopard bra, fingered the soft cups, imagining Kim's breasts filling them. For her he'd even become a pervert, very much enjoying fingering her underwear. He should be ashamed. But by now he was too drunk and too horny to care.

He did manage to remember his mission and peer at the tag: 34C. He'd save that to his mental hard drive. Thirty-four and a capital C done in silky, sexy leopard.

Oh, yeah.

He was hard now. Couldn't help it. No matter how stupid and teenaged it was to be standing here pawing lingerie with a stiffy, he couldn't overcome the simple fact that he was a man and underwear was something women wore next to their priceless parts. And these were all Kim's.

He draped the bra over his shoulder, went for another drawer, hoping to score matching panties.

On the CD, "Gematria" ended. "Sulfur" began. *You don't always know where you stand.*

He knew. He was standing in front of Kim's underwear drawer, aka heaven.

Nathan snorted, even knowing the joke was way beyond lame. Maybe this should be his last beer. Speaking of which…he picked up the bottle from her desk and took a long swallow, exhaled in satisfaction.

Onward. Panties. *Nathan Alexander, famous lingerie explorer, continues his quest for the wild leopard bikinis.*

A second drawer slid open, releasing a breath of another perfume, one he'd smelled on her before.

Mmm. It was almost as if she was standing there. If he closed his eyes...

He wasn't going to close his eyes. Because in the drawer were panties. All kinds. All patterns. He poked around gingerly, hoping for the leopard pair, and found a length of perfume-saturated cardboard from a magazine that was responsible for the fragrance.

Scented panties. Women were amazing creatures.

Another pass and he struck leopard, drew them out reverently. "H'llo, beautiful."

They were tiny, nothing more than black ruffled strings forming their sides, the feral pattern a sexual contrast to their delicacy. Kim would look so hot in them. These with the matching bra and the black high heels she'd been wearing tonight, with her new haircut that framed her face in just the right way, and in her new, bolder makeup.

God help him. More torture. He did close his eyes this time, picturing her dressed exactly like that, standing at her bedroom door, beckoning him in, the bra barely containing her beautiful breasts, tiny panties interrupting and accenting the curving flow of her hips.

He groaned, dying to drop his now-tented boxers and jerk off, but even he had his pervert limits. Not in her room. Not around her underwear. Didn't he say he should be ashamed of himself? He wasn't.

No wonder she preferred Dale. Dale romanced her. Dale sent her flowery emails and took her out to expensive dinners, probably wrote her poetry. The only way Nathan knew how to approach women was sexually. He'd been taught nothing else, learned nothing else, and frankly, it had worked for him. But it wouldn't get him what he wanted from Kim.

And then, even in his alcohol and lust-hazed brain, it occurred to him that attraction was only half of what he felt, but it was mostly what he was showing her. He should take a page out of Dale's book instead of strutting around beating his chest like some prehistoric King Kong. No, he wouldn't write poetry—a man could feminize himself only so much—but he needed to do the obvious: ask the woman out on a date. It was so ludicrously simple, he was embarrassed not to have thought of it before. But his relationship with Kim had been stagnantly one-way for over a decade. And he was feeling his way through brand-new territory.

Excellent. That called for another drink, then back to this difficult work. He drained half of what was left in the bottle, while out in the living room his favorite track, "Butcher's Hook," blasted into the apartment. Beer set back down, he peered at the label printed in the back of her panties: size five.

Done. He had what he needed: pictures, keepsake and underwear sizes. Starting tomorrow, a new chapter in the seduction of Kim would begin, that had, for once, nothing to do with seducing her body. Okay, less to do with seducing her body.

Satisfied in at least one sense, he went to put the panties back into the drawer, but their perfume called to him, and he gave in, lifted the silken material to his face, breathed in the clean floral perfume, which so reminded him of—

Instinct warned him. Too late.

Leopard bra over his shoulder, leopard panties pressed to his nose and mouth, erection turning his boxers into one of the great pyramids...

And there in the doorway, staring at him in horror, stood Kim.

8

KIM WOULD HAVE BEEN pretty sure time had stopped, except the horrible metal music was still playing. She was standing staring at Nathan, who appeared to be getting himself off over her underwear. She couldn't imagine a single thing worse than—

Well, yes, she could imagine a lot of things worse, but this was—

Well, it was creepy.

And very difficult, with his boyishly handsome familiar face gazing at her with as much horror as she was gazing at him, to imagine that he was really some kind of panty fetishist.

At least he went for the clean ones.

She nearly laughed, and immediately blamed the alcohol and giddiness over a shot at a relationship with Dale. This was not a laughing matter.

The horrible band took a breath between songs, leaving a profound silence. Kim left her room to turn off the CD player. If she and Nathan were going to keep living together, they needed to talk about this panty thing, and she wasn't going to do it shouting over someone with hemorrhaging vocal cords.

The next guitar-torturing track started before she found the right button and replaced it with blissful peace.

Nathan emerged from her bedroom, minus her underwear and with his boxers in their normal shape, looking so painfully mortified her heart went out to him. "Kim."

"Nathan." She was calm, facing him, arms crossed over her chest. He met her eyes with an obvious effort. "Do I need to ask what you were doing?"

"Actually there is an explanation. A normal, rational one."

"Okay." She sat on the couch, glad to be the one in control for a change. "I'm listening."

He clenched his fists, stared at the ceiling for a few seconds, clearly in agony. "I can't tell you what it is. Not yet. But it doesn't come from any need to fondle underwear."

"No?"

"No." He spoke quietly, looking so bravely miserable that she wanted to put her arms around him and make it all better. But that was always her way, to make other people comfortable before herself.

"Did you try them on?"

"No!" He looked so outraged she had to hold back a giggle. She couldn't help it.

"Were you *about* to try them on?"

"No!"

She stifled another one. Fetish or no fetish, she was about to get her revenge for the way he'd toyed with her earlier. "Because I hear that's normal for some guys, you know. Doesn't mean they're gay. Necessarily. Though bisexuality is a definite possibility."

"I'm not gay."

"Okay. Um-hmm. Sure." She spoke oversoothingly, as if she didn't even begin to believe him. "But I've heard underwear fetishists can sometimes—"

"I do not have an underwear fetish, Kim."

She could barely hold back. "I read about one woman who resorted to putting mousetraps in her lingerie drawers."

"This won't happen again. It was a one time…thing."

He dropped his head in his hand, rubbed his forehead. "A misunderstanding. I don't get off on underwear."

"Okay." She nodded rapidly as if she were humoring him. He closed his eyes and dropped into a chair, the picture of despair. "It's just that you looked, Nathan, very much like you were getting off. There was this telltale sign that—"

"It wasn't the underwear."

"No?"

"No." He sat forward, rested his forearms on his thighs, hands dangling, and managed to meet her eyes more easily, which all of a sudden for no reason brought to mind the kisses he'd given her and how they'd nearly sent her to the moon. And then she couldn't help thinking of Dale's kisses and how they'd nearly sent her to the tissues in her purse. "I went into your underwear drawer for a practical reason I can't tell you. What you, um, noticed, happened because…I was picturing you wearing them."

A rush of pleasure ruined her toy-with-Nathan intentions, toppled her from her position of superiority. She could say nothing.

"I'm not gay. I'm not weird. It's not about underwear. It's about you. Okay?" He stood up, jammed his hands on his hips. "Are we clear about this now?"

She nodded, practically unable to breathe.

"Good." He spun on his heel. "I'm getting a glass of water. You want one?"

"Sure."

He was back in thirty seconds. She hadn't moved a muscle. He handed her the water, sat back down in the chair opposite the couch, drank a few gulps and passed his hand wearily over his forehead.

"Look. I'm attracted to you. It is what it is. I don't want to do anything that could ruin our friendship. Someday I'll be able to explain what you saw. I hope to God you'll think it's funny. In the meantime…" He blew out a breath. "How was your date?"

The date seemed miles away, some distant fantasy of

courtship, which interaction here with Nathan had taken over to become her evening's reality. Should that happen? "We had a good time."

"Are you seeing him again?"

"Yes." She'd been so happy when he'd asked, so full of joy when he said he could fall for her. Now she just felt tired, and wanted to crawl into her room and be by herself.

"You really like him, huh?"

She couldn't answer. She didn't know.

Nathan's expression turned tender, so tender she had to drop her gaze. "You look exhausted, Kim. Go to bed. We'll deal with all this crap tomorrow, okay?"

Oh, gosh. That was so much more threatening to her peace of mind than the grab-and-kiss maneuver. He'd read her face, acted like a protector, watching out for her, wanting her to get what she needed. What was she going to do about this man she'd invited into her life? "I am tired. It's been a long and confusing day."

"C'mon." He stood, crossed to her and held out his hand. She took it and let him pull her up.

"Thanks, Nathan."

He stayed close, not touching her, but it was as if there was a force field around them, keeping either one from moving away. "I'm sorry about my part in wearing you out today. I've had some confusion to deal with, too."

"It's okay." She mumbled the words toward his chest, not wanting to meet his gaze. Because this time she definitely could break.

"Good night." He cupped her cheek briefly and walked to his room, then turned back. "Oh, one more thing."

God help her. "What is it?"

"Saturday is supposed to be warm. I thought maybe you'd like to come kayaking with me on the Milwaukee River."

"Are you asking as a friend, or...more?" She found herself holding her breath, waiting for his answer.

"I think we need time to be friends. Time without underwear." His expression changed to startled horror when he realized what he'd said.

Kim giggled helplessly. "Tomorrow I am buying mouse-traps."

"No, no, I'll just keep my mouth shut for the rest of my life." Nathan rolled his eyes, but his grin was back, and she was very glad to see it. "See you in the morning."

"Good night, Nathan." She watched him disappear into his room, then drifted to the bathroom, brushed, washed and made it back to her bedroom, stupid with exhaustion and…whatever else she was feeling. Something warm and sweet and dangerous. Something she shouldn't be feeling for anyone but the man she was supposedly going to start dating.

She changed into her pajamas, closed her pawed-through underwear drawer, smiling and shaking her head. He could explain? She looked forward to that one.

Sliding into bed felt like the best thing that had ever happened to her. She stretched comfortably on the soft sheets, arranged her down pillows, made sure the blankets were covering both shoulders.

Finally, after this draining and bewildering day, a see-saw of emotions, of crushed and raised hopes, of attraction she'd wanted and attraction she didn't, she was where she'd been craving to be: safe, in bed, alone, free to daydream about Dale, about their next date, as she slowly drifted off to sleep.

But sleep didn't come.

And all she could think about was Nathan.

MARIE STRODE DOWN THE aisle at the Pick 'n' Save on Garfield. She'd been home all morning, restless and cranky, and finally decided if she had to stare at the walls of her house another second, she'd go completely mental. She'd been alone at the Roots Cellar Bar the previous evening. Quinn hadn't been able to make their usual Friday night dinner, and though she tried telling herself it was the end-of-the-week ritual she loved, not just seeing Quinn, being there on her own hadn't been the same. The drinks hadn't been as bracing, the food seemed less tasty. And reading her newspaper hadn't produced the kind of sparks that conversation with Quinn could.

Worse was the assumption, based on absolutely nothing, that in spite of his adorable attempts to make her feel attractive as a woman, Quinn had found female companionship for the evening he preferred. That he was making good on his promise to himself to find a serious girlfriend.

Fine. Marie had decided a while back that friendship with Quinn was better than not knowing him; she'd gone into this with eyes wide open. If she was feeling miserable over him now, it was her own damn fault.

So there. She'd beat herself up for a while. Super.

She was heading for the dairy aisle to get milk, and made the mistake of cutting through the frozen foods section. Namely, the ice cream section. Her steps slowed; her eyes peered through the frosted doorways to heaven. A pint of Ben and Jerry's Chunky Monkey would make a healthy and sustaining dinner. She'd pair it with a bottle of cheap wine, a tearjerker movie and call it a hot Saturday night.

Her hand reached for the door handle even as the sensible calorie-counting part of her brain cried a slow-motion *noooo!*

"Marie." His deep voice made her snatch her hand back as if she'd been trying to steal the crown jewels.

"Quinn." She smiled brightly, cursing herself for not showering that morning, for being so down in the dumps that she'd not even bothered with makeup or decent clothes. But then he'd seen her this way before—in fact, the last time she bumped into him here in their shared neighborhood. Maybe she could summon him from nowhere simply by looking like hell?

Not the superpower she'd choose where he was concerned.

"Mmm, Ben and Jerry's." His eyes had drifted to the forbidden fruit. "I'm a Cherry Garcia addict."

"I'm a Chunky Monkey." She cringed. *No kidding.* "Oh, *that* sounded great."

He was laughing, but not unkindly. Quinn was never unkind. "I'm going to leave that one out there to mortify you."

"Thanks. Really. Super. Did you have fun last night?" Somehow she kept the edge from her voice.

"Oh, yeah. You can't attend benefit dinners without having a great time. Especially eating badly cooked, tepid food listening to self-congratulatory speeches. Don't know when I've had so much fun."

"You didn't have a date to liven it up?" *Shut up, Marie.* For God's sake. What a masochist.

"Oh, yeah." He drew the words out. "One wild, red-hot babe I used to work with."

Marie nodded stiffly, a smile plastered to her face. She asked for it; she got it.

"Not *quite* old enough to be my mother, but close." He moved his shopping cart to let a young woman and her kids scoot by, while Marie tried not to be knocked over by a tidal wave of relief. Old enough to be his mother. This was happy news. "What are you doing this afternoon, Marie? Somehow it's a beautiful spring day and only the first of April."

"I was going to…" She searched for something to make her afternoon sound thrilling, but nothing came. "Just… be."

"How Zen." He grinned and touched her shoulder. "I was planning to stroll the length of Riverwalk. I've meant to for a while and haven't done it yet."

"Sounds enterprising." Riverwalk was an ongoing project by the city to construct three miles of walkway along the Milwaukee River where it flowed through the city. Marie had only explored the part that went through downtown, among bars and cafés, by the performing arts center and the Usinger's Sausage Factory. The many sides of Milwaukee.

"Want to come along? We'll end up in the Third Ward and can find some dinner since we missed our date last night. If you want to."

If she *wanted to?* She tried to look politely interested, when she wanted to throw her arms around him and scream *yes, yes, yes!* "That sounds like fun."

"Good. Can you meet in an hour or is later better?"

"An hour is fine." She could move heaven and earth in that time if it meant spending half a day with him.

And then the little voice inside her piped up, that irritating, sensible one that seemed always to be trying to ruin her good times. It warned that she risked diving into him too deeply. And the deeper she went, the harder it would be to surface again, without getting a serious case of the bends.

"I'll pick you up? I remember where you live."

"Great, yes." Marie told the voice to shut up for now. She'd already told Quinn she'd go; she could be sensible later. "See you then."

He started off, then turned back, with that killer smile lighting his face. "I'm glad I bumped into you, Marie."

"Same here." And how.

At the end of the aisle—she passed Chunky Monkey without another glance—she yanked open the door to the milk, hauled out a gallon of skim and practically ran to the front of the store, where she managed not to push people out of line so she could get through faster. One hour until he picked her up—Marie had some serious transforming to do.

Back home she jumped into the shower, allowing the voice to advise her that she was ridiculous, becoming so giddy over a friendly request for company, and that yes, she was asking for nothing but more heartache continuing to see him, especially in situations like this.

It didn't help. Going from the depths of this morning's lonely doldrums to the prospect of spending the afternoon with one of her favorite people? Who wouldn't be thrilled? She was allowed.

The last coat of mascara had just gone on when her

doorbell rang. She ran downstairs, grabbing a jacket for the inevitable plunge in temperature after dark. Wisconsin would be playing them all for fools if they thought temperatures in the seventies would last longer than a day or two. Snow was still a very real possibility. Frosts in May weren't unheard of.

But today it was truly spring, and Marie had no problem clinging to that.

They drove to Riverwalk's northern origin at Commerce Street and Humboldt Avenue, where the properties were primarily residential, parked the car and started walking along the concrete path next to the Milwaukee River, which was flowing swiftly from the snowmelt. Along the walkway, which used to be a railroad line, several modern condominium developments in various styles, spanning "intriguing" to "hideous," had been built to rescue the neighborhood from its rail yard past.

The sun was gloriously warm, and though it would be some time before trees started leafing, the day made it seem possible, which couldn't fail to lift Marie's spirits, even if she hadn't been walking next to George Clooney's twin.

"This is great, Quinn." She bumped into his hand and wanted to grab it and hold on.

"It is." He smiled down at her, obviously measuring his stride for her shorter legs, because otherwise she'd probably have to run to keep up. "I've been wanting to do this for a while. Funny how you have to goose yourself to play tourist in your own city."

"I had a college friend who grew up in New York and had never been to the top of the Empire State Building until I came to visit." She unzipped her jacket, already warming. "Have you taken a tour of the Miller Brewing Company here?"

"Umumblemumble." He pretended to be fascinated by the oddly shaped facade of a development they were passing.

"Ha! *I've* done that."

His head whipped around accusingly. "Was someone visiting?"

"D'oh!" She feigned dismay. "You got me."

They walked farther, occasionally clambering around unfinished portions of the walk, which was being completed in stages. This northern third, called the Beerline, would be the last part built.

"How's Kim's big bash coming?"

"It's coming. We decided to do a wall of Kim, showing her evolution from shy girl to fabulous hot mama."

"A wall of Kim. Featuring what? Pictures? Letters? Objects?"

"All of the above."

"That's a really nice idea."

"Why, thank you, Quinn." Marie beamed at him, wishing he wasn't so kind, so thoughtful, so handsome, so goddamn perfect. Even his tortured inner nature was sexy.

"Wonder what my wall would look like. Or no." He tapped her lightly on the shoulder. "Tell me what yours would look like. Starting young."

"Let's see. Young Marie." She rolled her eyes. "Chubby. Of course."

"Adorably dimpled."

"Dimpled everywhere. According to Mom I was a sweet baby, but didn't handle frustration well."

"That doesn't surprise me. Tell me more."

She was flattered. Who wouldn't be? "I was a good student, a good girl, occasional bursts of mild wildness, nothing unique."

"I doubt that, but okay." He pointed up ahead to a small hawk, swooping through bare branches.

"Oh, pretty." They stopped to watch it choose a limb, perch and settle itself. Marie had to swallow a lump in her throat. The bird? The man? The day? Maybe just hormones.

"I didn't mean to interrupt." He waited for another couple to pass them before he took off walking again. "You were telling me about Marie. Smart, well-behaved, most of the time. What about later? The dating years?"

"She had a bad tendency to get swept off her feet." Like now, only Quinn wasn't sweeping on purpose.

"The ex?"

"Yup. Back then I believed in love at first sight, and thought I had lived it."

"You don't believe in it anymore."

"No," Marie said firmly. "I believe in infatuation at first sight, absolutely. But love? Love is what's left over when all the initial excitement is spent."

They separated to pass a single walker. Quinn nodded. "It's hard to stay a crazed romantic after your marriage has failed. Because you know all that excitement and all those deep, fabulous feelings can change. That they can die."

"Yes." She turned, touched by the sadness in his voice. "That's it exactly."

"By the way, did you ever decide what to do with that ring?"

Marie snorted. "Not give it back to him. That's as far as I got."

Quinn gave her a wide grin. "Good for you."

"Thanks." That smile made her feel she'd scored a lot more than jewelry.

A breeze blew springlike scents of earth; a couple of kayakers paddled by them downriver.

"What's next on your wall? No, wait." He raised his hand. "Let me guess."

"Have at it."

"After the divorce, a momentary dip into depression, then out of the ashes rises the powerful phoenix of Milwaukee-dates.com and the remarkable woman you are today."

"Thank you. I wouldn't have put it quite that way...but yes, that's the gist." She was blushing at his compliments, hoping he'd blame her color on the exertion and the breeze. "Now take me on a tour of Quinn's wall."

"Quinn's wall, hmm." He pointed ahead. "Juneau Avenue.

We're getting to the second leg of the walk through downtown. Accounts for more people around."

"And boat traffic." More kayakers passing, and a small motorboat.

"Speaking of tourists, have you ever taken one of the dinner cruises down the river into Lake Michigan?"

"No, sir, haven't done that, either."

"Hmm." He glanced at her, then away. "The Cellar Bar might collapse, but let's do that one Friday night when it gets warmer."

"Nice idea." Warmer? Marie was plenty warm right now just thinking about him planning for the two of them that far in advance. "But don't think I haven't noticed you avoiding answering questions about Quinn's wall."

He gave her a rueful look. "Can't get anything by you, huh?"

"Nothing. Give."

"Okay. Let's see." He stretched his arms over his head, then resumed their natural swing. "Boy Quinn was a handful. According to Mom I never stopped running except when I was asleep."

"Poor Mom."

"Then my parents divorced and I graduated to the sneaking years, the stealing years, the brushes-with-the-law years."

That surprised her. "Which brings you up to what age?"

"Four."

Marie cracked up. God, he was fun. "And then what, a six-year-old's tale of Life in the Big House?"

"Oddly, in high school I straightened out some, which I credit to Mom remarrying a strict but great guy. I found I actually liked school, and that while some women loved bad boys, there were plenty who were attracted to relative stability, too."

"I take it that clinched your transformation."

He bumped her purposely. "There you go again. Typecasting."

"Sorry. Go on." She wanted to skip ahead of him like a demented Dorothy on her own yellow brick road. Something about walking with a man—no, with *this* man, matching paces in the fresh air, talking easily—made her giddy with happiness.

"Then college, a good mix of fun and hard work, then moving to Boston, marrying, moving back here, divorce, pain, shutting self away, and now…"

"The great awakening." She smiled at him, enjoying his triumph.

"And the rest of the wall remains to be filled."

"What would you fill it with if you could choose now? Obviously, you want a new woman."

"Obviously."

"What else?"

"Honestly, Marie, I'm happy with the rest of my life. I love my job, I love making money, I have a great circle of friends. It's just that wo-oma-an."

His voice growled sexily on the word and made her go shivery. Whoever that wo-oma-an was, she'd be one lucky you-know-what.

Another kayak pulled into her peripheral vision. Marie turned to look, and did a double take.

"Holy kayakers, Batman. Kim!" She walked to the railing and made a megaphone with her hands. *"Kim!"*

Her friend turned. So did the guy in the kayak alongside hers. Who was *that?* Her brother? He wasn't on the Milwaukeedates.com site. Totally adorable.

"Hey." Marie waved with both hands. The boats maneuvered closer.

"Marie!" Kim was beaming, eyes lit, her new haircut blown into a beautiful tousled mane. Marie had never seen her look like that. She was radiant. "This is Nathan."

"Hi, Nathan." Marie gave a friendly smile, mind whirling. Nathan, the womanizer? He better not be the cause of Kim's radiance. She'd get her sweet, trusting heart splattered all over their apartment. Marie should not have sent him to check out Kim's underwear.

"Marie, nice to meet you." From his position in front of Kim's boat, his face out of her line of sight, he gave Marie a sly wink. "Kim's told me great things about you."

"That's sweet of her." She wished she could say Kim had been doing the same about Nathan. Marie gestured to Quinn. "This is Quinn Peters, a friend from my neighborhood."

"Nice to meet you, Quinn." Kim was looking at him exactly the way you'd expect a woman to look at Quinn.

"Hi, Kim, Nathan. Nice to meet you both." His deep voice rang easily over the water. "Having a good ride today?"

"Beautiful." Kim beamed at them. "It could not be more perfect."

"No kidding." Nathan turned to smile at her. *Whoa.* That was not the smile of a predator, that was the smile of a boy badly smitten.

So…did this crush go both ways?

Marie would have to have a chat with Kim soon.

"Have fun!" The kayaks had caught the current and slipped downstream. Marie waved to them until they were out of earshot. "Am I dreaming or was there enough heat there to set both boats on fire?"

"I'm surprised they're not ash already."

"Hmm. And she was too intimidated by Troy? That kid is beautiful."

"Oh, well, sure." Quinn laughed derisively. "If you like that young, virile and handsome thing."

"Not me." Marie blinked sweetly at him. "I like the *mature,* virile and handsome thing."

"Really." His gaze intensified. "I like that about you."

She refused to read anything into the exchange, ignored that her heart was beating faster, and turned to keep walking, thinking about Kim and Nathan, how happy they looked, how natural they seemed together. Quinn had sensed it, too.

What happened to the ordinary, dull man Kim wanted?

Maybe enjoying the dates with Troy and Dale had bolstered her self-esteem, made her broaden her search? That would be wonderful. Because Marie had seen in this business that if people came in with too narrow a focus on what they could or couldn't attract, that limitation often became a self-fulfilling prophecy.

Marie had told countless clients, including Kim, that if you visualized what you wanted, even if it seemed an impossible fantasy at first, and got used to thinking of yourself as deserving, then when you went after it…

The realization was so blinding, Marie had to force herself to keep walking, because what she really wanted to do was stop and stand there with her mouth hanging open, maybe smack herself on the forehead a few times. Then a few times more.

Because the most obvious example of someone closing herself off to the type of man, or in this case the *actual* man, she really wanted, was the woman Marie saw every time she looked in the mirror.

"We're still missing one thing on the topic of our walls." Quinn's voice jolted her back to reality. She needed to stay calm enough to finish this walk, keep chatting with him in a friendly and casual way so he wouldn't suspect that a thunderbolt had just shot through her. She needed time to live with this, to sort out what she was going to do.

"What's that?"

"What would you want next on your wall?"

She shrugged, as if she couldn't imagine, when the answer roared in her head so loudly she wouldn't be surprised if he could hear it.

You.

9

SATURDAY TURNED OUT to be one of those miracle days that almost never happened in Milwaukee that early in the season, especially downtown, where Lake Michigan, still cold from the long winter, could keep the air temperature a good ten degrees cooler than inland. Spring came a full week or two later lakeside than in the rest of the state.

But Saturday brought April into Wisconsin with a burst of unseasonably warm temperatures that were enough to make the winter-sick residents giddy. And enough to make Nathan actually organized. Kim had to say she was impressed. He'd reserved kayaks for them at Milwaukee's outdoor supplier, Laacke and Joys; planned that they'd leave his car at the end of their route, then drive to the beginning in Kim's; packed a picnic they could enjoy on the beach after their paddle— in short, he took charge in a way she'd never seen him do before.

Which was great, because her day had started out horribly. First a call from her mother woke her. Mom was an early riser but never seemed to comprehend that not everyone else was. She wanted Kim to know that one of Kim's classmates had been appointed VP of a Fortune 500 company, and one of Kent's old girlfriends had started her own company and was already pulling in half a million in annual sales. She wanted to know about men in Kim's life—Kim had told her nothing about Milwaukeedates.com, hadn't even told her about Nathan having moved in. Her mother asked what Kim was doing for her birthday, said she hated to think of her spending it alone with that computer. Thirty was such an important age, and how was her little business going, by the way? Mom worried about her future, she really did.

By the end of the call, Kim had been as rigid as an iron rod, one that someone had tried to stomp into the ground about a dozen times. Nothing could bring on heartburn like a call from her mother. All Kim's life it had been hammered home: nothing mattered but financial security. Husband cheating? Who cared, as long as his salary kept coming in. Work exhausting you to the point where it endangered your health? Oh, well! At least you had plenty of cash.

As if that wasn't bad enough, after Kim dragged herself through breakfast and powered up her machine, there had been an email from Dale that was so passionately over-the-top, she could only conclude that he'd been drunk when he wrote it, from Hong Kong or wherever he was now, and therefore it left her feeling more uneasy than romantic.

But wait! There was more! While she'd been sitting there feeling squeamish at Dale's certainty that the moon and sun set over her bed, another email had come in. This one from Emily, account executive at Soka Associates, the friend who'd tipped Kim off about Carter opening their website job for bidding. She said rumors were buzzing that Soka was reorganizing and that Kim's name had been brought up to fill the new interactive creative director post. A well-paying, prestigious job, a great opportunity for Kim, except that considering the change left a miserable, defeated taste in her mouth. Back to the grind, the politics, the backstabbing and low morale…

After that it didn't surprise her when she stumbled heavily through her dance class in a body that felt like it belonged to someone else. It was just one of those days.

Except it wasn't. Not anymore. Being outdoors without walls or worries after the long season cooped up in the apartment felt like being let out of jail. The afternoon with Nathan so far had been wonderful; Kim couldn't believe she'd lived in Milwaukee this long and had never been on the river before. In Wooster, Ohio, where she grew up, there wasn't a whole lot of water around, but she'd been kayaking once while visiting a friend in Loudonville, and had done pretty well. Today she was happy to find the strokes still familiar, the sensation of powering a boat so easily through the water exhilarating; paddling seemed to take hardly any effort. Granted, going with the current helped.

Best of all, Nathan had been nothing but polite and respectful, starting this morning when he'd hauled himself out of bed looking scruffy, sleepy and nearly irresistible. On the river, they'd chatted easily, pointed out sights to each other along the way, or drifted in companionable silence. She'd enjoyed his company more today than she ever had—which brought up its own set of problems that she refused to acknowledge. She was going to take on Nathan's philosophy: enjoy this day and leave analysis and consequences for another time.

Right now they were heading for a picnic spot on the near-deserted lakeshore, Nathan lugging a cooler, Kim hauling a fat canvas bag. She couldn't believe they'd bumped into Marie and that total catch she was with. If her friend had been keeping him to herself, she was in big trouble. No fair if Kim's love life was an open book—hell, Marie was helping write some of it—and Marie got to keep secrets. If she didn't spill, the girls would hear of this at their next Women in Power meeting, and take appropriate action.

Kim grinned just thinking about it. Everything was making her smile. The first days of warm weather were the best high that existed. She couldn't imagine how people in tropical and temperate climates existed without this annual rebirth. Of course, they probably couldn't imagine how anyone existed having to shovel hundreds of pounds of snow off every conceivable surface over and over, month after month.

However, in her book, days like today made all that more than worthwhile.

"How about right here?" Nathan jerked his head toward a spot no different from hundreds of others on the mostly empty beach.

"I don't know." She glanced over dubiously and pointed several inches to the right. "I kind of had my heart set on right there."

Nathan frowned. "This is going to get ugly."

"Compromise?" She pointed two inches left.

"I *guess* I can give that much." He set the cooler down, took the bag from her, and produced a worn comforter that he unfolded over the sand. "Have a seat?"

"Thank you. Mmm, I'm starving."

"Same here." He opened the cooler lid. "Peanut butter sandwiches, chips and Cokes sound good?"

"The best."

"Wow, Kim, I'm sorry." He looked crestfallen. "I don't have any of that."

"What…" She pushed him out of the way and peered into the cooler. "Oh, my gosh, Nathan! This looks amazing."

He grinned, adorably pleased with himself. "Glad you think so."

"Yum!" She started unpacking: French bread, olives, salami and ham, roasted peppers, tiny balls of fresh mozzarella sprinkled with basil, cherry tomatoes, Brie, marinated artichoke hearts, strawberries, chocolate chip cookies—"Nathan, you have outdone yourself."

"All I did was walk into Sendik's and buy." He reached into the bag she'd been carrying and brought out a bottle wrapped in a narrow brown bag. "The final touch. We'll have to keep it covered, but I couldn't resist."

"Oh, great idea." A bottle of wine! He'd thought of everything. She poked around farther in the cooler. Oops. Maybe not everything. "Corkscrew?"

His face fell. "Um."

"Plates? Glasses? Forks? Napkins?"

His groan made her start giggling. He was still Nathan, after all. "We'll manage."

"I can't believe it. I've violated the Manly Bill of Rights by not providing easy access to alcohol."

"We have our water bottles." Though hers was nearly empty.

"Wait! Hold everything." He dug in his pocket, triumphantly came up with a Swiss Army knife, twisted the corkscrew into the bottle and gave a yank. A satisfying thunk put a grin on his face. "*Now* I've thought of everything. Everything that matters, anyway. Let's eat."

Kim did. She ate until she was sure she'd doubled her weight. Sunshine, lake air and exercise did something magical to the appetite. Wine didn't hurt.

"You know how to have a good time, Nathan."

"Of course." He grinned his charmer's grin. "Story of my life."

"Right, I know, I know, and it's why you land a-a-all those women." She held out her hand for the wine, surprised when he didn't pass it over right away.

"I had four older brothers. I went to an all-male high school. My dad wasn't the world's biggest proponent of equal rights for women. Being around guys all the time meant once I passed puberty I didn't learn how to be friends with girls." He passed her the bottle. "Even our neighbors had boys."

Kim took her time drinking, nestled the bottle back into the cooler when she'd had enough. His words cast his attitude about women in a different light. When would he have learned about women as other than dating objects? Kim had been around Kent and his friends from the time she was little, and palling around with boys in their neighborhood had been second nature. If she hadn't had that experience, she might view men only in terms of dating, too.

"I guess I never thought about it that way. But in college?"

"I fell in with the same crowd. It was familiar. It was what I knew. You've met Steve."

She made a face. "Uh, yeah."

"I rest my case."

Kim laughed. "Well, it's not too late to change. You're friends with me."

He held her gaze to the point where she had to drop hers, suddenly uncomfortable with him again in a way she hadn't been all day.

"Another cookie?" He held one out.

She took it, not really needing more, but wanting to break the odd tension, even if it only existed in her head. "Thanks."

"Tell me about men in your life, Kim. And why you don't trust us."

"What makes you think I don't trust men?"

Nathan tapped his temple. "Instinct."

"Ah." He had good instincts. "Some unfortunate happenings…"

"Like?"

She gestured impatiently. "Like bad stuff. Men abusing my trust."

"Cheating on you?"

"No." She looked down at the soft blue comforter they were sitting on, nearly threadbare in spots, and absently wondered if it was one Nathan had as a child.

"They promised one thing, delivered another."

"In a manner, yeah."

"Promised love, delivered sex?"

Kim turned away from him, stared out at the lake, surprised by her urge to share the story, not sure why or if it was a good idea. "Why are you poking at this?"

"Because, Kim." His voice was deep and gentle behind her. "I'd like to know you better. Understand you better."

He wanted to understand her. She really wanted to tell him now, wanted more of this intimacy that had sprung up between them. And she wanted his reaction, for reasons she couldn't entirely grasp. "I thought this guy in college was really into me. It turned out he wanted to see if geeky girls were good in bed so he could brag to his friends."

"Bastard." Nathan's voice was no longer warm or gentle. Kim turned around and faced him squarely.

"Do you see what you do?" She was desperate for him to understand. "Do you understand that women aren't just 'women,' they're Kim and Marie and—"

"Of course I understand." Nathan's eyes were as earnest as hers. "But you're doing the same thing, Kim. To you I'm not Nathan, I'm 'man.' Man is untrustworthy, therefore Nathan is untrustworthy."

She opened her mouth for a searing comeback, then realized she didn't have one. "I don't think you're untrustworthy."

"No?"

Kim shook her head. She'd said the words to be polite, but it hit her that they were true, at least in his role as a friend. She wouldn't want to be in the position of having to trust him as a lover.

"But you wouldn't want to go out with me."

"Are you asking me to?" She reached for the wine in the cooler to cover a weird spasm of excitement.

"Uh, little awkward here. Rephrase. Let's say you had a single friend. Would you set her up with me?"

"Oh." She took a sip, was about to pass him the bottle, but took another. She was going to need it. "I don't—I'm not sure."

"Assuming I could convince you I'm not trying to have sex with every breathing woman on the planet, would there be something else in the way?"

"Uh." She wasn't sure how to respond. The objection was glaringly obvious to her, but there were probably flaws in her that were glaringly obvious to other people, yet which would flabbergast her. "What makes you think I have an answer?"

"I know you do." His gaze was direct; he seemed suddenly stronger, more mature.

She decided to take a chance.

"Well, maybe if you kind of…got things in your life… onto a more…" She sighed. "This is hard."

"Go on. You can't insult me."

She had a feeling she could. "Women want guys who are… Well, most women, I don't know about all, but—"

"Kim." He was quiet and steady, watching her thrash around. "Just say it. I won't break."

She smiled at the reference. Then took a deep breath and dove in. "Your life seems out of focus. We're past the era where women need men to provide for them, but those old instincts remain. Men on Milwaukeedates.com still post pictures of animals they've shot or killed, fish they've caught, like they're saying, 'I am man, I can provide.' You have this brilliant future ahead of you, a chance to make a real difference with the houses you're designing, and it's like you don't really want to do it."

She watched a bug travel up to the edge of the comforter.

Had the waves on the beach always been that loud?

Or was it the horrible silence after her outburst that made them seem that way?

She should not have had so much wine. It had absolutely erased her common sense.

"Nathan, I'm sorry. I shouldn't have—"

"No." He shook his head, jaw set. "You're absolutely right."

She stared at him. It was as if he'd turned into a different person. He seemed more centered, more solid, larger. No longer the horny frat boy. A man.

Come on, Kim. The wine had made her romanticize him.

Another blink and he was grinning again, back to the easy fun Nathan she lo—

Really liked.

"I'm going to go home and process that, but I don't want it to ruin our date."

"Our *date?*"

He rolled his eyes. "Yeah, I just said we were friends to put you off guard so I could try something. Come on, Kim, you know me better than that by now."

"Okay, okay." She laughed at his teasing, relieved at the release of tension, but not yet able to banish that momentary glimpse of Nathan the Man.

"Anyone ever tell you you're bristly like a porcupine, Miss Kimberly Charlotte?"

"Hedgehog. Porcupines have quills."

"For crying out loud." He offered her another cookie, took a bite of it when she shook her head. "Tell me what it is about the Carter proposal that's holding you up."

"Ugh." She fell back onto her elbows, admiring the view of the lake reaching out for the horizon. "It's a mess. You don't want to hear about it."

"I actually do. For reasons that might surprise you."

"Such as?"

"I'm betting…" He narrowed his eyes thoughtfully, gesturing at her with the cookie. "That you want it too much."

She nodded, surprised and buoyed by his perceptiveness. "Creativity is such a tricky beast. I'm trying to force it because this matters so much to me, because my company and career rest on whether I make this or not, and because there's a deadline in a week. I don't have any leisure or relaxing time to play with it, to have fun, which is when I do my best work."

He stopped chewing, then resumed more slowly. "Interesting. Why don't you try de-emphasizing the importance?"

She snorted. "Right. Who cares if everything I've worked for over the past five years turns to crap?"

"That's not what I meant." He closed the cooler, moved it out of their way and leaned back beside her. She didn't mind. It felt relaxed and right. "You have other options, besides despair and ruin. It's not a question of all or nothing."

Kim took a deep breath. "True. But it all got more complicated today."

She told him about Soka's offer, how important a move like that could be for her career, reputation and skills.

He frowned. "I thought you weren't happy there."

"Life isn't only about being happy all the time." Kim cringed. She sounded just like her mother.

"Yes it is. Screw Soka. Screw Carter. There are other companies out there. This is self-created stress based on some completely random idea of age thirty having to be some turning point in your life."

"Yes." She moved restlessly. "That's true."

"Let it go. Say to hell with all of it. Who cares? Find the joy in your work again. I'll be your caveman." He jabbed a thumb into his chest. "I'll get fish for our table and shoot things for you. We'll make it work, and be happy even if you don't get Carter, even if Charlotte's Web goes belly-up."

He was talking nonsense. They weren't a couple, they were roommates for a few weeks. And yet…while he was talking this nonsense, Kim felt as if some of the crushing weight of the world had been lifted from her shoulders.

"Maybe you're right. Maybe it would help to lighten up."

"Just being out here today will help. Refill your 'well' as all the creativity gurus say." He pulled the wine back out of the cooler and offered it to her. "And when all else fails, get a buzz on."

She giggled, tipped the bottle up, passed it back, not minding when their shoulders met and stayed pressed together. Not minding at all. She felt light and elated, and the mood had way too little to do with the wine. Nathan was a good guy. He'd listened and treated her problems with care and respect.

She flashed to the evening she'd spent with Dale, remembering how he sometimes ignored her interjections, how he hadn't wanted to hear about her work for Carter the first time around, how he'd listened absently when she brought it up again, trying to make it clear how important the job was to her. He'd taken her hands across the table, saying,

"You can do it, Kim. I believe in you." Then he'd changed the subject. She'd felt nothing but the weight of another set of expectations.

Movement caught her eye. A woman jogging on the beach, in a black exercise bra and tiny black shorts that exposed her waist. Her full breasts bounced with each step, her ponytail swung. She had a flawless muscled body that would look at home in the Olympics.

Beside Kim, Nathan became unnaturally still. She didn't have to look to know his eyes were following each stride, each swing, each bounce.

The jogger passed; Nathan's head turned, following her progress. Not a single jiggle was evident in her butt or thighs as she ran away from them up the beach.

Beside him, Kim felt utterly invisible. "Not leopard printed, but a thrill, huh?"

Nathan started, jerked his eyes guiltily away. "No, I was thinking…I mean, I wasn't thinking what you think I was—"

"Ha." She nudged him teasingly, nauseated from the wine. At least that's what she told herself was making her stomach sink and churn. "Relax. I get it. She was gorgeous."

He turned toward her. "Yes, but— No, I wasn't—"

"Don't worry." She put a maternal hand to his cheek, then wished she hadn't, when the stubbled strength of his jaw felt so masculine under her palm and fingers. "You can't help it. I get that."

"Right. I can't help it." He fell back on the comforter with a sound of total exasperation, then mumbled something she didn't bother asking him to repeat.

The woman's timing had been perfect. If Nathan had exhibited any more of that sweet, sensitive side, Kim could have been in trouble. But she knew what she wanted in a man, and she had seen a glimpse of that when Dale looked into her eyes and said, "When I'm in love, all other women cease to exist."

That's what she wanted. And even if it turned out Dale

wasn't the man for her, which she was seriously starting to wonder, in her search going forward, she wouldn't settle for anything less.

10

FROWNING, KIM CHANGED the red teapot from the red table to the blue one, absorbed in the creative process. She'd tried hard this week while Dale was out of town again to take Nathan's advice and get out of her own way, designwise. Whether or not it had worked, she wasn't sure, but she did feel that old excited buzz of being onto something good with this latest idea. It had come to her a few days earlier, as ideas often did for some reason she'd never figured out, while she was in the shower.

She'd found online pictures of fabulously funky circular tables in bright colors, each with a central chrome leg leading to a matching, smaller circle on the floor. On a series of those tables in different vibrant colors, Kim had arranged the new Carter2 table settings: china, stemware and flatware sometimes echoing the table color, sometimes contrasting. The effect was eye-catching, elegant and hip, exactly what she was after.

Was it good enough to stand out among the bids Carter was likely to receive? She wasn't convinced. However, with entries due on Monday, four days away, she didn't have a whole lot of time to fuss. At least she'd finally hit on the right feel, and the Carter execs would be able to see Charlotte's Web Design's work. If not this job, maybe another...

She heard Nathan's key in the apartment door lock and

glanced at her watch. Whoa. She'd been at this for hours. No wonder her shoulders felt as if they'd turned to cement. Usually she was good about remembering to take breaks and stretch.

"Hey, Kim."

She saved her document, pushed back her chair and wandered into the living room, eager to see him. Since their kayaking trip, she and Nathan had settled into real friendship, which she hoped would help prove to him that women could be part of his life without the hunt and capture mentality. He was spending more time at home and dedicating more hours to his thesis. Maybe he'd taken her remarks to heart about focusing his life, as she'd taken his about her approach to the Carter project.

"Hi, Nathan. How was work?"

"It was work." He held up two white paper bags. "I brought back dinner and a movie."

"Oh, what a good man." She yawned and raised her arms high. "I could use a break and I'm not sure there's anything in the pantry but a can of tuna and some pasta."

"I brought health food." In the kitchen, he opened the bags and unloaded burgers, fries and take-out frozen custard from Culver's, her favorite stand.

"Yum!" She picked up the DVD he'd put on the table. *Echoes*. She'd never heard of it. "What's the movie?"

"A recommendation from a friend. I haven't seen it." He stacked the take-out containers of custard and put them in the freezer. "Supposed to be very artsy."

"Really." She examined the cover dubiously. A couple in a rather provocative clinch, their nakedness hidden by darkness except for the smooth curves of shoulders and thighs. "Well, I guess we'll find out."

"I'm game if you are."

"Sure." She snitched a fry and chewed ravenously. "Mmm. The ideal thing following an entire day spent sitting in one place—ten thousand calories."

"Your brain burned at least that many." He brushed her

bangs aside and pointed to her forehead. "There, right there. Telltale scorch marks."

She laughed, still uneasy around him physically. That part, the undeniable attraction, she hadn't been able to conquer completely. Since Dale had calmed down and become less flowery and more normal in his emails, she'd tried to channel all that energy into hope that something could work with him.

"You want to eat first or get right to the movie?" he asked.

"How about burgers here, custard during the showing?"

"Good plan." He opened the refrigerator, pulled out a bottle of Heineken. "Beer?"

"Sure. I'm too burned out to do any more work today." She took the bottle after he opened it for her and gulped down a long swig. "Your advice has really helped, Nathan. I'm making progress. Not quite there, but nearly. And I'm almost having fun."

"I'm glad." He opened his beer. "I'm trying to apply the same principles toward working on my thesis."

"And?" She was excited for him. If he could get that done, it would be a huge load off his shoulders.

"Some progress." He held up his bottle. "We're celebrating tonight."

"Who is?" She sat at the table, pulling a burger toward her.

"You and me. It's our anniversary. A month and three days of living together."

She laughed and waited until he sat to clink bottles with him. "How about that. Here's to our anniversary, Nathan."

He clinked, picked up his burger and started unwrapping. "You know, I bought you a gift. Very, very expensive jewelry. Unfortunately, I lost it."

"Oh, gosh, how ironic." She balled up her wrapper and tossed it into the garbage. "I bought you a Lexus, but it crashed on the way to the dealer."

"Ooh, tough luck." He took an enormous bite of his burger,

which looked so delicious that she took an enormous bite of hers, too.

"Mmm."

He shoved a fry into his half-full mouth. "Mmm-*hmm.*"

Good idea. Kim copied him happily, thinking how terrified she'd been opposite Dale that sauce would drip off her fork or she'd drop food in her lap. How long before she got to a place with him where she could be completely comfortable like this? Maybe they'd get closer on their date tomorrow, since Kim would be going without makeup, dressed down, the way he wanted her. Though actually, she'd kind of gotten used to seeing herself in the mirror with a few minimal cosmetic touch-ups, and liked the change.

Nathan's cell rang; he reached into his pocket, checked the display and put the phone back. "Steve."

"Don't want to talk to him?"

"He's going out tonight. Wants company."

"And?" She ate another fry. "We can watch the movie another night."

"I'm not up for any more nights like that. At least not with him."

"Why?"

He shrugged. "Doesn't interest me anymore."

"Did you tell him?"

Nathan lowered his hamburger. "Are you suggesting I share my feelings?"

"D'oh!" She smacked her fist on her forehead. "What was I thinking?"

"I'll share them with you instead. I'm no longer interested in anonymous sexual contact."

"Wow." She was so surprised she put her burger down. "Why not?"

"Because I'm…" He glanced toward the window, then back toward her, obviously nervous. "No longer interested."

Kim snorted. "That's fact, not feelings."

"Okay." He set his face in concentration. "What I'm feeling is…"

Kim waited. "Ye-e-s?"

"A need."

"Okay." She nodded encouragingly. "A need. For something besides anonymous sex."

"Yes." He met her gaze, his dazzlingly serious; her heart reached out to him.

"You can tell me. It's totally safe."

He nodded solemnly. "I need…custard."

Gotcha. Again. Kim rolled her eyes. "Okay, okay, I get it. Women share feelings, men share facts. Let's have custard and watch the movie."

"See how easy that is?" He got up and went to the freezer, thumped their frozen custard servings down with a flourish. "Voilà. The final siege on our hearts this evening, Culver's daily flavor, turtle cheesecake. Only in the Midwest do they work on finding new ways to add more fat to fat."

"Amen." She lifted what was left of her beer. "Here's to fat."

"Another bottle?"

"Sure, it goes so well with custard."

He grinned at her sarcasm. "Yeah, sorry, I'm fresh out of *liqueur du turtle cheesecake*."

They went into the living room with their dessert and spoons, Nathan bringing along another six Heinekens, as well.

"You want the lights out?" She headed for the lamp, anticipating his preference for watching TV in the dark.

"Yeah. It's more like a movie theater."

"Okay." Kim turned off the light, settled onto the couch and covered herself with the blanket she kept there; she inevitably got cold watching TV, and would certainly get cold eating something frozen. While Nathan loaded the movie, she took her first bite. The custard was dreamy, cheesecake-tasting vanilla with bits of real cheesecake, sweet threads of caramel, chocolate chips and toasted pecan pieces. She was pretty sure she could feel her hips expanding as the creamy richness slid down her throat.

"Good?" He joined her on the couch, pried the plastic top off his cup.

"Orgasmic."

He opened a beer and handed it to her. "Good to hear."

"Want under the blanket?" She lifted the edge and held it toward him. "There's plenty."

"Sure." He sat close; she felt the warmth of his legs next to hers and wondered if she would regret the offer. It was oddly intimate, sharing a blanket in a dark room.

The movie started with a split-screen view of a man and a woman walking down a city sidewalk, heading toward each other from opposite directions. The next half hour was a bewildering collage of apparently unrelated scenes that depicted too many of the dramatic and complicated situations that kept the couple from meeting, which they were obviously destined to do.

Maybe he was just in her brain, but Kim swore the guy looked enough like Nathan to be his cousin. The woman was dark, exotic and extremely sensual, which meant Kim wouldn't be eligible for that role. The action played out over an insistently throbbing sound track with occasional throaty female singing in some language Kim didn't recognize, punctuated by ecstatic cries that sounded as orgasmic as the frozen custard, and were sort of embarrassing.

She and Nathan made nervous comments here and there, but gradually the movie became more coherent. The couple met, were attracted. Each had a significant other, but it soon became clear they weren't going to let that stop them.

Thoroughly engrossed, Kim finished her custard and her second beer, and took the third one Nathan offered without thinking, until she started drinking it, that she hadn't really wanted another one.

On screen, temptation was finally given the green light. The couple met in a darkened hotel room. For a long time they stood facing each other, fully clothed, including identical trench coats. The man undid the belt of the woman's coat and slipped it off her shoulders to reveal a tight scarlet cardigan, fastened top to bottom with tiny pearl buttons. Their profiles were barely visible in the dim light.

The woman reached out slowly and undid the man's belt, pushed his raincoat off his broad shoulders to reveal a black T-shirt stretched over his astounding physique.

Kim drank from her third beer, suddenly aware of Nathan next to her, and the fact that they were about to watch these two people…what? Fade to black? Make out? Have sex all over the screen? Gah, she hoped not the latter. With any luck the scene would hint at the passion then cut away to tasteful afterglow.

The hero reached for the heroine's sweater, started unbuttoning it from over her unfairly large breasts. Kim poured more beer down her throat, really uneasy now. Should she say something to break the tension? Suggest they fast-forward if the action got too steamy? Grin and bear it?

Beside her, Nathan watched, beer at rest on the couch's end table. If he felt at all uncomfortable he sure wasn't showing it. She wished she'd insisted they keep on the lights. This could get really awkward, the two of them sitting close beside each other under a blanket in the dark with sex happening a few feet away.

The sweater was peeled off. Underneath, the woman wore a black lace bra that cupped her full breasts, hinted at the darkness of her nipples. The man murmured to her, then the screen was filled with their lips meeting, separating, tongues visible.

Kim froze, kept her face to the front and darted a glance at Nathan. His index finger was playing with the top of his beer now, circling the opening.

The man kissed down to the woman's chin; she tipped her head back; her eyes closed in ecstasy as his mouth made its way down farther; his large, tanned hands covering the black lace holding her breasts, his tongue exploring the impressive cleavage between them.

Kim didn't move. A blush was heating her face, but there

was heating going on in other parts of her body, too. Beside her, Nathan shifted.

She closed her eyes. Then opened them again, because she didn't want to miss anything.

The man's lips tasted her nipple through black lace. Nathan blew out a breath. "Kim."

Her heart started pounding. "Yes?"

"This is…pretty hot."

"Ya think?"

"I didn't know it was going to be like this."

"Do you want to switch it off?"

"No." He turned, his face dimly illuminated by the light from the TV. "But I'm getting really turned on."

"Oh." She didn't know what else to say. "Me, too" would only cause trouble.

He turned back to the screen. She did, too.

The man's shirt was off. His body looked like Nathan's. The woman's bra was off. She did not look like Kim at all.

They stood facing one another, then the man brought his hands up to cup those incredible rose-nippled breasts with a look so reverent Kim got a lump in her throat.

His skin was darker than the woman's, his hands rough and masculine on her body.

Nathan let out a soft groan, shifted again on the couch. "Kim."

"What?"

"This might kill me."

Me, too. She couldn't admit it. "It's… I can see why."

"Are you feeling it?"

"Nathan…"

"Shhh, okay." He put his hand above her knee, squeezed reassuringly and let go.

She didn't want him to let go. Her knee burned where he'd touched her. She was getting terribly turned on. This was horrible. She couldn't stay here. She couldn't leave. She wanted Nathan to do to her what the guy was doing on screen.

The man had bent down, picked up the woman and carried her over to the bed; twisted so she landed on top of him. Her rich, dark hair tumbled over his chest; she kissed his sternum, following a path downward until Kim's eyes shot open. They weren't going to show *that*....

The camera switched to the man, the look of intense bliss on his face. Then a brief aerial shot of her between his spread legs, her hair providing tasteful cover; his hands on the back of her head, urging him on.

A half gasp escaped Kim; she couldn't help it. Her third beer went down. She was buzzed, horny as hell, vulnerable to the guy next to her. This was torture. This had the potential to end up somewhere she didn't want it to be.

A new shot with the man on top. Kissing those breasts, traveling down to her stomach and beyond. The motion slowed; he reached his target, hovering over her off-camera thighs with a hungry gleam in his eye.

Oh, no.

His tongue emerged from his half-open mouth. Even his tongue was sexy. He lowered his face.

Kim shifted, straining her hips up against the seam of her jeans. New shot, aerial again, floating in a wide circle, the man's head between the woman's legs, his hands on her breasts.

"Kim."

"Yes."

"I can't take this."

"Should I turn it off?" She was whispering.

"No."

"What are you going to do?"

"Are you turned on?"

She closed her eyes, bit on her lower lip. "Yes."

His breath drew in sharply. He said her name on the exhale.

"Nathan, it doesn't mean I—"

"Undo your jeans."

"I'm not going to sleep with—"

"I'm not asking you to." He was fumbling under the blanket. A zipper went down. "We'll each take care of—"

"*No.* I'm not sitting here masturbating next to you."

"Look." He nodded to the screen. His hand moved under the blanket.

She should be turned off. She should be priggishly horrified. She should throw back her side of the blanket and stomp off righteously to her room.

Yet the knowledge of what lay under Nathan's side of the blanket, the idea of him touching himself, getting more and more turned on, was so arousing she felt she could come just by squeezing her thighs together.

"Kim." He turned and gazed at her. What must be his, er, free hand, emerged from the blanket and followed a path from her temple to her cheek. "I won't touch you. Unless you want me to."

"No. No." *Yes. Yes, please.*

He turned back to the movie. The man was on top now, moving slowly, making love to the irresistible brunette, his pleasure and hers revealed in their expressions, the motions of their hands, the soft moans and cries. Then the camera switched, and he was kneeling behind the woman, who was on her hands and knees, his buttock muscles rippling through the forward-back motion of sex. The woman's breasts swung free, along with her rich mane of hair; her mouth was open in ecstasy.

"Kim." That whisper again, devil on her shoulder.

"What?"

"Come with me." His fingers touched her thigh lightly, thumb moving back and forth, then his hand slid upward, brushed across her hip and disappeared, leaving a trail of fire in its wake.

On screen the woman was now on top, sitting upright, her strong thighs gripping, rising up and down, her breasts swaying. The man's hands reached to cover them, his fingers playing skillfully. She tipped back her head, arched her spine.

Nathan gave a low groan; the blanket moved faster. Kim gave in.

Jeans unsnapped. Unzipped. Her hand reached down, fingers started working. Beside her Nathan moaned in time with the man clutching the woman's hips, thrusting up inside her, their bodies shrouded in shadow.

Kim's breath turned to panting. She needed more room, more access. She leaned back hard on the couch, pulled up her leg, spreading farther.

"Oh." The syllable escaped without her permission. She was aware Nathan had lost interest in the movie, was watching her face, watching her pleasure herself, and that knowledge kicked her arousal into higher gear. She was going to come for him. She was going to come big and drive him into completely insanity.

She rubbed harder, whispered only for him, "I'm almost there."

"Yes." He barely made a sound, as if someone were strangling him.

She closed her eyes, arched and let herself go, sighing in pleasure at the exact same time the woman on screen reached her own release.

Nathan let out a stifled moan; Kim opened her eyes, wanting to share his moment, and found him still watching her. She held that gaze until he finally came down, laid his head on the back of the couch, breathing powerfully.

On screen, the heroine was now in her office with a pile of files, talking on the telephone about a matter of urgent company business.

Kim had no idea what to say. How had this happened? Why hadn't she been thinking of Dale and their reenergized connection? Why only being with Nathan? Pleasing Nathan? Wanting to be made love to by Nathan?

She forced back her panic. It was okay. They'd both gotten carried away. Nathan hadn't touched her, nor she him; this changed nothing between them. Consenting adults, friends, turned on by a movie, were open and liberated enough to take care of it. A practical solution. Much better than sitting there getting so horny they did something together both of them would later regret.

"Kim, look at me."

Her panic came back, an instinctive fear that she couldn't ignore. What did he want? Was he going to say some horrible line from the *Man's Guide*? *Don't get any ideas that this meant something.* Or *that was hot, could you go get me another beer?*

She couldn't bear it.

"Look at me?"

She looked, but it was like dragging her gaze through Super Glue. His expression was calm, thoughtful, curious, almost hopeful. What was he feeling? She couldn't ask, He'd never tell her. He probably didn't even know.

This man would never tell her the sun rose and set over her bed.

She needed *right now* to stop wanting him to.

"You okay?" The tenderness in his tone undid her. It was all she could do not to break down and start bawling.

"Sure. Tell your friend that was some movie." Her voice cracked. Her lip started trembling. She looked away with the excuse of zipping her jeans. He picked up the remote and turned the movie off, leaving the room dark except for the streetlight glow through the unshaded windows.

Silence. Silence so profound she had to look back at him. He swallowed, appearing uncertain now. She couldn't stand it.

"What's the matter, nothing in your guide covers what to say after getting off with your female roommate?"

He didn't crack a smile. She wasn't joking. Still he said nothing.

"Well, this was great. Let's not do it again." She got up off the couch, headed for her room.

"Why not?"

She turned back. *Why not?* "Because, Nathan, oddly

enough, in sexual matters, women prefer to feel at least the tiniest bit special."

"You were right there with me, Kim. Every second."

She sagged against her doorway. What was wrong with her? She knew what she was doing when it happened; now she was acting as if it should have meant something. "You're right. I'm sorry. I don't know why I got so upset. It was just... unexpected, I guess."

"It was definitely unexpected." His voice turned hoarse; he cleared his throat. "I'll never forget what you looked like when you came."

She studied him, trying to interpret the emotion she glimpsed behind those words. But, as usual, understanding what Nathan was feeling was an exercise in frustration.

Though come to think of it, understanding what she was feeling right now about Nathan wasn't going much better.

All she knew was that something had started while they sat together in front of that scene, something that probably had its origins the first time he kissed her. And she wasn't at all sure now that it could be stopped.

NATHAN LAY IN BED, a lost cause, since at two in the morning he wasn't even close to sleeping. On the one hand memories of Kim haunted him, of the way she'd abandoned herself to the erotic images on the screen, the way she'd ditched her shyness and reserve and become a totally sexual creature.

He'd probably never sleep again.

On the other hand, her parting shot. *Women prefer to feel at least the tiniest bit special.* The irony was sickening. She had no idea. And that was the problem right there: she had no idea. His bumbling attempts to show he wanted to become the man in her life had been inadequate. He should have made love to her tonight. He should have told her how he felt. He should have...

Should have, should have. Was that the state of his life? Was that the defining characteristic? Twenty-six years old and only thinking about what he should have done? Should have finished his thesis by now. Should have gotten a job in his field. Should have been working harder. Should have, should have.

He was making himself sick.

Kim had made it clear what she wanted: to feel special. To have a man she could rely on, a mature, ambitious guy with his house in order, one able to communicate clearly what he thought and felt. And what had Nathan done? Kissed her a few times and whacked off next to her. Sure, that made her feel special. Mature and ambitious? He drank too much beer and watched too much TV. Communicate clearly? When that woman had jogged by them on the beach, he'd been staring, yeah, stunned that he felt nothing, no desire to pursue, no immediate fantasy of what she looked like under her clothes. He'd watched her the way you watch a painting in an art museum. Lovely, but not something you want or have to have in your life. Had he told Kim any of that?

No.

Tonight on the couch had he told her what he felt, what it had cost him to hold back from touching her?

No.

Nice. Very nice.

He turned over and stifled a roar of frustration into his pillow. *Idiot.*

He was still acting like a college frat boy. He'd hung on to that part of his life instead of moving past it, going out with Kent and Steve, frozen in adolescent boob-worship.

Kim had shown him that his path, one he'd always wanted to walk, had been crippled by immaturity and fear and lack of any appropriate male role model. No more. Starting tomorrow he was going to be man enough to take that path. Sprint down it instead of walking, to make up for lost time. Clean up his act, figure out what was going wrong with this thesis project and finish it, send out résumés, lay off the partying and start life in earnest. Show Kim he was a man to be trusted and respected. And then maybe loved.

Nathan got up, turned on his light, walked over to his

computer desk. There was enough other crap on it to fill a moving box. No wonder he never got anything done.

He cleared the mail, the laundry, the Kleenex, the cell charger...

Under a pile of books he found the envelope with the pictures from Kim's album, including the two of her with her dollhouse. He took them over to his bed, where the lamp was on, sat down and looked at the house's magnificence, at the proud little girl standing next to it, the girl who'd grow up to lose it, and to become the woman he was falling in love with.

And he suddenly knew exactly what he wanted to give her for her birthday. To show her how he felt. To show her he listened. To show her exactly how special she was to him.

11

"KIM, I HAD SUCH A wonderful evening with you." Dale grabbed her hands. They'd had dinner at Lake Park Bistro, one of Milwaukee's best French restaurants, which had totally taken Kim aback because she'd thought the whole point of the evening had been to go casual. She would have been more comfortable better dressed in a place like that. But Dale had reacted to her brown twill pants and cream sweater as if she were a Playboy bunny in a bikini. Wasn't that what she wanted? A man who appreciated her for what she was and nothing more?

Yes. It was. She'd just try not to think about how she'd felt last night on the couch with Nathan for those few minutes. Confident, wild, uninhibited, as if some sexual beast lurking inside her had been set free.

After dinner, she and Dale had a romantic, if slightly freezing, walk by the lake, and he'd driven her home, parked near her building and walked with her to the front entrance.

"You are the most amazing woman. Smart, sexy, beautiful. I can't believe my luck."

"Dale, thank you, I had a wonderful time." She smiled, wishing she could feel a hint of wild thrills and fireworks, but so far, this man didn't light her up. All evening he'd been the perfect date, attentive, complimentary, not a great listener, but that could come. What was missing? She couldn't name it. Maybe it was just her mood. She had the Carter proposal finished, in an envelope waiting to mail, and hadn't sent it. The design was good, but not good enough. Sometimes she wasn't even sure it was worth submitting.

On top of that, Emily's prediction had come true. The CEO of Soka had called that morning with a job offer. Interactive creative director, in charge of an entire new department positioning Soka to compete in the booming landscape of online marketing and advertising. She'd be able to hire her own designers, be responsible for bringing in new business. The salary was more than she'd ever made in her life, and included benefits and bonuses. She'd be a fool to turn down a chance like this right before her thirtieth birthday deadline.

"Omigod!" The high-pitched voice was followed by a squeal. "I totally know what you mean!"

Three hot young things approached on the sidewalk, vastly underdressed for the weather, obviously on their way to a bar or party. They passed close by, a jumble of long limbs and overexposed cleavages.

Dale didn't even glance over, didn't take his eyes from Kim's face for a second. "I am traveling again, but I want to see you when I'm back."

He didn't even glance! Kim felt a small rush of giddiness. That was something. "Yes, I'd like that, too."

"You are so many things I want. I feel really hopeful about the two of us."

"Oh, that is so…nice." Her giddiness felt a bit squashed. She was so many things *he* wanted. Didn't he worry what she was feeling? Did he even think about it? She'd told him about Soka and he'd offered his warmest congratulations, dismissing her objections to going back to office work, saying not to worry, she'd get used to it. He'd sounded like her mother.

"Kiss me." He leaned down; she rose to meet him. The kiss was more on target than last time, very nice, really. She even got a small tingle. But she didn't want to rip his clothes off and climb on for a ride. Because he was wrong for her? Or because he wasn't?

"Mmm." He kissed her again with more passion. That was better. She liked that. That held promise.

Another kiss. Pressing her close. His body was softer than Nath—

No. She was *not* going to think about Nathan, not while in another man's arms. That wasn't fair or right.

"Dale." She lifted her face and smiled. "I'd invite you up, but…"

"But?"

"My roommate…" She laughed awkwardly.

Dale looked incredulous. "I thought you lived alone."

"I did. I will again. It's temporary."

"And…she doesn't allow you to have men in your apartment?"

Kim blinked. *Uh-oh.* She had seriously walked into this one. "He."

"You room with a *guy?*"

"Temporarily." She cleared her throat. "He's a friend of my little brother's."

"Three years younger, not that little." Dale's eyes narrowed. "All those emails to me, you never mentioned him?"

"I just…" She shrugged helplessly. Why hadn't she told him? "It didn't seem important. He lost his lease. He's with me until he can find another place."

"Okay." Dale was studying her, suspicious now, looking for clues. "What were you inviting me up for that this man can't tolerate? And why does he have a say in any of this?"

"He doesn't." Kim lowered her eyes miserably. There was no reason she couldn't have men up to her apartment. She just wouldn't be able to handle the awkwardness of Dale being there when Nathan walked in after his shift. Not after what had gone on between them last night. "I assumed if you came up, we'd…continue what we started down here."

"And he wouldn't be okay with that? Why? He's in love with you? You're in love with him?"

"No. *No.*" Her voice grew shrill. What the hell could she say? That Nathan was violently opposed to kissing before marriage? This was horrible.

"It sounds as if there's something you need to figure out here, Kim." Dale spoke quietly, the hurt obvious in his sweet brown eyes.

Kim's stomach bottomed out. "No, there is nothing."

He wasn't persuaded. She could see the uncertainty in his face, and she didn't blame him. She wasn't persuaded, either.

"Good night, Kim. I'll email you while I'm gone."

"Yes, please. I'm sorry about this…misunderstanding. Really."

He kissed her—on the cheek—and saw her safely into the building. Inside the elevator she slumped against the wall. What was she going to do? How did she get herself into such a complete and utter mess over a guy who didn't deserve her?

Up in her apartment, she went straight to the telephone and dialed Marie.

"Hey, Kim! I was just about to call you."

"Yeah? What's up?"

"Candy is having the girls over to her house next Saturday night. Even Darcy can make it."

Saturday was Kim's birthday, but why not? "That sounds great. Can I bring anything?"

"Uh, to an event Ms. Party Planner is throwing?"

"Right." She got down a tall glass from the cupboard and filled it with ice. "Stupid question."

"How was the date tonight?"

"It was okay, until I told him he couldn't come up because my roommate wouldn't like it."

"Nathan?"

"Marie…" She filled her glass from the tap. "I don't even know why I said that."

"Because you knew he wouldn't like it?"

"Why should he care? More to the point, why should I care? And then poor Dale wanted to know why I couldn't have men in my own apartment and I just stood there like an idiot and had no answer for him." Tears started and she angrily wiped them away.

"Hmm. Any chocolate in the house?"

She grimaced. "I couldn't fit the tiniest crumb in my stomach. He took me to Lake Park Bistro. We had a nice evening until I ruined it."

"Okay. What does your instinct tell you about Dale? Right for you? Or not?"

She bit her lip. "It tells me he's the type I should want."

"That's not your instinct. That's your intellect, judging what you 'should' want or feel, not telling you what you do."

"My instinct is completely screwed. After Tony I refuse to trust it anymore."

"I bet it told you Tony wasn't right, too. You will always know when you're working against your instinct because it will feel wrong. You'll be anxious and upset instead of nervous and excited. Think back to that night you and Tony got together. You were at a party first, right?"

"How do you remember all this?"

"It's my job. Go back and think."

She took a sip of water. Okay. Back to the party before she gave herself to Tony. Or more accurately was taken by him. "I remember being uncomfortable at the party and drinking too much. Annoyed that he was paying so much attention to this other girl with the depth of a sheet of paper."

"That's instinct right there."

"But when we were together after…" She put the water glass down. "I felt great. It was the best sex I ever had. I felt wild and free and spontaneous and invincible."

"I think you need to sit down and have a long listen."

Marie's gentle voice made Kim start to relax. "Listen to what your instinct is really telling you about what you want. Forget Nathan. Forget Dale. Just ask it and listen."

"Like some meditation thing?"

Marie snorted. "Yeah. SMT. Some Meditation Thing."

Kim couldn't even laugh. "What if it tells me I want Nathan?"

"Then ask why. What is it you feel around Nathan that you don't feel around Dale? Make it about you, not the men. I promise it won't steer you wrong. You have all the answers you need right inside you. You just need to be patient and listen."

Another tear fell, but with this one came a sense of relief. She had something to hang on to, some hope of directing herself out of this chaos of emotion. "Has anyone ever told you that you're a genius?"

"Only six, seven times a day."

This time Kim could laugh, and her self-absorption lifted enough for her to remember. "Oh, my gosh, Marie, you have to tell me who that was with you on the Riverwalk."

"Quinn Peters. He's a friend. Now listen, because I'm going to give you one more piece of advice."

Ha! Marie dodged that one. Kim was going to have to keep at her. "More advice? I'd rather hear about—"

The front door opened. Kim started and put a hand to her chest. Nathan was home early. Thank God she didn't have Dale up here.

"Marie," she whispered.

"I want you to pay *close* attention to Nathan."

"Shh." She shrank away from the kitchen door. "He's home."

"*Hello? Kim?* We're on the *phone?* He can't *hear* me."

Kim rolled her eyes. She wasn't going to explain how Nathan got her so damn flustered. Or how she couldn't get the image of his face when they were together on the couch out of her head. "Sorry, duh. Just…hurry."

"Okay. Here it is. I think the guy is seriously into you. I

mean seriously. He was looking at you on the river as if you could walk it."

"He— No, no, I—"

"Hey, Kim." Nathan moved past her, opening the refrigerator for his evening beer.

"Oh, hi, Nathan." She sounded so oddly robotic, he stuck his head back around the door and did a double take. She turned away.

"Take it from me, Kim. The man is either crazy in love with you, or well on his way to being there."

Kim gasped, face flaming scarlet. "Don't say that."

She peeked over her shoulder to see Nathan reemerge from the refrigerator with a bottle of cranberry juice, scowling.

Cranberry juice? Were they out of beer?

"I, um, have to go now."

Marie chuckled. "Give him a close look. Give your feelings for him an even closer look. I suspect you'll be very surprised by what you—"

"Yeah, I *really* have to go."

"Okay, okay." Marie was laughing harder. "See you next Saturday."

"Right. Next Saturday. Bye." Kim hung up and took a deep breath, aware her face was still on fire. She could barely look at Nathan. "Hi."

He banged his glass on the counter. "That your *boyfriend?*"

"That was Marie."

"Oh." He looked sheepish for a second, then poured juice over ice. "Sorry."

"You're home early."

"Yeah." He put the cap back on the juice. "I gave notice at work. Both jobs."

"You *what?*" She took a step toward him. "Did something happen? Are you okay?"

"Fine." He was looking at her over the rim of his glass. Something else was different about him. He seemed older, or taller. The same way he'd been on the beach, only that had been a quick flash and this had been evident the second he walked in the room, and was still firmly with him. "I'm going to work full-time on finishing my thesis, sending out résumés, getting my career under way. I had a meeting with Dr. S. about local firms who might be interested in my designs. There are three or four of them, all places I'd love to work. He's really behind me."

"Wow. *Wow.*" She stood there wanting to hug him, not sure if she should touch him after Marie's comment, and realizing the nice simple confusion she'd felt earlier was amateur hour compared to what she was feeling at the moment.

"Come with me." He beckoned to her and walked out of the kitchen.

She followed blindly, unable to think past staying upright. "Where are we going?"

"My room." He shoved open his bedroom door. "Take a look."

She peeked around the jamb, not sure what to expect.

"Nathan, my God." He'd cleaned. Seriously cleaned. Not a speck of laundry, not a paper out of place, even the windows sparkled. "You've gone all House and Garden."

"And." He pulled a BlackBerry out of his pocket. "Check this out. This baby will keep me organized. No more missed appointments. No more screwups."

She couldn't believe what she was seeing. He'd taken her advice. He'd changed. For her? Was Marie right about his feelings? Kim could barely take the concept in. It seemed so…not Nathan.

He moved next to her so they could both see the screen, so they were touching side to side, so she could feel how solid he was, solid and tall and wonderful-smelling. Her instinct was certainly telling her something now. To lean against him and let him hold on to her until her world righted itself.

"See my new calendar? Pull up tonight and…look. I have a hot date."

"Oh." She stepped away from him, tried to swallow but her throat wouldn't let her. "New girlfriend?"

"Nope. I've known her since tenth grade." He was grinning at her. She wasn't grinning back.

"Long time." Her voice cracked again. "Old girlfriend?"

"Nah. She's my roommate."

"Your roommate." Kim murmured the words, unable to feel anything anymore. Not relief. Not joy. Nothing. She must have blown a circuit somewhere in her brain.

"Kim." He waved his fingers in front of her face to snap her out of her zombie state. "You in there?"

"I think so."

His grin faded into concern. "Hey, what's wrong?"

"Soka called and offered me the job. They want an answer right away."

"Oh, man." He pressed his lips together. "Why this week? That's all you need. Did you mail the proposal yet?"

She shook her head, not trusting herself to speak. He hadn't offered congratulations. He understood. The relief was so great, she nearly toppled forward into his arms.

"Okay, look." He took hold of her shoulders, made her look at him. "That settles it. You need to get out of yourself. Forget Soka. Forget Carter. Forget everything. We're going dancing."

"We are?" She felt numb, ghostly.

"That's what it says." He held up the phone. "You think these things lie?"

"Nathan…I just had a date." And she was emotionally burned out. Too much coming at her at once.

"Sure, but it's only ten o'clock. Nightlife is just starting, and this is exactly what you need. Go get dressed. Put on something sexy."

She lifted her hands, let them slap down, a spark of life returning. She hadn't been out dancing in a long, long time. "What's wrong with what I'm wearing now?"

"That?" He looked her current outfit up and down and dismissed it with a shake of his handsome head. "That's not who you are, Kim."

"It *is* who—"

"No." He touched his finger to her lips, reminding her of that day—how long ago?—when this deeper awareness of him had started, when she'd assured him his touch wouldn't break her. Now she was pretty sure it could.

"I want you to wear something sexy, Kim, because that's who you are to me."

12

THE MUSIC WAS HOT, the room hotter, and Nathan was a great dancer. Kim hadn't had this much fun since she didn't know when. Maybe since she was out kayaking. Was that her instinct telling her what she wanted? She didn't know. She'd had too much to drink. On top of the bottle of wine she'd split with Dale earlier over dinner—he drank most of it—she'd now had two mojitos, which went down way too quickly, even though she'd gulped ice water in between to keep herself hydrated.

Right now she was feeling no pain at all. Dancing like a crazy woman in her little black dress, which had made Nathan's eyes pop practically out of his head, which made her feel as if she were some kind of siren. In fact, he'd barely taken his gaze off her all evening. They were burning up the dance floor, burning each other up.

A new song came on. She gyrated shamelessly, flinging her head right and left, hands reaching for the ceiling. Nathan moved closer, put a palm on her hip, following her movements with his fingers and with his eyes. Was she dating Dale? She didn't care. Was Nathan wrong for her? She didn't care. Was she faced with either selling out her life's dream to Soka, or sticking around to watch it go down the toilet? She. Did. Not. Care!

All she cared about was the beat, the crowd, music loud

enough to lose herself in, the bodies around her, everyone as into the abandonment of selves and inhibitions as she was. A guy and his girlfriend got between her and Nathan and the four of them danced for a while; the girl put her arms around Kim as if they'd been friends since birth, and they danced together, undulating bodies to the pulse of the music, woman on woman.

Kim loved this night! She loved everyone! She loved life!

She would probably be seriously hungover tomorrow.

Who cared! Not her. Not-not-not.

Then the body in front of her was Nathan again, and she thought that was just fine, too. Man on woman. Woman on man. All good!

The music went on, the noise got louder, the dancing got wilder. Finally Kim's buzz started wearing off, her breath started running out; her legs began to feel rubbery. She met Nathan's eyes, pointed to the tables. He shook his head, pointed to the exit. Kim nodded and followed him through the crush of bodies, gripping his hand like a lifeline.

They poured out into the gorgeously cool night air, restoring freshness and oxygen to lungs and to blood.

"Oh, that's nice." Kim opened her arms wide and inhaled ravenously.

"Hot in there."

"Jungle-y." She stumbled over something on the sidewalk that probably wasn't there. "Whoops."

"Good thing I'm driving, sweetheart."

"Am I your sweetheart?"

"Of course." He took her arm and she let him, even though she wasn't more than mildly drunk by then. But it was a good, solid mild-drunk and she was enjoying every fizzy second.

They drove home, Nathan laughing at Kim, who kept changing the radio station until she found something she could boogie to in the front seat. They had so much fun together, whatever they did. Her instinct knew that much.

Back home, they raced for the elevator, got impatient waiting for it to come down, and chased each other up the stairs, arriving inside the apartment breathless and giggling.

"Oh, that was fun, Nathan! I could drink three gallons of water, though. I think I lost twelve pounds." Kim tossed her bag onto the couch, kicked off her heels and went into the kitchen to get ice water for both of them.

"I need a shower." He came in behind her, stretching his shirt away from his body.

She held out his water. "Same here. Yuck."

"Want to take one together?"

"I think not."

"Bummer." He took the glass from her, drank it down, refilled it and emptied that one, too. She gulped hers, watching him surreptitiously. His hands were sexy. His swallowing throat was sexy. His mouth was sexy.

He wanted her. She wanted him.

Like crazy.

Maybe Dale would make a better partner, maybe she should hang in there and try harder to fall for him, but tonight she only wanted Nathan, because with him she felt sexy and wild and completely free.

"You want to go first?"

"Hmm?" She had no idea what he was talking about.

"Shower."

"Oh, yes. Thanks."

He tossed his ice into the sink, gave her a devilish look. "You have five minutes, then I'm coming in, ready or not."

She banged her glass down and sprinted for the bathroom in mock panic, forgetting until she was naked and soaping that she hadn't brought in a change of clothes.

So? She'd wrap a towel around her. It covered only slightly less than her dress had, who cared? She didn't. Not tonight. Tonight she was an Amazon princess, a wild forest girl, a… disco queen and…whatever else.

Shower done, hair washed, she grabbed her towel, brushed her teeth with lightning speed.

"Finished!" she called out. "Did I make it in five minutes?"

"Am I in there yet?" His voice was right outside the door.

"Don't think so."

"Then you did."

"Good." She opened the door and smiled sweetly at him. "Your turn."

"Whoa." His gaze traveled over her. "Nice outfit."

"Thanks. Made it myself." She stepped past him and went to her room, hearing the water again pouring into the tub. She toweled her hair, and was about to put on her usual flannel pajamas when she stopped. Nothing about flannel said Amazon princess. Flannel cried out old Kim and she wanted to stay new Kim. Tomorrow she'd be sensible again, sensibly face all the choices and pressures ahead. She didn't want to be sensble yet. Self-indulgent, and to hell with consequences.

Way back in her closet hung a blue satiny nightgown with matching robe that her mother had once bought her as a birthday present, even knowing Kim's preference for pajamas. Kim had never worn it, but tonight she would, and thanks, Mom. Because tonight was a night for lingerie.

The material felt slippery, cool and wonderful against her still heated skin. She pulled on the robe and checked her reflection. Mmm, nice. The color matched her eyes and emphasized her slender figure in all the right places.

"Kim." A tapping sounded at her door.

Gah! She backed away. He couldn't see her like this. He'd think—

He'd think what? That she looked nice? Sexy even? He might want to make love to her. How about that? She stilled, her heart beginning a slow, steady thump. "Yes?"

"I'm not sleepy yet. If you're not, either, thought you might want to hang out for a while."

Before she could change her mind, she marched to the door and flung it open. He was wearing soft shorts that showed off his powerful thigh muscles, and a T-shirt that did the same for his biceps. His hair was wet and tousled, his skin golden, his eyes vividly brown, surrounded by dark lashes.

It took her five seconds to be able to speak, which was fine, because he looked as taken with her body as she was with his.

"I'm not sleepy, either."

He gestured to her gown. "I've never seen that."

"I've never worn it."

"What's the occasion?"

"Tonight."

He nodded, hands on his hips. "Want to hang out in the living room?"

"Dirty movies?"

"None. I promise."

Neither of them moved.

"Kim." His voice was low, throaty, that tone that got her so worked up, undoubtedly perfected on dozens of women. She knew what was coming. "Can I come in?"

She didn't let herself think that she'd had a date with another guy earlier, that he had every expectation of seeing her again, that she would hurt him if he knew what was going to happen tonight. She didn't bother doing anything but feel, and what she felt was the certainty that if she didn't let Nathan in right now, she'd burn up and be nothing but ashes by morning. "Come in."

He took a step forward; she didn't move back. His arms went around her waist, and he lowered his head to kiss her. Everything that had been missing from Dale's kiss was there, every firework, every flash of heat, every wild and confusing and exhilarating feeling.

The kiss deepened; he backed her into her bedroom, aiming straight for the bed. No, she hadn't expected him to mess around. This was Nathan's expertise; he was in his element, and she was about to find out what who-knew-how-many-other women had found out about him. How he tasted, how he moved, how his body looked and felt and satisfied.

She didn't care, because tonight it was about her and about Nathan. Because instinct told her Nathan was what she wanted. Nathan and the gift he could give her, of feeling like the sexiest woman in the world. Even if it was just for tonight.

Kim fell back onto the bed and lay there, watching as he stripped off his T-shirt, lowered his shorts. He was beautiful naked, his body muscled, lean, well-proportioned, his erection clean and golden like the rest of him, its tip faintly blushing. She wanted to feel the baby-soft skin covering it, the iron hardness underneath.

He was scanning her body. Undressing her? Calculating his next move? Then his gaze met hers, something sweet and hot swelled in her chest and she knew that she'd been right before, about his touch. If he lay over her, looked into her eyes, if he made love to her with any tenderness, she'd break.

She hauled herself up, slid to the edge of the mattress and took him into her mouth, surprising him so much his body jerked back. Then he relaxed and let out a heavy sigh of pleasure. This was good. This wouldn't break her.

His hand stroked her hair; his hips kept subtle time with her rhythm. He smelled citrusy from the shower, his skin smooth and dry at first taste, then slick under her tongue. She cupped his balls, stroking their softness, loving the power and the safety of having him like this.

With her lightest touch she grazed the length of his penis with her teeth, then sucked more firmly, enjoying his gasp, the tough work of his breath, the way she knew she was driving him mad.

She pulled back and fisted him, kept the rhythm going, then applied her lips only to the magically soft tip, while her hand kept working, bringing him in and out of her mouth as she stretched and manipulated the skin over his cock.

His groan increased her own passion and she quickened

her rhythm, loving the wet sounds, the hard, sexy length of him, the way he responded to increases and decreases of the pressure under her palm and the movements of her tongue and lips.

"Kim." He was barely able to speak. "You're going to make me come."

"Is that a problem?" She looked up slyly, took him deeper into her mouth.

"That's...up to you."

"No problem," she whispered.

He sucked in air, gripped her head, pushed so that she no longer felt totally in control, so that he went deeper into her mouth than she would have thought possible. She took him all, let him do what he wanted, her lips tighter and tighter until his fists clenching in her hair and the salty spurt to the back of her throat let her know he'd gotten there.

She felt satisfaction and triumph, and tenderness that she shoved away, reaching back for the Amazon inside her, the one who could be intimate with a guy and not fall madly in love. Because Nathan's other women, the others who had done exactly what she just had, were in the room with them. She couldn't forget.

"You are—" Nathan lifted her to the opposite side of the mattress, breathing hard, and climbed into bed "—the sexiest woman I've ever known."

She didn't buy it. Not for a second. But it was absolutely what she needed to hear, lying there among all his ghosts.

"And, Ms. Kimberly, I am going to get you back for what you just did to me."

"Oh, no!" She pretended panic. "Have mercy!"

"None." His warm hand slid over the slippery material of her gown. When he reached the hem above her knees, he reversed direction, sliding her gown up. Her struggling stopped. She drew in a long breath of pleasure and anticipation.

He kissed her stomach, once on each pelvic bone, then along the elastic of her panties across her lower abdomen, hesitating one, two, three torturous seconds before pressing his mouth between her legs, his breath hot through the thin cotton. She made herself lie still, absorbing the sensations. Nathan opened his lips, gave her biting kisses, the indirect stimulation making the rush of arousal even more powerful. Her climax started building; Kim held it off, wanting to stay on the edge, loving the feel of his tongue moving against her, pressing and releasing, pushing into her as far as her panties would allow.

He slid a finger under the material, let it glide over her swollen clitoris, once, then again. "Do you like that?"

"Yes." He already knew the answer. She was panting, gripping the bedspread under her, straining her hips up to his mouth. He pulled the elastic aside and buried his tongue inside her, licked up to her clit, back down inside her, and back up to stay.

Her orgasm hit so fast she barely had time to react, the burn shooting her through with impossible pleasure. Blissful contractions came in waves, again and again, then slowly, slowly down.

Kim let go of the bedspread. Let her hips relax. Let herself breathe again.

"Nathan." She'd done it. She'd survived. Her heart was still intact.

"Mmm?"

"I think I enjoyed that."

He laughed, repositioned her panties reverently and slid off the bed. "Me, too. Stay here."

"Like I could move?"

He chuckled, left the room, came back with two big glasses of ice water. "Drink?"

"Mmm, thank you, yes." She sat up and gulped thirstily, still tasting him, not sure what to expect now. She'd made it this far, but felt a little shaky. He'd want to leave now, right? Wasn't that what his type did? That would be best. She'd have time here on her own to recover, and figure out what consequences this night would bring to their friendship and to her heart.

He emptied his glass, reached for hers and put them both on her night table, crawled back into her bed, put his arm around her and pulled her against him.

Uh-oh.

"Now. Kim."

"Mmm?" She tensed, wary of whatever he was about to say.

"We are going to solve all your problems."

She lifted her head. "What, now?"

He pushed the bangs from her eyes. "You know a better time?"

"Uh…" Actually, no. This was fine. Second to him leaving, but fine. As long as they were just talking. "I guess not."

"So. What do you want most?"

She snorted. "That's easy. A way to win the Carter bid and save Charlotte's Web."

"Okay. Easy." He trailed his fingers down her bare arm. "I'll give you that."

"Yeah?" She smiled into his beautiful eyes. *Don't get used to this, Kim.* "Gee, that would be super swell, thanks."

"I'm serious." He squeezed her hand. "Let's figure out how you can win it. Tell me what you've got for Carter."

She rolled away to lie on her back, staring at the ceiling. "You've seen the website I designed. Which I love."

"Same here. You think it's missing something. Tell me what."

"Something. Some extra special…thing."

"Okay. Let's take this apart. What do customers want?"

"China and crystal."

"Why?"

"So their tables will look nice. So they can have fancy beautiful parties. So people will be impressed by them. So they can be like Mom and Dad."

"Why should they pick Carter?"

She counted off on her fingers. "Best quality. Good name.

Beautiful products. Cutting edge. Impressive pedigree. Will make their tables look fantastic."

"How can you let them know all that?"

She moved restlessly. "Carter reputation takes care of most of it. A great view of the products on the website will help, too."

"Yeah, you've done that with your design. But that still doesn't show how it will make their own tables look. For example, I use software that shows a model of the exact building the client wants so he or she can see it."

Her brain turned that concept over for one…two…*bingo*. She sat up abruptly, twisted to look at him. That was it. Exactly. "*Yes*. Yes, I can. I can do that. Nathan, I love you."

His face brightened comically. "Really?"

"I'm serious. That's *it*, Nathan." She pounded her fist on the bed. "That's totally *it*. I can create a program where people can upload pictures of their tables or entire dining rooms or kitchens or whatever, and they can try out the place settings online, right there, to check colors and sizes. The coding would be complicated, but it wouldn't be anything I'd have to work out for the bid. I could just put in a quick paragraph mentioning it. I can do it right now, in half an hour, tops. Get the whole thing in the mail tomorrow by the deadline. Oh, my God!"

She was standing next to the bed; she had no idea how she got there. "You are brilliant."

"Not me. You thought of it." He was grinning, laughing, looking as happy as she felt. "Congratulations, Kim. You'll win for sure."

"It's perfect. It's fabulous. It's—*oh!*"

She was back in bed, lying on top of him, but she knew how she'd gotten there. He'd lunged over, snagged her around the waist and brought her back horizontal with him. The kiss he gave her was long and sweet, with promise of more passion. By the time he released her, she was breathless from a different kind of excitement. "We've finished working, Kim.

Your problems are all solved. Charlotte's Web is saved. Now we celebrate."

"No, no." She tried to wiggle free. "I'm on fire for this idea now. I want to go right away and make changes to—"

Another kiss, during which he rolled them with slow, powerful grace, and then she was on her back and he was on top, and her arms went around his neck because there was nowhere else they could go while she was being kissed like that.

"I want you on fire for me." He was hard again; she parted her legs to let him settle between. The hot bulge of his erection pressing against her made her desire start climbing again, and with it her fear. She'd survived round one. Barely. But having him make love to her face-to-face…

"Come on, Nathan. We did this already." Her voice nearly gave way.

"Not *this*."

"We shouldn't get too involved. You're my roommate. You're my brother's friend. You're—"

"We're already involved." He grinned sweetly. "Deal with it."

"Involved how? Sex whenever you want it and nothing else?"

His grin faded. "Not nothing else."

"What else? Exactly?"

"Kim." He made a sound of frustration. "Nowhere in the *Man's Guide* does it give instructions for discussing the existence of any 'something else' that might go with sex. I love being around you. You are very sexy to me. That's not going to change tomorrow."

How about the next day? She didn't bother. It wasn't fair to press him for feelings when he was so badly equipped to express them. "You are such a guy."

"I am." He kissed her. "And you are *such* a hot woman."

"Nath—mmm." He'd begun a rhythmic push that made his erection strain to be inside her, stopped only by the stretching barrier of her panties. "If we're going to do this, we need a condom."

"Oh, Kim." His lips left a line of passionate kisses on her throat. "Could you maybe break the mood a little more?"

Kim burst into giggles. "Just being sane while I can be."

"You're right." He dragged himself off her, disappeared, presumably into his room where he probably used an entire dresser drawer for his stash.

She sat up, needing this time to regroup. What had Marie said? *You will always know when you're working against your instinct because it will feel wrong. You'll be anxious and upset instead of nervous and excited.*

How did she feel?

Kim took a deep breath. Nervous, yes. Excited, yes. None of this should feel as fun and good and right as it did, but if Marie knew what she was talking about, this was truly what Kim wanted.

Nathan barged into the room, showered the mattress with the contents of an entire box of condoms, and sat next to her, grinning wickedly. "Happy now?"

She laughed, likely harder than the situation warranted, but yes. She was. Nervously. "I'm very happy, thank you."

"Good." He got that adorably evil glint in his eyes. "Can we do it now?"

Kim gave him a shove that toppled him over, though she suspected if he didn't want to fall it would have been like shoving the side of a cliff.

He bounced back up, then pulled her down with him, and for a long time there was just kissing, long, passionate kisses alternating with gentle brief bites, now sweet, lip tasting lip, now hot with tangling tongues. His hands were still, his body relaxed on the mattress, but his mouth never stopped moving.

Right away, a test of her strength and decision to go forward. Kissing Nathan like this was so intimate, and so romantic. She kept being jerked out of nice safe arousal by sweet pangs in her chest, by warm thoughts in her brain, thoughts of wanting to be treated like this, cherished like this, revered like this forever. But Nathan had only promised her tomorrow. She wasn't fool enough to believe he could change overnight. She needed to stay solid, remind herself that her kid brother's crazy friend happened to have grown up hot enough to set forest fires with his body, and leave it at that.

Finally, when she didn't think she could stand another kiss without falling crazy in love with him, he moved from her mouth and used his very talented lips and tongue to pay homage to her breasts. Much safer. That she could enjoy with her nerve endings and ignore with her heart.

She moaned, encircled his head with her arm, kissing his soft, shampoo-scented hair. His hand snaked down between her legs. He found her plenty ready, but that didn't stop him from stroking her, making love to her with his fingers until she was shaking with impatience. Her fingers scrabbled around on the mattress until she found a condom, which she very unsubtly shoved at him.

Nathan didn't need persuading, but put on the condom while she stripped off her damp panties. He moved over her; she spread wide, waiting for the first delicious thrust, the first joining. It had been a long time.

Nothing happened.

She saw him looking down at her with an expression of such tenderness that she gave a tiny gasp.

"Kim."

Danger. Whatever he was going to say, she did not want to hear it. She reached between his legs, took hold of his penis and guided it toward her.

"Look at me." Even in his soft whisper, the command was unmistakable.

She obeyed, and regretted it when that tenderness was still there, when it took on new depth as he pushed inside her.

"Nathan." His name was a protest, a plea, a surrender. She didn't know what she wanted or what she was trying to say. Only that this man was reaching a place inside her that hadn't been reached in a long time, and she wasn't talking about the sex.

He gathered her in his arms, started to move, and helplessly she wrapped hers around him and joined his rhythm.

Then there was nothing in her world but Nathan, nothing but the slow slide of him inside her, stretching her, filling her, creating friction that would end up tearing her apart. Already she was building, reaching toward her climax, even at this slow, steady pace.

His body was so clean, so smooth, so male. How would she ever look at him now and think of anything but this? She was nearly lost, probably had been for a while. Marie had seen it. Dale had sensed it.

Nathan murmured something she didn't catch. She turned, and found his mouth again, and if kissing had been romantic before, it was twice so now with their bodies joined like this.

Oh, Nathan.

No, no, no. Falling for him would be like falling for fog— now you see it, now you don't. It might show up for a few days, then disappear again, misty and indistinct, impossible to hold or keep. Saying he was changing wasn't the same as changing. He'd only promised tomorrow...

She moved her hands down his strong back, the smooth line of his buttocks, felt the powerful muscles clench and release, shooting her desire higher. She trailed a finger down the cleft between, as far as she could reach, then back, then in again.

His rhythm quickened; his breathing in her ear became irregular and hoarse. She pulled her knees up, shifted so she could reach a little farther, press more deeply.

He ground his pelvis against her, increasing the friction; a light sweat broke on her body, her orgasm signaling its approach, and her breath came in bursts. She moved her hips more vigorously, inviting him even deeper. Her climax started, hesitantly at first, then increasing to a roaring wave that went on and on. She forgot where she was, lost all sense of herself, hearing herself gasp out little cries, aware of Nathan's body tensing, his thrusts becoming more forceful, increasing her pleasure impossibly more as he pulsed inside her.

Slowly, regretfully, she returned to reality, stunned and breathless. Nothing in her experience had ever been like that. She'd orgasmed not just with her vaginal muscles but with her whole body, with her brain and her heart and her soul.

Nathan.

He lifted his head, and she was looking at the same shell-shocked expression she knew she was wearing.

Keep it light.

"Wow." She smiled, skimmed her hands over his back. "I can see why you don't have trouble getting women in bed with you."

His mouth stretched into a strained grin. "Yeah?"

"I imagine it's harder getting them out."

"Well." He touched his nose to hers. "I don't want *you* to get out."

She laughed. "It's my bed. Why should I?"

"Right. Right." He shook his head, as if to collect himself. "You are incredible, Kim."

"Thank you." She smiled as if he'd told her she made good omelets, and moved, grimacing slightly as if he were crushing her, which he wasn't. The truth was, his body smelled good and he felt good, and she wanted to snuggle next to him and sleep there all night.

But if she did that she'd be fully in love with him by morning. She needed to get away from this spell he'd cast over her, needed space to think through what she wanted. This night had blindsided her. How much had he really changed? What would she be risking by showing him more of her heart, knowing how hard it was for him to show his? Only time would tell how he felt about her. And if he stayed in her bed much longer, she'd do something she might always regret. Like tell him she loved him. Like suggest he move in permanently. Freak him out entirely with typical female demands for commitment when he was just taking baby steps toward getting his life together and growing up.

He kissed her forehead, pulled out of her and grabbed some tissues to dispose of the condom, got up to throw them out. Then, hands on his hips, he stood next to the bed, looking down at her, strong, proud, naked and totally unself-conscious. While she, in contrast, had pulled up the sheet to cover herself, an absurd gesture given that they'd spent the past hours sharing every inch of each other's bodies. But she felt emotionally naked.

"You want me to go back to my room." It wasn't a question.

She smiled cheerfully, her heart sore and fragile. "We'll both sleep better. But, Nathan, really, you gave me such an awesome night tonight. Hope for the Carter bid and two orgasms that nearly took my head off. You're wonderful. Thank you. I was in bad shape and now I feel really great."

He nodded as if she'd given him the answer to a question he hadn't asked. "Right. Sleep well."

"You, too!" She hated the chirpiness in her voice.

For an agonizing few seconds longer he hesitated, seemed about to say something, then changed his mind and left the room, unaware that he'd taken a sizable chunk of her heart along with him.

13

NATHAN WOKE UP WITH that horrible heavy sensation in his chest that meant something bad had happened. A few seconds later, he remembered what it was: Kim. The most amazing sex of his life, during which he'd been thinking weddings, house shopping and babies, and she'd been thinking hey, great lay, thanks.

How many women had he done this to? A few. He recognized the signs retroactively: facial expression plummeting from smile of pure happiness to stoic awareness of impending rejection. He'd felt it happen to his own face the previous night, and until that moment, he had no idea of the pain that went with it. He, Steve and Kent used to laugh, *Ha-ha, women think sex means more than it does, ha-ha*. Kim couldn't have taught him a better lesson or struck a more powerful blow for womankind if she'd sawed off his balls with a dull bread knife.

Oof. He cringed. *Forget that image.*

Well, guess what. He'd read the last page of the *Man's Guide* now and was on his own. Any doubts he'd had about being in love with Kim were put to rest when he'd made love to her. The actions were familiar, the orgasms spectacular, but they didn't even scratch the surface of what he'd felt, how entirely different the act had been from anything that had come before.

But if Kim could go through lovemaking that intense and act as if it was just another roll in the sheets, then he was nothing more than an erect dick to her. Maybe a good friend with an erect dick.

Nathan pushed himself out of bed, aware that at the moment he was a crabby, confused, unshowered guy with an erect dick. He wanted to go into Kim's room, gather her sleepy, beautiful body into his arms and feel her there with him, make love to her again.

Like that was going to happen.

What were his options? Move out? Stay here? Keep away from her? Try again?

He didn't know. He was entirely inexperienced in matters of love. So inexperienced that though he'd undoubtedly fallen for Kim the first time he saw her back in tenth grade, it had taken him over a decade to figure it out. Nice going.

His computer was still on; after leaving Kim, he'd worked late into the night on his thesis. Making up the dollhouse plans had been a revelation. He'd wanted to have them for her birthday, so he—or someone—could build her a replica if she ever decided she wanted one.

In the process, though, something remarkable had happened. The little house's elegant simplicity had been a joy after the pressures and expectations inherent in his master's work. When he'd finished and turned back to his thesis, in a lightning bolt of recognition he'd realized his project was a Frankenstein mishmash of green certified products, from mandatory environmental window shades to geothermal heat beds, one "green" element after another stuffed into the design until it was sinking under its own weight. He'd lost sight of the beauty that was necessary, lost sight of design integrity, of the people that would inhabit the place. He'd been thinking only of budget and the LEED platinum rating he'd promised his advisor and his ego.

To hell with it. He wanted to be an architect, not an engineer, build houses people would want to live in. Inexpensive and environmentally sound, yes, but they also had to be homes.

Compromise was in order, downgrading the LEED level to gold, silver, whatever it took to sacrifice the least and satisfy the most.

Finally, his path moving forward was clear. He would finish this project, get a job and learn as much as he could. Someday he'd be in a position to put everything he had into finding materials that could be recycled, begged, borrowed— no, not stolen—so that all his buildings would be LEED platinum and inexpensive *and* attractive.

One step at a time. He promised himself to live slower and think more often of the consequences of his actions before he got into another no-way-out bind. Like the one he hoped to God he hadn't gotten himself into with Kim.

He took a shower, thinking admittedly less noble thoughts about her, her breasts, the smooth, muscular curve of her ass, the way she gave those sexy gasps when she was getting close to coming. The way her skin tasted, the way her wetness tasted, the way her body squirmed under his tongue's touch, the look on her face when she went over the top.

Somehow he managed to keep from coming under the spray, in case a miracle happened and she woke up wanting him again. Ever the optimist, he even stuffed a condom into the back pocket of his jeans.

He was doomed. He should have himself shredded and woven into a doormat to be delivered here anonymously so she could wipe her feet all over him.

Toweled off and dressed, he strolled—very nonchalantly, in case Kim had gotten up while he was in the bathroom— into the kitchen. No, she wasn't up yet. He made coffee for both of them, thinking it was too bad his supply of Alterra beans would dry up now that he was officially unemployed, and settled down with the previous day's newspaper.

Kim's door opened. Her steps shuffled sleepily to the bathroom, then back. Silence for a while, then he heard them again, coming toward the kitchen. He tensed, rattled the paper so she'd know he was in there and pretended to be absorbed reading.

"Morning."

"Oh, hi." He didn't sound convincingly surprised even to himself. "Sleep well?"

"Not really." She passed him on her way to the refrigerator; he wanted to reach out and hug her close. "I couldn't sleep after you left so I put in the new material for the proposal. I'll get it in the mail today and it will arrive Monday, deadline day."

Even in his off mood he couldn't help being happy for her. He looked up from an article he wasn't reading to give her a congratulatory smile and thumbs-up, noticing she'd changed out of the sexy gown and into her usual sweats and sweater. She still looked incredibly hot to him. Would she ever not? He doubted it. "Carter will give it to you. You're the best."

"If I do get it, it will be because of your idea." She took out a carton of orange juice.

"Kim, it was your idea. You deserve all the credit."

"I wouldn't have thought of it if you hadn't made me talk it through."

"Okay, you owe me."

She laughed, pouring her juice, completely comfortable around him, as if nothing had gone on between them.

Damn it.

He went back to not reading his paper. Live slow. Play it cool.

A phone rang; Kim grabbed her cell, which she must have left lying on the counter the previous night.

"Hello?" She look startled, then laughed incredulously. "You're calling me from Japan?"

D was for disembowelment, dismemberment, death and Dale.

Nathan wanted to shove back his chair and stalk out of the kitchen, but that wouldn't fit in too well with his decision to play it cool.

"What? Oh, no." She glanced at Nathan, biting her lip, looking anxious. "No, nothing like that."

He stared as she turned away, head bowed to one side. She seemed to want to fold over, retreat into herself. What was this guy saying to her? A rush of protectiveness made Nathan want to grab the phone away and tell Dale what he could do to himself.

"No, it was great, really. I know. I'm sorry."

Nathan wanted to growl. She sounded like a guilty teenager talking to her angry father.

"I have some good news. I got exactly the idea I need to make the Carter proposal work." She sounded timid, as if she wasn't sure she should be telling him. What the hell was that? "Yes, it's pretty great. I'm excited. All I have to do now is—"

A long pause. Nathan forced himself to unclench his teeth. The guy interrupted in the middle of Kim telling him about one of the most important parts of her life?

"Really? You did? That's terrific."

He stopped pretending to read. Stopped pretending he wasn't listening. Glared at her back. The asshole had manipulated the conversation so that now she had to congratulate *him?* How much time had he given her achievement? Three seconds?

"No, it's really not like that." She moved into the living room, her steps heavy, head down. "No. Yes, I, um, I do, too."

Nathan froze, black hatred boiling in his chest. Yes, he had admitted he needed practice living slow and being cool. But did Dale just tell Kim he loved her? Was that what she was answering? *I do, too?*

No. No way. Kim couldn't fall for that creep. Not when he beat her down like that. And she wouldn't have let Nathan into her bed if she was in love with someone else.

Steady.

"Okay, well, I'm glad you did. Right. Have a great rest

of the trip. I'll see you when you get back. What? Oh, no, of course you can. Yes. Bye!"

Nathan put down the paper, took a sip of coffee. One look at her perplexed face and he knew there was no way he could sit here and pretend that her happiness wasn't more important than his. "Dale?"

"Yeah." She went to the counter, drank the glass of orange juice she'd poured earlier. "He's in Japan."

"Ah." Sip of coffee. Trying to keep this casual. "And how is Mr. Dale?"

"Busy."

"You disappear when he talks to you."

She looked annoyed. "Yeah, well, I didn't think it would be that comfy for either of us if I talked to him in here."

"That's not what I meant. You disappear. You wilt. You shut down. Your voice drops. You lose your spark." Nathan was angry, and sounded it.

She put her glass down on the counter with a sharp thud. "That's ridiculous."

"Like a girl in the principal's office."

Her eyes flashed fire. "You are absolutely out of line—"

"There." He got up from his chair, pointing triumphantly. "Right there. It's all back now. With him, you're not Kim, you're anemia personified."

Her eyes narrowed dangerously. "*Excuse* me?"

"You're not the hot woman I saw on the dance floor and you're sure as hell not the woman I was in bed with last night. What the hell do you see in this guy? Why do you want someone who beats you down like that?"

"He does not beat me down. He's a sweet man who—"

"Isn't even happy for you about one of the most important things in your life right now." Her angry expression faltered, all the encouragement Nathan needed. "He didn't even react."

"You couldn't hear what he said."

"I could hear you turn into a pale imitation of yourself for a guy who wants you only for his ego trip."

"And what do *you* want women for? An orgasm or two, and then thanks and buh-bye?"

How could she still think that after last night? "I listen to you. I want to get to know you as you. I really care about your successes and your—"

"Oh, right, the perfect man." She lifted her arms, let them slap down on her thighs. "And I should go out with someone like you who—"

"Yes." He stood up. "Yes, you should."

For an incredulous second she froze, blinking up at him.

Maybe he'd made a mistake, but it was too late to turn back, and then, suddenly, he didn't want to. No more bullshit. No more games. "Have you kissed him yet?"

"That's none of your business." She took a step back, nearly to the wall.

"I take it that's a yes." Nathan moved opposite her. "How was that?"

"None of your business."

"Was it anything like when you kissed me last night?"

She tried to back away farther; the wall stopped her. She started looking panicked. "Last night was fun, Nathan, but we need to forget—"

"Was it like this?" He pulled her close and found her mouth, held nothing back, indulging the wild heat and chemistry that sprang to life between them in an instant.

She pushed weakly at his shoulders, but he knew her real strength and persisted, seducing her with his lips over and over until she relaxed her arms and clutched at him. Almost beyond reason, he leaned her back against the wall, shoved his thigh between her legs, kissing her until she made a whimper of arousal and surrender that hardened his cock as if it was programmed to respond to that sound.

"When he kissed you was it like that?"

"No," she whispered.

Vicious joy. *No.* Then a flood of masculine triumph, a primitive need to restake his claim. Nathan pulled her away from the wall, twisted her around, put a hand to the back of her neck and bent her over the table, loosening his hold for a second to make sure she wasn't struggling. No. She lay there, cheek to the smooth wood, breathing heavily.

If he thought he was hard before, he'd just redefined the word. Two seconds to put his hands to the waistband of her sweats and yank them down. Two more for the panties. Her ass taunted him, firm and golden, fuzzed with tiny blond hairs like a ripe peach.

He groaned and dropped to his knees, buried his face between her legs, tasting and tonguing, hands on his fly, unsnapping, unzipping, shoving his jeans off, rolling the condom on.

Back on his feet, he took hold of that gorgeous ass, one hand on either cheek squeezing the firm muscle, spreading them wide, taking his fill of the view between before he guided his cock home and watched himself disappearing inside her an inch at a time, pushing deeper, pulling out, pushing deeper yet, nearly coming just from the sight.

She was tight, not quite ready, and the friction was unbelievable. If he was hurting her, she gave no sign.

"Yes-s-s-s," she breathed.

Oh, man. He had to stop his movement, regain control. *Five-four-three-two-one.*

He thrust again, slow and hard, letting her know who was boss.

"Oh, yes-s-s-s."

Again he stopped, panting with the effort not to come. Who was he kidding? She was the boss. He was the junior apprentice, about to shoot inside her prematurely like an inexperienced teenager.

"Give it to me, Nathan."

Her whisper undid him. He gritted his teeth, braced his legs and gave it to her for as long as he could stand it, thrusting hard, his balls slapping on her thighs; she cried out in pleasure-pain, urging him on, goading him, her beautiful face pink with pleasure.

Finally she propped herself up on her forearms and took control, pushing her ass at him, breasts swinging, arm muscles contracting, hair a wild sexy mess.

There was no way he could hold back. He came in a long burst of pleasure that seemed to come from deeper inside him than anything ever had.

Then she was touching herself and the sight was so hot he stayed hard, keeping his in-and-out rhythm until she came, watching her back muscles contract as she arched, feeling her vaginal muscles pulsing around his penis.

Oh, man. He wiped perspiration from his forehead. So much for playing it cool; she was too hot and he wanted her too badly, loved her too deeply to stand by while she wasted herself on a jerk who didn't deserve her. Nathan had been that kind of jerk, so he could recognize them. But he had a hell of a lot more to offer her than Tokyo Dale.

He pulled gently out of her, hating to break the contact, and helped her straighten. "You okay?"

"I'm fine." She didn't sound fine.

"Want more juice? Water? Coffee?"

She shook her head, biting her lip, and he had the sudden shocking realization that she was about to cry.

"Kim." He took her into his arms, horrified at what he'd done. "God, I'm so sorry."

"No, no." She burrowed against him, thank God. "It's not your fault. I wanted you. I'm just..."

"Confused? Overwhelmed?" He stroked her hair gently. "Sore?"

She gave the hint of a giggle against his chest. "All of the above. Nathan...I think we should stay away from each other."

"Why?"

Her face creased into a sad smile that nearly broke his heart. "I'm not really sure."

He kissed her soft mouth—gentle, nonthreatening kisses. The kind of kisses a man gives to a woman he loves.

"I have an idea."

"Mmm?" Her arms crept around him. He'd never felt anything so sweet. If this was how she planned to stay away from him, he could handle it.

"Let's not stay away from each other. And not try to define this."

"Oh, Nathan." She sighed. "You mean do whatever we feel like regardless of the consequences?"

He cringed. "Do you have to put it like that?"

"I'm sorry. I have to figure some stuff out. And it's really hard to do when you're..."

"Jumping you every chance I get?"

She shrugged. "Yeah."

He nodded. Another lesson in patience for Nathan. If staying away from her was what it would take to win her, then even though it might kill him, he'd do it.

He let go of her, feeling as if she'd be pulled away from him by invisible hands the second she was no longer secured against him. But he also understood that though he wanted her in his arms more than anything else, he wanted her there only by her own choice.

DREAM DANCE STEAK WAS one of the most expensive restaurants in Milwaukee. Kim sat numbly opposite Dale while he paid the waiter what must be an appallingly high amount, and thought about how she'd rather be on Lake Michigan's shore eating food without plates or forks, drinking wine without glasses and having nothing to wipe her mouth with. How she'd rather be anywhere but here. How she'd told Dale she didn't want to eat out, that they needed to talk, and he'd argued back that they had a reservation and there was nothing they couldn't talk about over a good dinner.

Except the fact that she didn't want to see him again.

Not hard to see why she'd resisted her feelings for Nathan for so long. He wasn't exactly Mr. Constancy when it came to women. And yet...she believed they'd shared something in the kitchen that went beyond wild sex. She sensed that he'd been struggling to let her know he cared. As soon as she'd had time to be alone and examine her own feelings, those feelings had felt safer coming out of hiding. She was in love with him. Against her better judgment, against everything she'd experienced with guys like him in the past. Whether this was a good thing or yet another colossal mistake that would end with her heart crushed like a bug, she had no idea.

One thing was for sure, though. It hadn't just been Nathan's competitive ego talking when he said Dale was domineering. What she'd thought was her nerves on other dates revealed itself clearly as some weird submissive pall he cast over her. Worse, Nathan had caught on in twenty seconds, listening to one side of the call from Tokyo, that Dale wanted her around only to reflect his own magnificence, that he wasn't really interested in getting to know her at all, while Kim was only just figuring it out.

"This was such a lovely time, Kimmy."

She gritted her teeth. "Thanks for dinner, Dale. It was delicious. And sorry, but I'd rather be called Kim."

"Not Kimmy? I like it. It suits you." He smiled as if her objection was not only wrong, but on its way to being overruled.

"Not Kimmy. Just Kim." She wasn't smiling in any way whatsoever. Tonight her fantasy man of the past seemed only pudgy and overbearing.

"Is everything okay?" He pocketed the signed receipt their waiter brought back. "You're not yourself tonight."

She wanted to say, *No, Dale, the problem is that I am myself.*

Of course she didn't. Because that wouldn't have been like the herself he wanted her to be. However, if she was sitting across from Nathan, she'd be able to say it in a heartbeat. And he'd take it in stride and answer seriously.

"I'm okay. Shall we?" Finally. The dinner had taken approximately a month to finish. A different woman would have insisted they skip it. She could be that different woman with Nathan.

"A stroll in the moonlight is exactly what you need." He patted her hand. "Fresh air will do you good."

He was right. Fresh air was exactly what she needed. And the biggest, most wonderful breath of fresh air, as far as she was concerned, was Nathan.

Outside, they started walking to the car, which wasn't much of a stroll, but she'd take it.

"Dale, I need to say something."

"Of course, Kimmy."

She resisted punching his soft gut. Just barely. "I don't think this is going to work out between us."

"What?" He stopped walking, clearly aghast. The streetlight glinted off his glasses. "What do you mean?"

"I mean I've really enjoyed getting to know you, but I don't think I want us to move forward as a couple."

His brows dropped like anvils. "It's that roommate."

Bingo. "That's only part of it."

His face darkened further. "You're sleeping with him, aren't you?"

"No." Splitting hairs to spare his feelings. She had, but she wasn't. All week long, Nathan had honored her request to stay away from her, though there had been several times she'd nearly weakened and gone into his bedroom. Begging. On her knees.

"Bullshit."

"What?"

"Bullshit you're not sleeping with him. You've been sleeping with him all along. What kind of idiot do you think I am?"

She didn't think it would be a good idea to treat that as anything but a rhetorical question. "No, I haven't been, Dale."

"I know his type."

That stopped her. "You've never met him."

"I had him looked into."

"Looked *into?*" Her mouth dropped open. "You had Nathan investigated?"

"I had my suspicions, Kim. I'm not going to be played for a fool again."

Any sympathy she might have had over the "again" part of that line was washed away by a flood of outrage that he'd hired someone to pry into Nathan's life and hers. And yes, also some guilt. She had slept with Nathan while Dale trusted that he and Kim were building toward a committed relationship.

Except if he'd really trusted, he wouldn't have hired a detective.

"The guy has a track record a mile long. Women all over the place. He'll get tired of you in about a week and it's on to the next one. It's been his pattern. And not many of the women had very nice things to say about his methods. There one minute, gone the next." Dale stuck his face close to hers. "You think you'll be any different?"

Boom. There it was. Every fear, every piece of baggage, every ghost that still haunted her, and every bit of her difficulty trusting.

"I don't know." She could barely hold back tears. "But it doesn't change the fact that I don't think you and I are—"

"Yeah, yeah, so you said. Come on, I'll drive you home."

The ride back to her apartment was the most horrible, silent, miserable time she'd ever spent in a car. She practically leaped out of the vehicle when they reached her building, and Dale certainly made no move to get out and walk her to the door. When she attempted to apologize through the passenger window, he rolled it up and drove away.

Oh, for—

Fine. Go. Good riddance.

Inside, she took the elevator up, nervously twisting her keys. She'd need to tell Nathan what she'd done tonight. He would be happy. He'd been down on Dale from the beginning, down on the whole idea of her dating. And instinct—which, thanks to Marie, she'd been trying hard to listen to—told her it wasn't only out of concern for her welfare. Maybe he really did care for her?

He'd been keeping up with his efforts to stay what she'd dubbed Nathan the Man. His thesis was moving forward again; he hadn't missed any appointments; he'd been drinking substantially less, keeping his room and their common areas tidy, helping with the cleaning—an amazing transformation.

She'd changed, too. Around him she was able to be the kind of bold, sexy woman she'd never thought she could be. Maybe—she was really dreaming now—maybe they could establish a wonderful and healthy relationship, the kind she'd always dreamed of but had never been able to manage. Maybe if she got the Carter bid or, if worse came to worst, she took the Soka job, and he got a good position with an architectural firm, they could find a nicer place to live. Together. If he really cared about her…

She was giddy with optimism by the time she got to their apartment door. It wasn't that late. Not ten yet. Maybe he'd want to go out dancing again. Maybe he'd want to stay in and dance horizontally, nyuck, nyuck. She pushed the door open quietly, hoping he was on the couch and she could jump him.

No. In his room, then?

No.

Kitchen?

No.

A note was on the table. "Out partying with Steve and Kent, back late, possibly not until tomorrow."

The hand holding the note started shaking. Kim sank into a nearby chair and read it again, her heart in free fall.

She knew what happened when he was out with Kent and Steve. The beers would pour in. The inhibitions would leak out. The women would be there, young, wild and willing. Steve would encourage him. So would Kent. Nathan wouldn't want to look like a wimp in front of his friends.

Plus, he thought Kim was out with Dale tonight; why should he behave himself?

Possibly not until tomorrow.

Immediately, an image of her mother came to her, sitting up late at night all alone, pretending nothing was wrong, that it was fine her husband wasn't there again, that she knew where he was and with whom, and it was all on the up-and-up.

Kim folded her arms on the kitchen table and buried her head in them. What had she been thinking? How had she allowed something as stupid as a fantasy to creep into the reality of who Nathan had always been?

She couldn't even think about having a relationship with a man she couldn't trust.

14

MARIE STEPPED BACK from the wall of Kim and nodded in satisfaction. "I think it's perfect."

"Yes!" Candy stood next to her, wiping a smudge of glue from her nose. "It is perfect. I'm so glad we did it ourselves."

Marie stepped back to get the full effect. With the guys' help, they'd taken pictures and hangings down from one wall in Candy's living room, moved chairs and a table down to the basement and hung up poster-board panels. But when Kent and Justin had started randomly throwing on the memorabilia that Kent and Nathan had collected—from Kim's apartment, a jumbled mess in a box Kent retrieved from his place, and a frighteningly organized assortment from Kim and Kent's mother—Candy and Marie put their feminine feet down.

After sending the boys away with assurances they couldn't have done it without manly assistance, Candy and Marie had gone to work constructing a timeline. Pictures of Kim as a baby, as a little girl next to a fantastic dollhouse, as a young girl and teenager; letters she'd written from camp, from college; dried flowers from her high school graduation, prom, the opening day of Charlotte's Web; funny emails Kent had saved and printed out; her first baby shoes, her first toe shoes, a high-heeled black sandal they'd badgered her into buying on their recent outing.

Marie stopped by the last item, sent over by Nathan and prominently displayed: architectural plans for Kim's lost childhood dollhouse. The guy had to be in love with her to do something that sweet. Marie understood Kim's fears over falling for a player, boy did she ever, but she hoped Kim would give him a chance.

A long sigh preceded her millionth time check of the afternoon. Marie was a nervous mess over her regular Roots Cellar date with Quinn that night. She was going not as a friend, but as a woman.

After her lightbulb moment on the banks of the Milwaukee River, she'd gone home and done some listening to her instinct, which told her loud and clear that Quinn was what she wanted. Romantically. Sexually. The whole enchilada.

She couldn't in good conscience encourage Kim to go for it with Nathan and not take that risk herself. She'd chosen tonight for no particular reason except she'd decided there was no point waiting. Tonight she'd start showing Quinn she could be more than a friend. Tonight she'd start trying to interpret various signs that he could be interested as encouragement, instead of trying to find every possible reason she might have misunderstood his signals.

And if the effort was a complete disaster, so be it. Life would go on. The very next night, she'd be back here, surrounded by friends celebrating Kim's thirtieth birthday. Maybe she'd even try dating. Maybe she was more ready than she thought.

"Okay. Let's see." Candy fished a worn piece of paper out of her apron pocket and consulted it. "Computer cake's baked. I'll frost it tomorrow. Custard in the freezer, sandwich fillings ready, her favorites, egg salad and salami with cream cheese. We'll put those together tomorrow, too. Chips, soda, beer, wine, all those are coming with guests. So on, so on, yadda yadda, I think we're good!"

"You've done great as usual, Candy. Thanks for your hard

work." Marie glanced at her watch yet again, though she knew exactly what time it was. She had one hour to go home, change into a brand-new outfit bought for the occasion, and show up slightly late to be sure he'd already be there. Maybe she could manage five minutes of deep breathing so she didn't hyperventilate. "I should get home."

"Going out tonight?"

"To a neighborhood bar. A regular Friday night…gathering."

"Sounds great." Candy put the list in her pocket, then dug it out again. "Oh, I need to wrap Kim's underwear. Leopard print for our wild jungle beast. She is going to die."

Especially with Nathan right there imagining her wearing it.

"She'll love it. Have fun." Marie hugged Candy and grabbed her bag, saw herself out into the chilly afternoon and drove home, seriously risking a speeding ticket.

One hour. Less now.

In her room, she shed her jeans, sweater and comfortable walking shoes and marched determinedly to her closet where the dress of seduction awaited. Not that she'd ever look like the kind of woman Quinn regularly, er, associated with, but compared to her usual, Marie would be hot tonight. The outfit had taken two exhausting days to find. Marie was adamant the dress be sexy without looking as if it were trying to be, and sophisticated without being fancy.

Finally, in a small downtown boutique she almost passed by, she'd struck gold. No, not on the clearance rack, but some things were worth paying for, and this was one of them. The dress had a white cotton knit bodice that crisscrossed over her chest, exposing more cleavage than she was used to, but not more than plenty of woman out there showed on a regular basis. A band of solid blue hugged under her breasts; from there a blue-green floral skirt flowed to just below her knees, camouflaging and concealing in all the right ways. She'd even found a pair of blue high heels, which added important inches to her height, and which she could actually walk in instead of teetering.

Maybe she was being silly putting so much emphasis on one night and one dress, but too bad. This was how she wanted to try. If Quinn had decided to pursue a girlfriend, it was time she let him know she considered herself in the running. And if he rejected her, okay, she'd show him in word and action that she accepted his decision, and wouldn't let it ruin their friendship.

After she died a little.

The dress wouldn't be wasted. There would be other men to wear it for, other occasions. She'd rebuilt so much of her life after the divorce, making all her own decisions. This time she'd be making her own relationship decisions, too.

The dress went on smoothly; she zipped it up and smiled happily at her reflection. She hadn't imagined how flattering the style was for her coloring and her figure. This was a dress she could wear confidently, and which might even turn a few heads. Including Quinn's.

Makeup went on lightly; no need for overkill. Panty hose, shoes, very simple jewelry so as not to look overdressed, including the ring she'd finally called Grant to tell him he wasn't getting back. Another victory. More porgress. She wanted to wear the ring and enjoy it without being haunted by pain or memories.

A critical last once-over, and she tugged up the neckline, worried about overexposure. In the next second, she let it go back down. What the hell? Might as well give him an eyeful. She'd never met a man who objected.

There. She was ready.

She was beautiful.

She was sexy.

She was terrified.

No, none of that. Marie picked up her new purse—yes, a blue one—and strode to the front door. She called goodbye to Jezebel, who meowed to wish her luck, grabbed up a light jacket—blue!—and headed outside, wondering if this was how Cinderella felt before going to the ball. And how Marie Antoinette felt on the way to her beheading.

Marie marched out into the evening, thinking confidence, thinking success, visualizing Quinn's face lighting up at the sight of her, visualizing his eyes darkening, visualizing him taking every opportunity to touch her while they chatted, visualizing herself receptive, not overeager and not at all nervous.

Oh, God. Could she do this?

Of course she could! She'd been doing nearly the exact same thing every Friday for weeks now, without the cleavage and flirting. Cleavage did its own work. Flirting wasn't hard, especially with someone as charming as Quinn.

She reached the restaurant, took a moment to steady her breathing, to stand straighter, hold herself taller. She'd go inside the main restaurant, down the stairs to the Cellar Bar, greet Quinn, casually take off her jacket and perch gracefully next to him as if this were the same as any other Friday night they'd spent together.

Or wait, maybe she should take her jacket off sooner, and float downstairs with it draped over her arm, in case he was watching for her. A movie-star entrance.

Okay. Here goes.

She opened the front door and sauntered in, head held high. At the top of the stairs, she took off the jacket, slung it over her arm and poised her hand elegantly on the railing.

The first step. Second. She wasn't tripping, wasn't shaking too badly. This was fine. Another step. Another. Now the hem of her dress could be seen. Step. Step. Now the waist… the cleavage, step, step, and the full picture.

Marie kept an unconcerned look on her face, staring straight ahead, when she was dying to turn and peek. Was he watching? He'd certainly be there by now. She'd been careful to calculate that much.

At the bottom of the stairs she turned to face the bar.

Yes.

He was there.

With a woman.

His arms were around her, and he was whispering into her ear. She was dark, slender, beautiful.

Quinn finished whatever he'd said and she laughed, gazing up at him with clear adoration while he gazed back with equal tenderness.

Marie froze. She couldn't move. Not forward. Not back. He took the woman's hand in both of his and leaned forward, speaking earnestly.

Slowly, Marie backed up. Slowly, she turned. Moved back up the stairs slowly, not wanting to call any attention to herself, though it didn't look as if Quinn was aware of anything but the woman with him.

As soon as her head was out of sight, Marie sprinted up the rest of the flight, executed a few moves worthy of a running back to avoid waitstaff and patrons in the restaurant, and burst out into the cold, damp, unpleasant April evening. Alone.

She reached home and kicked off the damn shoes, in which she'd twisted her ankle twice hurrying on the uneven pavement. Up the stairs, into her room, purse tossed onto her bed. The jacket came off, the dress came off, Grant's ring came off. She washed off the makeup, came up from the bowl of the sink with her face streaming water, got an eyeful of her sorry, sodden state, and burst into tears.

Half an hour later, her sobs had quieted and she'd already started working on her self pep talk. Disappointment was natural. But she'd built this fantasy all by herself out of nothing, and someday it would go back to being nothing. Quinn wasn't the last man in the world, he was the first. The first to get her out of her lethargy, out of her relationship coma, to awaken in her the desire to share herself and her life with someone again. That was important, that was a good thing. She was grateful to him for that.

The rest of her plan would go forward. Tomorrow she'd be at Kim's party. Sunday she was visiting a college friend in Madison. Monday she'd think about signing up for a dating site—sadly not Milwaukeedates.com, that would be unethical, but one of the big ones. There were men out there who would appreciate her smarts and independence, who didn't have Quinn's relentless need for perfect faces and bodies. Who'd have fewer commitment issues, less baggage and plenty of other good traits.

Feeling a swelling of strength, she splashed water on her face again and dried it, picked up Grant's ring—no, her ring—from her dresser and shoved it back on her finger, admiring its glitter. This wasn't the end. This was the beginning. The beginning of the second phase of Marie's love life. And she was ready.

From her phone in the next room, she heard the beep of an incoming text message. Candy, most likely, with more party needs.

She went into her bedroom, dug her iPhone out of her purse, peered at the screen and held it, staring. From Quinn.

Hey, where are you? Get over here, I want you to meet my sister.

NATHAN RAISED A BEER he didn't need to his lips. His sixth? Seventh? He didn't know. Too many, though he'd been at it since… He peered at his watch. Whenever. Was it really that late? He wanted to know if Kim was back from her date. He wanted to know that she'd had a terrible time. But she might not be back. She and Dale might have had a fabulous, romantic evening, and she might have decided to end it naked and sweaty in his bedroom.

Pain stabbed Nathan so hard he nearly moaned.

There was no way he could have sat home tonight in their living room alone, waiting for her to come home. Or not come home.

So he was sitting on the floor in Troy's living room in his ritzy house in a ritzy neighborhood, watching some stupid made-for-TV movie with Steve, Kent and Justin, Troy's friend and coauthor and fiancé of Kim's friend Candy. Nice guy. Oh, and Dylan. Dylan was lying by Nathan's side. Dylan was a dog. A very cool dog.

"Nathan."

"Huh?" He blinked blearily around the room. Someone talking to him?

"Nathan, man, you have been a complete lame-ass all night." Steve stuffed a handful of popcorn into his mouth. "What is *up?*"

Nathan turned to Steve, who'd had two beers to every one of his. Maybe that's why he looked sort of blurry. "Not much. I'm in love."

The words spilled out of his mouth. He had definitely not been planning to say them. But there they were. A relief, actually.

"Man, you are pathetic!" Steve jiggled more popcorn in his palm. "The same one from that day at Wolski's? *Angelina?*"

"Not *Angelina*." Nathan imitated his derisive tone. "She's a fantasy. I'm in love with a woman. I want to marry her."

Those words had definitely not been planned. What the hell was this beer made of? He'd barely slept the night before; that had to be compounding his, uh, condition.

But marry her? He wanted to marry Kim?

Yeah. He did.

The room had gone quiet. Kent turned off the TV.

"What did you just say?" Steve's hand was frozen halfway to the popcorn bowl.

"I'm in love." He got unsteadily to his feet. Dylan did the same, but he got to wag his awesome tail. "Crazy effing in love with her."

"Aw, *man*." Steve threw his hands up to his forehead in despair, as if something truly nightmarish had happened, like the Packers' quarterback had been sacked. "You idiot. I told you, keep the balls to yourself."

Justin gave Steve a withering look before turning to Nathan. "What makes you think you've been hit?"

"Other women were like…" He frowned, trying to get his brain to cooperate. "What's that stuff magicians use that flares up, then disappears?"

"Flash paper." Kent had done props for musicals in high school. "Burst of fire and it's gone."

"Right. That's what women have always been for me. This is more like…" He paused, hand moving up and down like a chopping ax, trying to come up with the image he wanted. "It's like a long, slow burn."

Justin was nodding. "That's exactly what it feels like. A long, slow burn that never goes out."

"Gimme a break." Steve waved them away like a bad smell. "That's fairy-tale bullshit."

"Then you've never felt it," Justin said, with considerable acid in his tone.

Silence. It occurred to Nathan that none of them had ever taken Steve on like that, no matter how much they disagreed with him.

"Who is it?" Kent asked. "Do we know her?"

"Yeah. We do. Especially you." He gave a harsh laugh. "It's Kim. Your sister."

Kent stood up. He'd look threatening except he'd fallen asleep earlier and still had ink from a magazine picture decorating his cheek. "What the f—"

"Kim?" Troy lifted his beer. "Kim is awesome. Nice, funny, hot…"

"Then why didn't you go out with her again?" Justin asked. "I thought you were going to."

"I was." Troy flashed a glance at Nathan. "She, uh…I didn't want— It was complicated."

Nathan peered at him curiously. Something weird about that excuse.

"Oh, no." Justin pointed his bottle accusingly at Troy. "Don't tell me it's still Debby."

"Not Debby." Troy shook his head emphatically. "She

called me again and I blew her off. Marie Hewitt from Milwaukeedates.com has been talking to me about new matches. I'm over her, really this time, and looking around."

"Good man." Steve crunched another handful of popcorn, pieces of which fell from his lips to the carpet. Dylan moved in for cleanup duty. "You gotta keep those balls where they belong. Unlike *some* of us."

Justin rolled his eyes. "Steve, my guess is that you were either hurt badly and haven't stopped pouting yet, or you're gay."

The guys hooted with laughter. Nathan decided Justin was a great guy. He loved him. He loved everyone, but mostly Kim. And not Steve, who'd turned an unbecoming shade of purple and had risen to his feet.

"You want to say that outside?"

"Jesus, Steve." Kent sounded as disgusted as he looked. "You need to get over yourself."

"He called me gay."

"You've called people worse."

"Time to go home, Steve." Troy stood and opened his front door. "That crap gets you thrown out of this house."

Steve walked threateningly toward him, but as he approached and had to tip his head back farther and farther to keep looking Troy in the eye, he apparently changed his mind, turned around, grabbed his jacket and left, muttering obscenities.

"Nice guy," Justin said. "I can see why you hang around him."

"Yeah, maybe that needs to change." Troy shut the door with a flourish and aimed a kick after it.

"Nathan." Kent turned to him. "What the hell are you doing with my sister?"

"Everything."

Kent's eyes narrowed. "You better—"

"Making dinner. Helping her with her work. Taking her kayaking. Trying to become a better man for her."

"Oh." He deflated a little. "That's it?"

"That's all that's your business."

"If you hurt her…"

"Ha! If anyone is going to do any hurting here, it's her. I'm gone. I'm history. This is it."

Dylan came back to stand by Nathan, as if he knew Nathan needed support.

Good dog. Nathan should get a dog. But he wanted a Kim first.

Justin was looking thoughtful. "Have you told her?"

"I want to tell her. I tell her everything except that. I met with my thesis advisor today and he said I'm finally on the right track, but I can't even tell her that, because she's out with some other jerk tonight." He squinted, considering how that sounded. "I mean, some jerk."

"Oh, man." Troy shook his head. "Killer."

"You have to tell her." Kent swooped his beer emphatically through the air. "She has a hard time trusting guys. Especially guys who screw around."

"Don't sleep with her," Justin said. "Let her know she's different from the others."

Nathan didn't move a muscle.

"Oops. Too late," said Troy.

"No way." Kent appeared flabbergasted. "Kim and you… really?"

Nathan scowled. "I don't want to talk about it."

"No, no." Kent made placating gestures. "It's just that she wouldn't… I mean unless… Geez, she must like you. Some, anyway."

"Some. Nice." He rubbed his forehead. "She pulled way back after."

"Tell her how you feel," Justin said. "That's probably what's wrong. She needs to hear it."

"I don't know." Nathan's heart twisted. He sat back down on the floor. Dylan put his head in his lap. "She could be on her back with this Dale dude right now."

"No way." Kent shook his head. "She isn't like that."

"Have you seen her recently?" Nathan snorted. "She's changing."

"How so?" Justin asked.

"She's acting...sexier. Dressing that way. Makeup, too."

"You mean when she goes out?" Justin tipped his beer up and took a swig.

"No, around the house, too. And when we went out dancing, you should have seen her. She never used to, not when I first moved in, anyway. But not that long after."

"Hello?" Justin tapped his head. "Anyone home?"

Troy was grinning. "Sounds to me like you're in."

"I'm calling her." Kent pulled out his cell, started dialing.

"No." Nathan struggled to his feet. So did Dylan. "No. I don't want to know—"

He told himself to shut up. Of course he wanted to know.

"Hey, Kim, it's your brother. Where are you?" His face broke into a wide grin. "Yeah?"

Nathan felt as if his head were on the chopping block and the executioner was making up his mind whether to pick up the ax or not.

"Yeah, we're at Troy's having beers. We were at Wolski's earlier. What?" Kent listened, then clapped a hand over his mouth, trying to get laughter under control. "No, no, nothing like that. We're just hanging out. How was your evening?"

Nathan stared as hard as possible at Kent, as if Kim's words could pour out his ears and across the room to Nathan's.

It didn't work.

"Ooh, *that* good? I know, I know. Okay, yeah. Take care."

That good? What did that mean? His beers started turning to foam in his belly.

Kent hung up the phone, looking smug as hell. "Well. She's home."

"What did she say?" Nathan's voiced cracked like an adolescent's. "Did she ask if I was here?"

"Yes, she asked if you were here."

"I'm going to her." Nathan grabbed his coat, tried to put it on, but the sleeve holes seemed to have moved. Oh, well. He'd carry it instead.

He'd taken four steps toward the front door when strong hands landed on each of his shoulders.

"I hate to stand in the way of true love." Troy, on his right.

"But you're not really in great shape to drive." Justin, on his left.

Kent burst out laughing, as if it was the funniest thing he'd ever heard. "You are so busted. But they're right. Dude, you can't drive like that."

"I'm fine." Troy and Justin let go at the same time and he staggered forward. "Sort of fine."

"You can stay here tonight," Troy said. "Any of you can stay. There's plenty of room. I even have bacon and pancake mix for breakfast."

Nathan groaned. "I can't wait all night."

"For bacon?" Troy looked confused.

"For *Kim*."

"You'll survive. It's **not** bad news, I promise." Kent slapped him on the back; Nathan barely escaped more stumbling humiliation by grabbing one of Troy's chairs. "And no offense, but you might not want to declare love in the shape you're in right now."

"You're right." Nathan sighed mournfully. "I probably stink."

"Like a skunk," Troy added helpfully.

"And you look like hell," Justin said.

"Not to mention you might puke." Kent squeezed his shoulder. "Not a good accompaniment to 'I love you.' Wait until morning."

Nathan screwed up his face in distaste. "Morning isn't going to feel good, is it?"

"Skip morning. Sleep until noon." Troy brought out a glass of water from the kitchen. "I'll put you upstairs."

"Noon." Nathan nodded, bumped fists with Justin and Kent, and followed Troy up the staircase, feeling like a pathetic stray. "Thanks, man."

"You're welcome." Troy put the water down next to the bed. "She seems worth getting it right for."

"Troy." He bit off a yawn. "Why did you really not call her again?"

Troy shrugged. "That day playing basketball I could tell you were into her. I thought I'd step aside."

"Wow. Thanks, man." He peered groggily at Troy's handsome face. Definitely a good guy. "I hope you find someone, too, because it mostly feels like absolute shit."

Troy burst out laughing. "Not for long, dude. Sleep and you'll get it straightened out. Tomorrow you can give her the best birthday of her life. I'm sorry I'll miss it."

"You're not going?"

"I have a date. Sleep well. The bathroom's down the hall on the right. All I ask is you don't turn the wrong way, because that's my room." Troy tapped on the wall, grinning, and left.

Nathan made it down the hall, turned right, brushed his teeth with toothpaste and his finger, drank the water Troy left, stripped off his clothes and fell into bed.

Best birthday of her life… Wait, how was he going to do that?

His eyes shot open.

He had a pretty good idea.

15

KIM OPENED THE apartment door. "Nathan?"

No answer.

She strode into the living room. *"Nathan?"*

Nothing.

She checked his room to see if he was taking a nap.

No.

Where was he? Still at Troy's?

She headed to her room and dumped her shopping bags on the bed. Apart from not seeing Nathan, Kim had managed to enjoy her birthday so far, which last night she wasn't at all sure she would. Finding out Nathan hadn't spent his evening trolling for women helped a lot, though she was discouraged by how quickly her fears had surfaced. She wanted to trust him, but would have to learn to, which would take time, with no guarantee of success.

How much of her life did she want to invest in the hope of him?

That morning, after her dance class, she'd gone for a long walk by the lake in the cool April breeze, knowing if she stayed home she'd spend every minute fidgeting, wondering when he would be back. Not far from where she and Nathan had picnicked after their kayak trip, she'd stopped and sat quietly in the sand to see if some wise inner voice would give her the answer, as Marie said it would.

The first inner voice she heard was her stomach telling her loudly that she hadn't eaten enough breakfast. Not exactly what she had in mind.

But then she'd opened herself up to listening, really listening, thinking about what Nathan had done for her, how she lit up like the Fourth of July at the mere sight of him, how much confidence he had in her and in her talent, how when she was with him she felt like the person she'd always wanted to be. Strong. Beautiful. Sexy.

She'd asked herself whether she should give up on him, and immediately felt angry and anxious and upset. Should she stay and see what could happen between them in the long term? Nervous. Excited.

Okay, Marie. On your head be it.

After the walk, she'd met her mother to have lunch and go shopping. They'd actually had a pretty decent time. For once the clothes Mom wanted to buy her were pretty close to the ones Kim wanted to wear. Even at lunch, when she said her choice right now was between the job at Soka or the contract with Carter, her mother had refrained from making any snotty comments about Charlotte's Web.

Now, to make the day perfect, Kim wanted Nathan. She checked the answering machine: two messages. One from a college roommate and one from her aunt who refused to call cell phones, both with birthday wishes. Only two? She checked her BlackBerry, and remembered she'd turned it off while she was by the lake, and had forgotten to switch it back on.

Five voice mails. Eagerly, she dialed into the system. One from Kent, one from Dad in Ohio, two from high school friends, all four wishing her happy birthday. The next message was from her mother.

"Hi, sweetie, happy birthday again. I just wanted to say how much I enjoyed lunch and how very proud I am of you and what you've accomplished..."

Tears came into Kim's eyes. *Oh, Mom.* This was a new—

"...Now how about finding yourself a man to settle down with?"

Kim chuckled, wiping the tears away. *Guess what, Mom?* She'd found the man. The settling down part...remained to be seen.

Last message: from Emily at Soka.

"Where are you? Why aren't you picking up? Call me ASAP. I have insider news from my contact at Carter."

Kim let out a shriek, fumbled to call back and had to start over.

Emily's cell rang. Rang again. *Come on, pick up.*

"Hey, Kim, where are you?" Contact! Her friend's voice was casual, not brimming with excitement, but not oozing sympathy, either. What did that mean?

"I'm home." Kim put a hand to her chest, trying to calm down. "What's the news from Carter?"

"Meet me at Harry's Bar and Grill in ten minutes?" Still a carefully neutral tone. "I'll buy you a drink for your birthday."

"Uh. No." The hand on Kim's chest turned to a claw. "I am not waiting that long for you to tell me."

"Sure you are."

"Emily!" Kim had to work hard not to bellow. "You can't do this to me."

"Ten minutes."

Argh! She checked the clock on Nathan's TV. "I have a dinner party to go to. How about you just say 'good news' or—"

"See you there." She signed off.

"Em—" Kim let out a roar of frustration. Fine. She'd go to the damn bar.

Phone shoved into her pants pocket, she grabbed her jacket and ran for the elevator.

NATHAN OPENED THE APARTMENT door. "Kim?"

No answer.

He strode into the living room. "Kim?"

Nothing.

He checked her room to see if she was taking a nap.

No.

Where was she?

She hadn't been home earlier, either, when he'd first come back from Troy's. At that point he'd been glad she wasn't around. He hadn't wanted her first birthday sight of him to be unshowered, with death-breath, in yesterday's wrinkled clothes.

He'd woken up early that morning, hungover as he deserved to be, and had struggled out of Troy's guest room to use the bathroom. Luckily, no one else had been up yet, and he'd managed to sleep for another three hours. After bacon and pancakes—at lunchtime—Tylenol, a lot of water and good strong coffee, he'd felt halfway human.

Then Kent took pity and let him know Kim not only hadn't had anything like a hot date the previous night, but she'd told Dale she didn't want to see him anymore, which was undoubtedly the biggest reason Nathan had started feeling better. Better and more optimistic about Kim's feelings for him. Staying distant and friendly for the past week had nearly killed him.

Now, with the dollhouse plans completed and on the wall of Kim at Candy's house, he'd put another plan into motion this afternoon, a plan that would guarantee Kim understood how he felt about her, even if he couldn't bring his stupid guy-self to say it.

He hauled out his cell and dialed her number, praying she was planning to come home before the party. He wanted to drive her there, to see her alone and, if everything worked out, a lot more than that.

She picked up on the fourth ring. "Nathan, where are you?"

"I'm home." His voice automatically gentled and deepened; his body relaxed. Kim was like a drug to his system.

One with frequent Viagra-like side effects. "Where are you?"

"Having a drink with Emily at Harry's."

He frowned, checked his watch. "What about tonight?"

"There's time."

"Not much." He was supposed to make sure she got there on the dot of six, and if she pushed it too close, his plan would have to be postponed. And wasn't this a switch, him worrying about being late, and Kim not caring. "I'll drive you to Candy's. I'm going that way anyway. And I'd like to see you on your birthday."

"I'd like that, too." Her voice did the same gentling and deepening as his, making his chest tighten with happiness. And hope. And fear.

"Come home, Kim."

"Ten minutes?"

"Ten minutes." He ended the call in a goopy trance that shattered when his cell rang again.

"Mr. Alexander?" The deep, accented voice of the man who'd waited on him at Stein's.

Perfect. Nathan's heart started a strong, solid beat. "It's ready?"

"It's ready."

"I'll be right there." Nathan checked his watch again. He could just make it. He shoved his phone in his jeans pocket, grabbed his jacket and ran for the elevator.

KIM BURST INTO THE APARTMENT. "Nathan?"

No answer.

She darted into the living room. *"Nathan?"*

Nothing.

What the heck? She'd just talked to him. Where was he?

Giddy with excess energy, she ran into her bedroom to change into a teal knit dress she and her mom had bought: knee-length with a scoop-neck front and plunging V-back. What a birthday it had been already! Apparently Emily's

Carter informant had spilled on Friday that the bid candidates had been narrowed down to two: Kim and Soka. That morning, Emily's boss had called to tell her Soka wasn't getting the contract. Which meant, as far as Emily was concerned, Kim was.

Of course, Emily knew how much Kim wanted this, and what it meant to her, and had wanted her to find out on her birthday. Plus she'd been terrified Kim would accept the job at Soka before Carter got around to calling.

Until Kim heard officially, she was going to have a hard time believing it, though Emily wasn't the type to repeat unsubstantiated rumors. But after so long dreaming and hoping, it was almost too much to take in. Assuming this all worked out, Charlotte's Web was saved!

Giggling nervously, Kim closed the door to check out her reflection in the new dress. The outfit clung in all the right places, forgave in all the others. A simple silver chain necklace, her favorite dangling silver earrings and just a touch-up of mascara were all she needed. Happiness and excitement had made her eyes large and shining and put flattering color in her cheeks.

Where was Nathan? She wasn't going to tell anyone else about the Carter job until she got the official notice, but she had to tell him. The minute he laid eyes on her he'd know something was up, anyway; he read her so well. And he'd helped her so much getting that final piece for the proposal, he deserved to know.

She laughed at herself, and nearly brushed mascara onto her eyeball. Yeah, he deserved to know because he'd helped. Right. She wanted him to know because she was crazy in love with him and wanted to share everything.

If only she could be sure he felt the same way. He desired her, yes, liked her, sure, but love?

Her cell rang from the pocket of her discarded pants; Kim rushed to answer while putting in the second earring. *Yes.* It was Nathan. She couldn't wait to tell him her news.

"Hey, Kim. I'm downstairs."

"Five minutes?" Her hair could use brushing.

"You're gorgeous." He sounded impatient and tense. "Come now."

"What's the big rush?"

"I haven't seen you since yesterday, and if I have to wait any longer I might die here alone in the street."

Immediate warm and fuzzies. He was right; her hair looked fine. Though whether she was dressed to the nines or un-made-up and in sweatpants, he seemed to think she looked perfect.

For how long?

"I'll be right there." She grabbed her jacket and flew down the stairs, out of the building and over the sidewalk to where Nathan's car was waiting. And in it, Nathan, looking to die for in a white shirt and jeans with a brown suede, bomber-style jacket.

She slid into the passenger's seat, joy filling her as if she hadn't seen him in weeks. This was special, what was between them. He had to feel it, too. "Hi there."

He leaned toward her, his eyes lit by the evening and something that might have been joy also. "May I kiss the birthday girl?"

She didn't have to think that one over, but met him half-way in a long, slow kiss that left her melting in his front seat. There had been *some* reason Kim pulled away from him, *some* reason she'd decided there should be no more kissing... What was it?

Oh, yes. She'd been temporarily insane.

"I've missed this so much," he murmured. "I've missed *you,* Kim. It didn't feel right staying away. Like part of me wasn't there anymore."

Kim caught her breath, managing to stop short of an out-right gasp. Unless she was hallucinating, Nathan Alexander had just shared feelings. Tender, sweet feelings. For her. This day just kept getting better and better.

"I missed you too, Nathan." She had. Like crazy. "It was a complicated week."

"But we're okay now?"

"We're okay." They were more than okay. Or at least she hoped they were. A lot more.

"Thank God." He kissed her again, pulled away reluctantly and eased the car onto Oakland, heading north toward Shorewood. "Nice birthday so far?"

"Very nice." Kim suppressed a smile; she was about to tell him exactly how nice. "I had my dance class, went for a long walk by the lake, then met my mom for lunch and shopping."

"Fun. Pretty dress, by the way." He put his hand on her thigh, picked up the hem, rubbed the material between his fingers. How could she find fingers so sexy? "Soft. Nice color on you."

"Thank you. I was…" What? She had to clear lust-fog from her head to remember. "Oh, right. Then I came back home, Emily called and we went out for a drink."

"Yeah?" He stopped for a red light, turned to give her a searching look. "She have anything interesting to say?"

Kim smiled to herself. No, she couldn't hide a thing from him. More than that, she wouldn't ever want to. "Oh, not much. Just happy birthday and I'm getting the Carter job."

Nathan blinked. The light turned green. He accelerated, tires protesting, drove another hundred feet and pulled into a parking place on Capitol Drive, so fast the car bounced when he braked.

"Outside." He unbuckled his belt and shot from his seat.

Kim was barely able to unfasten her seat belt before her door was yanked open and strong arms pulled her up, out, then wrapped themselves around her.

"*Kim.*"

She laughed against him, hugging almost as tightly as he was, but not quite, because he was considerably stronger and nearly suffocating her. She didn't care. What was air compared to how she felt about him?

"Congratulations." He drew back, beaming into her eyes,

looking nearly as happy as she felt about her accomplishment. What more could she want in a man?

A small voice whispered the answer: *Commitment.*

"Thanks, Nathan. I'm not telling anyone else until I hear it from Carter, but I wanted you to know."

His smile faded, but not the intensity of his gaze. "Why me?"

Because I love you. She shrugged. "I knew it would mean something to you."

"It means a lot." He swallowed; his expression took on an odd urgency and something that looked like…fear? "But you're not supposed to give *me* a gift like that. It's *your* birthday."

She laughed, feeling a little uneasy. Something was going on, something really uncomfortable for him. Her instinct knew it, and according to Marie, her instinct couldn't be wrong. "I think it's fine to give you something on my birthday, Nathan. I mean it's not as if—"

"I love you, Kim."

She stared stupidly. She couldn't have heard him right.

"I love you, and I got you something, too." He fished in his jacket pocket, had a little trouble coming up with it, but once he did, her heart simply stopped beating.

A jeweler's box. Black velvet.

"Nathan." She nearly got dizzy. "What is this?"

"My balls."

"Your—" Her face froze in horror. "Uh. You want to explain that one?"

He winked, but his eyes were more vulnerable than she'd ever seen them. "It's actually your birthday present, Kim."

"Oh, my gosh."

"I know I'm taking a huge risk here." His voice broke; he ran his hand nervously through his hair. "We maybe don't know each other— We haven't really— But I couldn't see—"

"I love you, too, Nathan."

His mouth snapped shut. His turn to stare stupidly. "You do?"

"Yes." She was near tears, trembling, and so, so happy. "Yes. I do."

He took a long, slow breath, as if he'd been figuratively holding it for the past half hour.

"Open the box, Kim," he said hoarsely. "So I can ask you."

The tears came, probably ruining her makeup. A good reason not to wear any, except Nathan was about to ask her to marry him, and with life together ahead of them, she wouldn't have to worry much about tears.

With shaky fingers she opened the little box. Even knowing what was inside, she found the sheer magical beauty made her catch her breath. Yes, it was a ring. Simple and beautiful, a diamond flanked by smaller twins in a beautiful twisted gold setting. "Oh, Nathan."

He dropped to his knees right there on the sidewalk, not taking his eyes off hers. Passersby and customers exiting The City Market holding cups of coffee began to gather.

"Kim. I've loved you since the first time I saw you a decade ago. From then on, I have never loved any other woman." His voice was strong, calm and sure. "And I know now that I will never love any other woman. You have made me into a better man and my life would be empty without you. Will you marry me?"

Squeals from a gaggle of young girls startled Kim, and she glanced over. Open tears from a mom pushing her toddler in a stroller. Gentle smiles from an older couple with linked arms. Gagging noises from teenage boys in the back. A young woman held up her cell phone to capture the moment; Kim's marriage proposal would likely be on YouTube by the time she and Nathan made it to Candy's. She didn't care. No matter how many people saw, this was only for her and the man she loved.

"Nathan." She turned back to him; he hadn't stopped gazing at her, and in that second she truly understood that he wouldn't look away from her again. "I have never loved a man as completely as I love you. I have never been the kind of woman I wanted to be until I met you. Yes. I will marry you."

She barely heard the cheers and applause from the onlookers. Nathan got to his feet and kissed her with a mixture of passion and reverence that nearly overwhelmed her, and that made the crowd cheer harder.

They lingered for a few minutes, accepting congratulations, until Nathan's phone rang. He glanced at the number and ushered Kim back into the car.

"Who was that?" She waved to the well-wishers through the window.

"Another part of your birthday surprise."

"There's *more?*" She smiled at him as he maneuvered the car back onto the road, this handsome, gentle, funny, lovely man she'd be proud, for the rest of her life, to call husband. "I'm in your hands."

"Putty in them?"

"Absolutely." She deliberately lifted the hem of her dress. "Do I really have to be on time for this party?"

He groaned and nearly missed their turn. "Don't do that."

"No?" She spread her legs, lifted her knees so her thighs were completely bared, leopard underwear making a brazen appearance. "I wore your favorite."

"Kim." He took one hand off the steering wheel, adjusted his pants. "I'm going to be on fire all night now."

"Yeah? You better not make moves on anyone else, wherever you're going."

"Actually." He pulled into Candy's driveway. "I plan to make a whole lot of moves on this party's guest of honor."

"What do you—" She glanced toward the house. "This is for my birthday?"

"Come inside and find out how many more people love you."

"Oh, wow." Kim choked up, thinking of the girls and

what great friends they'd been to her. Darcy, Candy, Marie—did anyone deserve this much happiness? She leaned over for another kiss from her fiancé, wondering if she'd ever get enough of them. "Promise you'll keep that fire hot for me?"

His mouth curved in the sexy grin she loved so much, which now belonged only to her. "Sweetheart, this fire's been hot for the past ten years, no way is it going out. Tonight, tomorrow, for the rest of our lives, it's going to be a long, slow, beautiful burn."

Epilogue

"HOW MANY WOMEN DO WE know who have two sets of leopard underwear?"

Kim laughed and shook her head at Darcy. "I don't want that passed around."

"I wish I'd been there to see Nathan's face when you caught him with his hand in your drawers." Candy snorted. "I imagine the explanation was kind of a relief."

"You could say that." Kim sipped her coffee. "Thanks again for the party, everyone. It will always be remembered as one of the best days of my life."

Kim was radiant. Seeing her beaming like that, even this early in the morning at their April Women in Power meeting at the Pfister Hotel, seeing her laughing loudly, making bold gestures with her hands—she was a different woman through and through, not just the makeup and hair.

"Turning thirty, winning an enormous contract and getting engaged in one day? Ha!" Marie winked at her. "I'd say you won't forget that soon."

"How soon do you start work on the website, Kim?" Darcy asked.

"Ugh." She pretended to look grouchy. "Right away. I'm nothing more than a slave now."

"Poor baby." Candy patted her hand. "Money, recognition, doing what you love… It just breaks my heart."

"I know, I know." Kim pressed a hand to her forehead, in a classic suffering-heroine pose. "Somehow I'll make it through."

Amazing change. She was confident, relaxed and in charge of her life. Marie couldn't be happier.

Well, she could. If she could make some progress getting Darcy matched up. Marie had considered and discarded most of the men on Milwaukeedates.com, even seen if any sparks could fly between Darcy and Kent—no, they couldn't—and was feeling desperate. How did you get a woman matched up who had no apparent interest in cooperating?

"Have you and Nathan set a date yet?" Candy asked.

"Probably Christmas. We'll be looking to buy a place, but want to see where he gets a job first. He has two interviews next week."

"Oh, a Christmas wedding." Marie said yes to more coffee from the circulating pot. "I love those. So beautiful."

"Fall wedding, Christmas wedding, I'm thinking it's your turn next, Darcy." Candy took the words right out of Marie's brain.

"My turn?" Darcy made it sound as if they were asking her to dive into a quarry with no water in it. "No, no. Thanks, really, I'd rather feed myself to sharks."

"What, happiness not your thing, Darcy?" Kim joined Candy in a fit of girls' club giggles.

"Happiness has more to do with finding yourself than finding a man." Darcy finished her serving of fruit cup and put her spoon down, obviously disgusted with the whole topic.

"Uh-huh. But sex with a man is a whole lot better than sex with yourself." Candy leaned toward Darcy, blinking innocently. "Don't you like sex?"

Darcy sneered, eyes twinkling. "You can do that all you want without getting married."

Ooh. Marie brightened, and not just because the waitress had set down a heaping plate of pastries at their table.

Maybe she was going about this the wrong way. Maybe

the trick to getting Darcy matched up wasn't enrolling her on a dating site and sending her out on endless coffee dates with Mr. Wrongs Darcy could easily dismiss.

Marie helped herself to a muffin *and* a scone. Maybe it was a question of finding a Mr. Right who'd move straight to seducing her.

* * * * *

Look for Darcy's story in
HOT TO TOUCH
by Isabel Sharpe.
Enjoy!

Harlequin *Blaze*

COMING NEXT MONTH

Available April 26, 2011

#609 DELICIOUS DO-OVER
Spring Break
Debbi Rawlins

#610 HIGH STAKES SEDUCTION
Uniformly Hot!
Lori Wilde

#611 JUST SURRENDER...
Harts of Texas
Kathleen O'Reilly

#612 JUST FOR THE NIGHT
24 Hours: Blackout
Tawny Weber

#613 TRUTH AND DARE
Candace Havens

#614 BREATHLESS DESCENT
Texas Hotzone
Lisa Renee Jones

You can find more information on upcoming
Harlequin® titles, free excerpts and more at
www.HarlequinInsideRomance.com.

HBCNM0411